MARISABINA R

HOUSE OF SPORTS

GREENWILLOW BOOKS
An Imprint of HarperCollins*Publishers*

House of Sports

The text of this book is set in Times Roman.

Library of Congress Cataloging-in-Publication Data

Russo, Marisabina.
House of sports / by Marisabina Russo.
    p.   cm.
"Greenwillow Books."
Summary: Through a series of triumphs and tragedies at home,
at school, and on the basketball court, plus time reluctantly spent
with his elderly grandmother, twelve-year-old Jim Malone
learns that there is a lot more to life than basketball.
ISBN 0-06-623803-X (trade)
ISBN 0-06-623804-8 (lib. bdg.)
[1. Basketball—Fiction.   2. Grandmothers—Fiction.
3. Interpersonal relations—Fiction.
4. Family life—New York (N.Y.)—Fiction.
5. New York (N.Y.)—Fiction.]   I. Title.
PZ7.R9192 Ho   2002   [Fic]—dc21
2001023039

10   9   8   7   6   5   4   3   2   1
First Edition

For Susan Hirschman

Jim woke up seconds before the clock radio went off. He looked at the red numbers. Five forty-five. Abruptly a husky voice pierced the silence. "Baby, baby, baby—" A shadowy arm rose from the other bed and slammed down the top of the clock.

"Whatsa matter with you?" said Pete, Jim's brother. "It's friggin' Saturday! Why did you set the alarm?"

"Sorry," said Jim, trying to remember if he had set it or not.

Pete muttered something and tossed over and soon was snoring again. Jim lay there with one arm across his eyes to block the creeping daylight. Pete's snoring sounded like the broken muffler on Dad's old Volkswagen.

"Stop snoring!" Jim yelled. Pete didn't answer.

Jim stared at the wall of posters at the foot of his bed. Only sports posters: football, soccer, baseball, and, most of all, basketball. He looked up at the ceiling. There in the gray light he could barely make out the smooth, shaved head and the long, outstretched arms. Impossibly long. Jim often stretched out his own scrawny arms while lying on his bed and tried to imagine being as big as Michael Jordan.

Dad was tall, six-four. He said Jim had lots of growing to do. But Mom! Mom was a shrimp. Jim hated it when his grandmother Nana, Mom's mother, said, "But, Jim, you're already as big as I am, and you're only twelve." Nana was even more of a shrimp than Mom!

There was no use trying to go back to sleep. Today was Saturday, but it was the most important day of the year. Jim couldn't stop thinking about the tryouts. He could see the shiny gym floor, hear the squeak of his sneakers, feel the pebbled surface of the ball hitting his palm as he dribbled downcourt. The coaches were sitting on folding metal chairs behind the basket. They were watching him approach. He pulled the ball back, then spun up like a corkscrew to lay the ball softly against the backboard before it dropped quietly through the net. *Swish.* A perfect layup. Today were the tryouts for the travel basketball team. The old days of town teams when everybody played, even Gary Bushnell, the spazziest boy around, were over. This was the next step, a team that played the best teams from other towns. Jim had to make this team. He had lived his whole life for this day.

Jim got himself out of bed. It was cold. The window over Pete's bed was broken, the wood rotted away. A pane of glass was missing, and Mom had taped a plastic bag from a package of English muffins over the space. It made a soft flapping noise.

When Jim pushed open the swinging door to the kitchen, he heard Jake yelping in his sleep. Jake, a yellow Lab, had his bed under the kitchen table. Jake was the warrior, the old fella, the great one. He had led a long, adventurous life: coming home with a porcupine quill in his nose, dragging a deer leg up to the back door, being caught by the animal control officer and sent to the shelter ten miles away. Jim crouched down to rub Jake's belly. "Hey, big fella!"

Jake raised his head and looked at Jim. In the old days Jake would have jumped up, banging into the table leg, wiggling his whole body with his wagging tail.

"You're so lazy," said Jim. "Look at you!"

It was light outside. Jim pulled on his thick, white basketball shoes and laced them loosely. He grabbed his windbreaker from the hook by the door. Then he rolled up the bottoms of his pajama pants.

"Come on, Jake," Jim said as he unlocked the door. Jake stretched and yawned. "Let's go," said Jim, clapping his hands. "Time for some hoops."

The sky was a flinty gray, and a woodpecker was drumming away up in the maple tree. No cars were driving by, no snowblowers, no planes over the house, just the steady staccato of the busy woodpecker. Jim picked up the blue-and-white ball that was lying in Mom's snow-covered flower bed. It was the ball he had won last summer at basketball camp for being the MVP of his team. He held it in both hands and tossed it up a few times. It was cold and heavy. He dribbled it into the driveway over to the chalk marks still visible from yesterday's game of Horse. He set his feet, brought the ball up to shoulder height, and arced his wrists and hands as he released the ball in the direction of the basket. It hit the front of the rim and bounced out toward the flower bed. Jim ran to grab it, then took a quick jump shot and swished it. "He jumps, he shoots, he *scores!*" Jim sang out. Over and over, shooting from every side, listening to the wind in the trees, which sounded like cheering fans. He called to Jake, who was rolling on his back in a patch of wet grass, "Watch this, old fella!" Jim played until his hands were numb from the cold.

When he went back inside, Jim found Mom up making coffee. "You're the early bird this morning," said Mom. "I thought you wanted to sleep late?"

"Not today," said Jim. "Today's the tryout. I've gotta be ready."

"Jim, it's only seven o'clock! The tryout's not for three more hours!"

"So?"

"Take it easy, Jim," said Mom. "You don't want to wear yourself out."

"Mom, you never played sports. You don't understand. You have to get yourself psyched, pumped, ready to explode!" Jim didn't want to hurt Mom's feelings, but let's face it, she was not an athlete. She was an artist! She spent all day in her little studio, wearing one of Dad's old shirts, painting pictures, listening to that old-time music. When Jim and Dad were watching basketball on TV, Mom would come in and say something stupid like "Look at those uniforms. What a great color, kind of a cerulean blue."

"Hey, big shot, I understand plenty," said Mom. "Don't forget, I used to be really good at archery when I was a kid!"

"Archery, a big-time sport. Yeah, Mom, you were the Gail Devers of archery!"

"No, I didn't say that," said Mom. "I just meant that I competed, and I remember how I felt. I remember getting nervous. Just for that, I challenge you! To a match in archery. You name the place and time."

"Mom, there are no archery ranges around here," said Jim.

Mom laughed. "Lucky for you!" she said, pouring herself a glass of orange juice. "How about some pancakes?"

Pete was still sleeping when Jim and Dad left for the tryouts. Pete was in high school. He loved to sleep. But Jim was kind of glad Pete wasn't around to say something sarcastic like "The outside shot's gotta hurt. . . . You know you don't have one!" or "They're looking for height, you're no Shaquille O'Neal! You're a little kid, and that's gotta hurt." Pete always said these things in a low voice so no one could make out what he was saying except Jim.

Mom would get furious. "Stop all the constant chatter unless you want everyone to hear it."

Driving over to the Pigeon Hill School, Jim's old elementary school, Dad said, "Remember what I told you, don't shoot from down by your hip. Bring that ball up here." He pointed to his chest. "And remember you have to dazzle 'em with your skill—your quick hands, your jumping. Don't try to overpower the other guys. You're too small. Go around them."

Dad had played basketball in high school. Jim had seen the black-and-white photographs of the team in Dad's old yearbook, the yellowing newspaper clippings. Dad looked a lot like Pete, same long, skinny face, same floppy right ear that stuck out more than the left, same pimply forehead. In the last year Pete had grown five inches! He was almost as tall as Dad. But even though Pete watched lots of basketball on TV, he couldn't care less about playing sports. He liked to read and listen to music and play his guitar.

"I know, I know," said Jim. He was looking out the window at the passing houses: the green bungalow where Mrs. McCormick, his third-grade teacher, lived; the yellow ranch house where his best friend, Josh, lived; the firehouse; the town hall; and down the hill to the low brick school. There were a lot of cars here already. I hope I'm not late, he thought. There was Frankie Bellini getting out of his van. Frankie was the biggest, strongest kid in the seventh grade. His legs were already hairy, and he had shoulders almost as big as Dad's. All he has to do is not fall down and he'll make the team, Jim thought.

"Look at the size of that kid!" said Dad. "He's not trying out, is he?"

"Yeah, Dad, he is," said Jim.

When they got to the lobby of the school, they found a table set up for registration. There was a long line. Jim looked around. He recognized some of the guys, but there were many he'd never seen before, kids from the other side of town.

"Hey, Big Foot, whaddya think?" It was Josh, his black, curly hair standing out from his head in all directions as if he'd just gotten out of bed.

"Piece of cake," said Jim, trying to sound blasé.

"Definitely," said Josh.

It was Jim's turn to register. A woman wrote down his name and phone number and gave him a piece of paper with the number 27 printed on it in thick black Magic Marker. "Pin this to the back of your shirt, sweetheart," she said, clicking her gum. "Next!"

In the gym all the boys lined up in numerical order. There were two coaches sitting on chairs with clipboards. A teenager with a shaved head and a black warm-up suit stood on the court and called out the name and number of the first player. It was Kenny Gaynor, a tall, skinny kid Jim remembered from the town league.

"He's got no hands," Jim whispered to Josh. "Remember him? He always goes down before he goes up."

Kenny had to dribble to one end of the gym, do a layup, and take five shots from five different spots on the arc. Then he dribbled to the other end where the coaches were sitting and did the same thing. He made four out of ten shots.

"Cut," said Josh.

"No, man, he's too tall," said Jim. "You'll see. They'll keep him."

Kenny stood on the side while the next boy did the same thing. It was Danny Patton, this chubby kid who always seemed to be smiling. He dribbled slowly down the court, walking along, concentrating on the ball as though he were afraid he might lose it.

"He's outta here!" whispered Josh.

"You've got that right," said Jim.

When there were six players, they were divided into two teams of three and played a minigame under that basket for a couple of minutes. Immediately Danny made a good pass right to Kenny's hands. Kenny bobbled the ball but managed to hold on. He brought the ball down for one dribble and had it swatted away by another kid.

"They can't take him!" said Josh.

"Oh, yes, they can. Except for Frankie he's the tallest kid here. You'll see," said Jim. "Height rules in basketball." He remembered Coach Boylan from the camp last summer. One afternoon Jim was walking down the hall from the gym for a drink of water when he heard Coach's voice coming from his office. "Honestly, Mrs. Wright, Claude has wonderful movement and anticipation, but he's not that tall, and he won't be getting that tall from the looks of it, and in Division One ball you need the height. You can't teach height. It's there or it isn't. Just like you can't teach speed or heart."

When those six players sat down, they began calling the next six and so on until it was Jim's turn. As he trotted out onto the hardwood, he didn't feel nervous at all. He pushed the ball ahead, using his stronger left hand, and went in for an easy left-handed layup. He worked his way around the arc, remembering what Dad had said about bringing the ball up higher, and made four out of five. Then back to the other end, where the two coaches were both writing something on their clipboards. Again four out of five. Jim tried not to smile. That would make him look like a show-off.

Josh was the sixth player, and he rushed his shots, making only five out of ten, but Jim knew he was usually better. In the 3v3 they were on the same team. Jim passed to Josh, who gave the ball right back to Jim, who was cutting through the middle for a layup. Then Jim passed to Josh, who made a clean outside shot. Jim and Josh had been friends since kindergarten. They had played millions of hours of basketball together, first on a little orange-and-blue plastic hoop in Jim's room and later during recess in the playground and after school in each other's driveways.

When the teenager blew his whistle, Josh slapped Jim's hand. "Good as gold," he said without smiling.

"Okay, fellas, come on in," said one of the coaches. He was the shorter one, with thick brown hair that looked like a toupee and a beaky nose. "My name is Mr. Mondini, and this is Mr. O'Malley. We're the coaches for the seventh-grade travel team." Mr. O'Malley was a little taller than Mr. Mondini, and his red hair was cut close to his scalp. "We saw a lot of good things out there. Most of you guys obviously know how to handle a basketball, but unfortunately we can take only twelve players on this team. You will all be getting a phone call tonight. We'll be calling back about twenty of you for another tryout tomorrow." Mr. Mondini paused and looked around at the boys. He had small eyes, and he squinted a little, so it was hard to tell whom he was looking at as he scanned the crowd. He didn't smile. Mr. O'Malley grinned nonstop, but he didn't say a word. "Good luck to all you guys," Mr. Mondini finally said.

"Okay, I've counted sixteen for sure, but I can't figure out the other four," said Josh as they walked to the doors. "Let's see, there's me, you, Frankie, Kevin, Matt, Corey . . ."

Jim wasn't really listening to Josh. He was thinking about how long it seemed until tonight. He had to be one of the twenty. But he was small. He could only really play the point. He knew that. Actually, Josh was even smaller, but Josh was stronger; he already had muscles you could see in his arms. It didn't seem fair that you could be terrible but tall and that that automatically held a spot for you on a basketball team as long as there weren't any other really good, really tall kids. When you were short, you were competing with the whole world.

"Jim, what do you think?" It was Josh's voice insistent in Jim's right ear.

" 'Bout what?" Jim said, suddenly noticing they were outside.

"Marty? You think he'll get called back?"

"Maybe," Jim said. Right now all he wanted to do was go home. Sometimes Josh could be annoying. He talked too much.

"I'll call you," said Josh, and he sprinted down the parking lot to his mom's waiting station wagon.

Jim was looking across the parking lot when he heard Dad walk up behind him. Jim hadn't even noticed him back in the gym. "Nice shooting, Tex," said Dad as they headed for the car.

* * *

At dinner the rule was no one could answer the telephone. "That's why we have an answering machine," said Mom. When the phone rang, though, everyone stopped talking and chewing and listened to see who it was.

Pete got the most calls, especially on Saturday evenings.

Beep. "Hey, Pete! It's Betsy. Wuzzup? Just wanna know what you're doing tonight. Call me."

Beep. "Pete . . . heard there's a party at Fletcher's. Give me a buzz. Later!"

Beep. "Pete, Nick here. Wuzzup? Just chillin'. Call me."

"Hey, Pete, *wuzzup*?!" said Jim with a laugh. "That's all your friends ever say? 'Wuzzup, man?' "

"Shut up," said Pete without looking up from his food.

"No fighting at the dinner table," said Mom.

Mom made a big deal about dinner every night. They always sat in their dining room. Mom always lit candles on the table, and Dad always played records. Mom and Dad were so out of it, Jim thought sometimes. In their own little dreamworld. Having an answering machine was a big deal for them. They didn't have any of the stuff all his friends' parents had: no microwave, no computer, not even a CD player. Instead they listened to these scratchy old records. Dad used to play in a rock band when he was young, and sometimes after dinner he played along with the records on his trumpet. That's when Jim and Pete had to run upstairs and close the door to their room and blast their CD player.

"I think Nana is going to come up tomorrow," said Mom. "Just for the day. It's supposed to be beautiful, and I think she needs a day out of the city."

"Again?" said Jim. "She was here last Sunday."

"So?" said Dad. "She's your grandmother, and she enjoys seeing you guys."

"Yeah, Jim, whatsa matter with you?" said Pete. "You don't like Nana or something?"

"Anyway," said Mom, "I have to call her right after dinner."

"Mom, do you think I could use the phone first, just for a couple of minutes? I have to call Nick back so I know what we're doing tonight," said Pete.

"As long as you keep it short," said Mom.

"Wait, Mom, you and Nana can't blab away tonight," said Jim. "I'm expecting a call about basketball."

"If they get a busy signal, they'll call back, honey, don't worry," said Mom. "More pasta?"

"Why can't we have call waiting like Josh's family?" said Jim.

"I've only been suggesting it for about four months now!" said Pete. "Dad, whaddya think?"

But Dad was humming along to the music, his head nodding in time to the beat. "Wait, listen to this riff," he said, pointing to the ceiling. A solo saxophone filled the room. "That's gorgeous," Dad said with a smile. "Now, what did you say, Pete?"

Just then the phone rang again. "Mom, I'm done," said Jim. "Please can I get it? It might be for me!"

"No! Dad's still eating," said Mom.

Beep. "Pete, hi, it's Amy. Are you going to Fletcher's tonight? Can you guys pick me up on the way? Puleeeze! Thanks. I love you! Call me."

"I *love* you, Pete, mmm, smoochie smoochie," said Jim, making kissing noises.

"Oh, shut up, you little excuse for a brother," said Pete.

"Can I be excused?" said Jim. "I'll load, you scrape," he said to Pete.

Mom shook her head. Sometimes Jim knew they had just worn her out. "Okay, okay, you're both excused." Mom and Dad liked to sit at the table by themselves, talking and laughing.

In the kitchen Pete threw scraps to Jake, who barely moved to eat them.

"Don't give him so much. You'll make him sick," said Jim.

"He's getting so old and fat," said Pete. "What's a few more scraps of chicken? Before he dies, I want to give him a real steak dinner with a potato and everything."

"Don't talk about him dying," said Jim. He couldn't even imagine not being greeted by Jake's snores every morning. Or seeing him lumbering up the driveway to meet the school bus.

Ring. "I'll get it!" Jim and Pete called in unison. Pete reached for the phone, but Jim pulled a spin move, got around him, and picked up the receiver.

"Hello."

"Jimmy, is that you? How are you, my darling?" It was Nana's deep, gravelly voice. Oh, no, thought Jim. Now I'll be on with her for an hour!

"Hi, Nana, do you want to talk to Mom?"

"In a minute, Jimmy," said Nana. "First I want to talk to you. Tell me what's new, how's school?"

Jim heaved a sigh. Pete was watching him and laughing silently. "Oh, I don't know, I got an eighty-five on my math test and—um, let's see, I'm captain of my volleyball team in gym."

"Very good. Will I see you tomorrow? I'm coming on the train. I'll bring you a surprise." Nana always brought shopping bags full of stuff, things she bought from vendors on the street, like Velcro wallets and sports hats, cakes and cookies from the bakery on her corner, bags of candy she bought on sale at the discount drugstore.

"Okay. Do you wanna talk to Mom?" said Jim, looking at the clock on the stove. Seven-fifteen. Mr. Mondini should be calling any minute. *"Mom! It's Nana! Hurry up!"*

Mom and Nana always talked on the phone for an hour. Actually, Mom didn't say very much. She mostly said, "Really?" or "No kidding," or "That's great, Mama!" Nana did most of the talking.

Pete had left all the scraped dishes in the sink. Jim finished loading the dishwasher. Then he stood there and stared at Mom, who was still yakking away with Nana. Jim pointed at the clock. Mom nodded back at him. He held up a copy of the sports section from the newspaper and pointed at a picture of a New York Knick going up for a slam dunk. Mom just smiled and nodded again. "Listen, Mama," she said, "Jim's expecting a call from his basketball coach. . . ." He's not my coach yet, Jim thought. "So okay, okay, that's good. Yes, I know this is the House of Sports. I'll see you at eleven tomorrow. Good night, Mama. I love you, too."

"Why does Nana always call this the House of Sports?" said Jim.

"Oh, she thinks you guys spend too much time with sports and not enough time going to museums. But she did wish you good luck!"

Ring. Jim answered it.

"Hi. Can I talk to Jim Malone, please?"

"This is Jim."

"Hi, Jim, this is Mr. O'Malley, one of the travel team coaches. How are you?"

"Fine," said Jim. Come on, come on, get to the point.

"Good!" said Mr. O'Malley. Then he stopped to clear his throat.

Yes or no? That's all I want to know.

"Well, Mr. Mondini and I were very impressed with your basketball ability today."

Another pause. Jim wondered, Am I supposed to say something? "Uh, thanks," he mumbled.

"And we'd like to know if you can come back tomorrow for the final tryout?"

"Why, sure, yeah," said Jim. He gave Mom the thumbs-up sign.

"Okay, it will be at two o'clock at the Pigeon Hill gym. We'll see you there."

"Great," said Jim. "Bye."

"Congratulations!" yelled Mom, wrapping Jim in a hug. He could feel the wooden beads on her necklace pressing into his cheek. He could smell that musk perfume she always wore. Then he felt Dad come around to hug him from the other side so that he was now like a piece of salami in a fat roll.

"Hey, I didn't make the team yet," Jim struggled to say over their arms. They were crazy sometimes. Luckily none of his friends was witnessing this craziness. Luckily Pete was in the shower.

Then suddenly, without warning, Jake hoisted himself up from his bed and let out a delighted yelp.

Nana was always the last person to appear coming down the stairs at the station. Mom and Jim sat in their car watching the arriving passengers: college kids with backpacks, young couples with bouquets of flowers, older people in long, dark coats.

"Why is she always the last one?" asked Jim. He looked at the car clock: 11:08. He wanted to get home. The final tryout was in less than three hours.

"There she is!" said Mom. Nana had appeared at the top of the stairs and stopped.

"Why is she just standing there?" said Jim. "Come on, Nana, let's go!"

"Honey, she's eighty-two years old. I think she's entitled to rest on the stairs. Why don't you run up there and help her with those shopping bags."

"But, Mom—"

"Go on," said Mom in her no-nonsense voice, the one she rarely used.

So Jim got out of the car and sprinted up the stairs to Nana. She was wearing her long fur coat and wool beret. Jim always thought she looked like a little bear in this coat. "Jimmy. Jimmy!" she called out. Why was she so embarrassing? Jim wondered. Why is she yelling? Does she think I'm going to miss her?

"Hi, Nana," said Jim. "Let me take your bags."

"Hello, my Jimmy," Nana said, grabbing him for a hug and hitting him with one of the bags at the same time. Nana always wore a lot of makeup, and after she kissed his cheek, Jim automatically rubbed it with the sleeve of his jacket.

"Oh, getting rid of my kiss? I see. I will not forget that!" said Nana, her German accent bending the *w* to a *v*. She laughed her husky, deep-chested laugh.

They continued down the steps, Nana pausing every fourth or fifth one.

"What a beautiful day!" said Nana, looking out over the parking lot. She took a couple of quick breaths as if she had just run a mile.

Why was Nana always so slow? Ever since her heart attack two years ago, she never seemed to have enough air to breathe except when she was sitting. Jim took three more steps and halted.

"What's the hurry, Jimmy? Where's the fire?" said Nana as she navigated the next few steps.

Jim bit the inside of his lip, trying not to say anything fresh. Lately, when he became impatient, words just popped out of his mouth from somewhere deep in his throat before he could censor them. Dad had already punished him for calling Pete an asshole. It didn't matter that Pete had been needling him and chanting "loser" over and over in that Jim Carrey voice during a particularly ferocious video game. All Dad had heard as he passed the family room was Jim's raging reply.

That was the trouble with parents, Jim thought. They came in at the end of a fight and automatically blamed the first person they saw. And if they blamed you enough times in a row, then they started to have this preconceived idea that you were always the one who was causing the fight. Pete was such a goody-goody, with his perfect grades and his neat desk. His teachers loved him, said he was so polite, "a pleasure to have in class." Only one teacher had ever written that about Jim. Mostly they said things like "Tries hard but finds the subject difficult" and "Needs improvement."

When they finally reached the last step, Nana had a faint mustache of sweat over her upper lip. She smiled as though she was very proud of herself.

Mom was standing there. "Mama, why don't you just take the elevator?" she said as she bent down to hug Nana.

"Why, you think I'm an old lady?" said Nana indignantly. "Dr. Mazer says I need exercise every day!"

"I know, I know," said Mom in the voice she only used with Nana. It was a soothing voice but with an edge of sarcasm. Nana and Mom sometimes seemed to be on the verge of an argument, but Mom usually backed down.

"Here you go, Mama. Can you get in the car all right? Is the seat too far back?"

"I'm okay. Stop fussing over me," said Nana.

Mom shrugged and said nothing.

"So what's going on today in the House of Sports?" asked Nana as they pulled out of the parking lot.

"I have a basketball tryout," Jim said.

"What was that?" said Nana, twisting awkwardly around in her seat.

"Jim's trying out for the traveling basketball team, Mama," said Mom.

"Always sports, always more sports," said Nana. "What about music? A concert wouldn't hurt, would it? An opera, maybe? A museum once in a while? You come stay with me, Jimmy! We'll have some fun. Enough with the sports already."

"Okay, Nana," said Jim as he stared out the window. Nana didn't understand that sports were the only thing he was any good at. He hated sitting still. Reading bored him. How could Nana understand? She was from another planet really, coming from Germany with her funny accent, her fancy teacups and porcelain, the lace doilies on her tables, the big console record player in the middle of her living room where she listened to opera. Jim loved his grandmother, but she was so old. And even though she claimed she had been a swimming champion in Germany before the big war, Jim never really believed her.

After lunch Nana sat on the couch staring at the basketball game running across the television screen. Dad was sitting next to her.

"Can we get anything else on this TV?" Nana asked. "Or does it only show sports?"

"Nana, this is an awesome game," said Jim. It was the biggest rivalry in the ACC, Duke versus North Carolina, the best game in the best college conference.

"Only three minutes left," said Pete. "Here we go . . . nice foul! Come on, you know he's their best foul shooter! Show some self-control out there!"

"Who are you talking to?" asked Nana. "They can't hear you, Peter. This is a crazy family. *Ganz verrückt!*" She closed her eyes and rested her head on Dad's shoulder.

Mom came in and pointed to her watch. "Ready, Jim?" she asked.

Jim stood up and watched one more play. The point guard for Duke brought the ball down the court, pushing hard to his left, then faked a pass, spun around, and drove to the basket. The ball went in, and he was fouled. "Awesome move," said Jim.

"Yeah, can you do that one, Jim? Huh?" said Pete.

"Let's see you even make one simple layup," Jim shot back.

"Okay, fellas, that's enough," said Dad.

"House of Sports . . ." murmured Nana without opening her eyes.

"Let's go, Jim," said Mom.

Mom didn't say a word the whole way over to Pigeon Hill. She hummed softly along with an old bluesy song that was playing on the radio, a song Jim had recently heard over a car commercial on TV. Actually, Jim was happy Mom was taking him. She wouldn't give him any advice or strategy for the tryout. She wouldn't come in with him the way Dad would and watch the first five minutes. Mom would merely pull up to the curb by the front entrance, pat his shoulder, and wish him a simple "Good luck, kiddo."

As he walked through the empty lobby of the school, Jim could hear the insistent squeak of sneakers and echoing thuds of many basketballs. Mr. Mondini was standing by the door to the gym.

"Hey, Jim, right?" he said.

"Yeah, Jim Malone."

"Here, sign in, then join the guys on the court," said Mr. Mondini. He wasn't smiling, but his half-moon eyes made him look sort of merry. "Get yourself warmed up."

Jim saw three groups of boys under three different baskets. Maybe he was late? Josh, wearing a Notre Dame T-shirt, waved him over to the group on the far side of the gym. There was Matt slinking around the outside of the crowd, Corey with his goggles strapped over half his face, Danny, and Frankie, rising above them all like the water tower behind the high school. As he jogged over to join them, Jim noticed another player he had never seen before, some fruit with a black pony- tail, but when the guy turned around, Jim realized it was a girl.

He stopped and muttered, "What the . . ." as Josh tossed him a hard, high pass that Jim missed because he jumped a second too late.

"Hey, Josh, I wasn't ready!" said Jim.

"You gotta always be ready in this game, Jim," said Josh with a snort. "What are you staring at?"

"Who's she?" asked Jim as he watched Ponytail make a smooth three-pointer.

"Mondini's daughter. I don't know what she's doing here—"

"Are we here to play ball or catch up on some gossip?" came Mr. Mondini's booming voice from the doorway.

Jim took off straight for the basket and leaped to make the next rebound. Focus. Focus. That's what Dad always told him. Do what you're there to do. Block out everything else. Focus. Jim dribbled, looking to pass the ball. Suddenly there was Ponytail clapping her hands over her head, calling, "Here, here. I'm open!" He hesitated. Should he pass to her? What is she doing here at a boys' tryout? Why doesn't she go shoot arrows at a target or swim a few laps? And as these thoughts passed through Jim's mind, Danny stripped the ball right from under his nose and made a layup.

Ponytail was glaring at him, her dark eyes flashing angrily. "What's wrong with you? Why didn't you pass me the ball? I had an open shot!"

Jim felt his face grow warm and the words "What do you know about basketball? You're just a friggin' girl!" rising to his mouth. A part of his brain was screaming, No, don't do it. She's the coach's daughter! but it was too late, the words were already spilling out.

"Okay, big shot. We'll see who makes this team," she said, and slowly turned away.

"Everyone in," called Mr. O'Malley. When they all had gathered around the two coaches, Jim thought, There have got to be more than twenty kids here! He stood next to Frankie and felt small, smaller than ever, as though he were growing down into the floor. All these kids except for Josh looked huge. They had muscles you could see. He felt a stinging sensation and then realized that Ponytail was staring at him, her eyes in squinty half-moons exactly like her father's.

"—hustle and skill. Speed helps, but if you don't show desire out there, I can tell you right now you're not going to be picked for this team." Mr. Mondini was talking in this sharp, no-nonsense tone, pausing to glance at his clipboard after each sentence. "Okay, we're going to run a few drills, and then we'll be scrimmaging," he said.

"Good luck," said Mr. O'Malley.

They started with easy drills that everyone could do, simple ball passes, bounce passes, then moved it up to passes with layups. They did dribbling drills and two players versus one. Mr. Mondini blew his whistle and told everyone to take a break and get a drink. Jim sat down on the floor with his back against the cool cinder-block wall. Josh crouched down next to him and took a long guzzle of water. "When we scrimmage, you've gotta skin Damian."

"Who's Damian?" Jim asked.

"That dork with the Webber jersey. He's the only other point guard–type player out here besides you and me," said Josh. "Just remember, he can't go left at all. Make him shoot from the outside, and it becomes a fifty-fifty ball right there. Oh, here comes Mondini . . ."

"Okay, we're going to have four teams, the reds, yellows, regular T-shirts, and skins. Here we go," announced Mr. Mondini. Mr. O'Malley stood next to him, smiling his catlike grin, arms folded across the chest of his T-shirt, which Jim just noticed was a tie-dye Grateful Dead shirt. Like something Pete would wear. What was the deal with these two anyway? Jim wondered. Mondini, the evil twin, in his black nylon warm-up suit, his squinty black eyes, and O'Malley, just a big kid.

"—and Malone," Mr. Mondini read off the last team.

Great. Skins. Just what Jim wanted, to have to peel off his shirt and let everyone see how bony he really was! He looked to see who his teammates were. A bunch of losers! This was a bad sign. Jim tried very hard to control his natural superstition. When a day was going badly, he felt there was some force of darkness behind it. Dad told him that was ridiculous, and Mom told him it might be true but you had to work against it. Only Nana seemed to know what he meant. Nana believed in witches. She thought she was one herself. She once told Jim a story about an American soldier giving her a ride after the liberation, when she was still weak from her time in hiding from the Nazis. He had tried to get fresh with her, and when she pushed him away, he had become fiercely angry, calling her names, telling her to get out of his jeep. She wished him bad luck as he finally drove off. The next day she heard he had been injured in a jeep accident on the outskirts of the city. "Other places, other people, the same thing happened. I don't know why, but it happens." Now Jim thought about Mondini's daughter in alarm. Could she be a witch? His insult might have turned all her evil energies against him.

The Skins were up first against the Yellows. The Yellow team had Ponytail and Josh. Josh was the man Jim had to beat. He could handle him because he knew all his moves. Ponytail was good: Her passes were clean and precise; she moved a lot and was hard to guard. The Skin who had her was a round, lumbering kid who never put his arms up. His belly hung over the top of his shorts. Ponytail and Josh played as if they knew each other and cut through the Skins like rabbits. When Jim cornered Josh, Josh leaned into him, and Mr. O'Malley blew his whistle for a foul on Jim.

"You've gotta be kidding!" said Jim under his breath.

"Aw, quit whining!" said Ponytail as she moved past him.

That did it. Jim was taking matters into his own hands. He left Josh and slid sideways, keeping his arms up as a wall between Ponytail and the basket. Just try to shoot over me, he thought, go ahead, I own you. Ponytail jumped and shot over Jim's hands, but the ball went whizzing past the basket and barely touched the backboard. Skins' ball. Jim told the fat kid to stay with Josh. He took on Ponytail for the rest of the five-minute scrimmage, tying her up, stealing a couple of balls, and using that spin move he'd been perfecting to get by her. She hung tough, and Jim forgot she was a girl or Mondini's daughter and just went into his playing zone, that place where he was focused only on the ball and the game.

Mr. O'Malley blew his whistle. "Okay, you guys, get a drink. Next two teams . . ."

As they walked off the court, Ponytail sidled up next to Jim. "You're pretty good for a boy," she said.

Jim looked at her. Her face was pink all over, sweat was running down the sides of her cheeks like sideburns, and a few strands of black hair had escaped from her ponytail, curling out like antennae. But she was smiling, and her teeth were white, and her eyes were suggesting a truce.

"My name is Lisa," she said, offering him a handshake.

J IM DIDN'T WANT to talk to anyone after the tryout. Dad was standing there by the door with his arms behind his back next to a couple of other fathers.

"Come on, let's go," said Jim as he brushed past Dad.

"Slow down there, guy, what's the hurry?" said Dad.

"I just want to get out of here." Jim's head was spinning. He didn't like the feeling he had in the pit of his stomach, a churning, uneasy feeling. Mr. Mondini had said he would call tonight. He had looked around at the players, but not once had he looked directly at Jim. The scrimmages had gone okay, but Jim's best playing had definitely been against Mondini's daughter. Maybe Mondini hated to see his daughter beaten? Jim only knew that Mondini's squinty eyes had avoided him. Jim was not in the mood for telling Dad every detail.

When they got to the car, Jim realized someone was already sitting in the front passenger seat. Nana!

"How was it, Jimmy?" she asked immediately as he slid into the backseat.

"Okay."

"Who was that girl?" asked Dad.

"Mr. Mondini's daughter."

"Is she trying out?"

"Yeah."

"How is she?"

"Okay."

"Just 'okay'?"

"Listen, Dad, I don't feel like talking right now," said Jim.

"A girl trying out for a boys' team!" said Nana. "Whoever heard of such a thing? Only in America."

"She's probably better than some of the boys," said Dad. "She looks like she can handle the ball. What do you think, Jim?"

"She's okay."

"Not as good as our Jimmy, though," said Nana. "You are going to make this team, darling, I know it. I feel it. *Nicht zu* worry. Just listen to your nana."

Why did Nana talk like that? Sometimes it was a forecast of disappointment like the time she had told Pete he wouldn't get Tracy Goble to go to the junior prom with him and sometimes it was a prediction of success like now, but the weird part was how often she was right. Jim could barely see Nana sitting ahead of him, so small and hunched. Without looking back, she held up her left hand and turned it toward Jim. It was a large hand for such a shriveled old person, with brown spots and purple veins and a fleshy palm. Jim knew she wanted him to put his hand in hers. He remembered all the times she had held his hand when he was tiny, a firm, bossy grasp to keep him from running off. He remembered all the clapping games she had played with him and Pete while she sang German nursery rhymes in her deep off-key voice. But now he looked at her hand in disgust. He didn't want to touch it. He was too big to hold hands with his grandmother.

"Jimmy, where are you?" she asked. Jim gently laid his left hand in hers and felt her familiar firm grasp. "You remember to listen to your old nana. I only speak the truth. I know a lot."

Jim thought, You know a lot, Nana, about running away from Nazis and being a mother, and you know about operas and classical music, but you don't know anything about sports. But he only said, "I know, I know."

They passed the turnoff for their road and headed straight down Route 56.

"Dad, you missed our road," said Jim.

"We're taking Nana to the station," said Dad.

"Can't you drop me off?" Another twenty minutes in this confined space with Dad and Nana and their annoying questions. Jim looked out at the darkening world. The lights were coming on in windows, and people were moving around their family rooms and kitchens.

"When I was young, I lived in a big apartment building in Leipzig," said Nana. "And my bedroom window looked out on a courtyard. I could watch all these windows, and I loved to guess what was happening in each apartment. Then one day I realized there was a young man who always looked back at me from his window. He would stand there buttoning up his military jacket and grin at me. He put on his cap and black belt. I could see his Nazi insignia on his arm. He had a little girl he would scoop up in his arms, and then they would wave back to me. My mother came in one day and saw this. Oh, how furious she became! She closed the big, heavy wooden shutters and warned me not to stand by the window. What did I know? I was just a kid. It was a game to me."

That's exactly what Jim meant about Nana. She had all these old stories about herself before the war and during the war, but she didn't understand anything about Jim's world, about sports, or about being a boy for that matter. She didn't have a clue about how it felt to go streaking down the court with the ball bouncing alongside you close and tight or the way you felt when your feet lifted off the floor and you were in the air, just you, the ball, the basket. Nana could not possibly imagine the disappointment of losing a close game in the final seconds, the replays of what you could have done or should have done, the flashing anger running up and down your legs as you stood there listening to the final buzzer. Mom always said, "Listen to your nana. She is very wise and smart. There is so much she will teach you," but Jim didn't get it.

"I will come for your first game, Jimmy, okay?" Nana said. "But before that, your mother and I decided next weekend you will come to see me in the city."

"What?" said Jim.

Dad shot Jim an icy glance in the rearview mirror. Dad's eyebrows were close together over his blue eyes. The message was clear.

"We'll do something fun, just the two of us. Maybe go for a ride in the park in one of those carriages, or go to an opera, eat in a restaurant. Finally your mother is letting you come to stay with me. I can show you off, my handsome grandson!" Nana said.

"Great," said Jim, not meaning it. When did you get old enough for your parents to stop making plans for you without asking? Who wanted to spend his weekend with his grandmother in a stuffy old apartment, riding around in a buggy, and going to listen to fat women with big bosoms singing in foreign languages? What were they thinking when they made these plans? And what about Pete?

"Is Pete coming, too?" Jim asked.

"No," said Nana. "He has his to finish his last college application."

Nana and Dad started talking about Pete and how great he was doing in school and how smart he was and what colleges he might get into, so Jim stopped listening and tried to imagine the phone call from Mr. Mondini. "Yes, Jim, we want to offer you a place on the travel team . . . but we can't because you were rude and obnoxious to my daughter, and anyway, you missed that easy layup during the scrimmage with the red team, so keep practicing and maybe next year." Then Jim saw the kids at school all saying, "Too bad about not making the team," and he wondered what he would do on Saturdays while all his friends were off at tournaments and he was just home watching the Knicks on TV.

"Aren't you going to get out and say good-bye to Nana?" The car door was open, and Dad was standing there. Jim was startled because he had lost all sense of where he was.

He pulled himself out of the backseat, unfolding like a measuring stick. Standing beside Nana, he felt tall. Jim remembered all the times he had stood on his toes to reach Nana's soft perfumed cheek to kiss her after he had opened a birthday gift from her.

"Good-bye, Jimmy," said Nana as she planted a kiss on his cheek. "Be good. Help your mother!"

"Sure, Nana," said Jim, patting her small, rounded back.

"See you on Saturday!" And off she went up the stairs with small, unsteady steps, one after another without a pause.

"Nana, what are you doing? Take the elevator!" called Dad.

"The elevator is for old people," Nana said without turning back.

"Run up there with her, Jim, until she reaches the top," said Dad.

The last thing Jim wanted to do was run up those stairs, but he sprinted up two at a time until he was alongside Nana. She was huffing and puffing and concentrating so hard she didn't even notice him beside her.

"Nana, slow down," said Jim, cupping her elbow in his hand.

Nana flashed him an angry look. "Why are they always so worried about me, like I'm about to drop dead?" she said. "Your mother and father are both the same. They act like I'm such an invalid." She spoke without looking at Jim but then stopped five steps from the top, catching her breath. "Don't tell them, but last week a couple of hoodlums tried to grab my shopping bag when I was going into the subway, and I just hit them over the head with the bag and they ran off. Don't tell your parents. That's all I need! They'll make me come live near you in some old-age home . . . and don't tell your mother that I was going to the subway. She'll have a fit!"

Jim started to laugh. "Nana, you sound like me and Pete!"

"Yes, we have a lot in common, so much you don't even know, my sweetheart. Okay, now go back down with your father. You shouldn't be running around here in the dark," Nana said. "See you Saturday!"

"LET'S GO, I'M going to be late," said Jim.

"Yeah, yeah, yeah," said Pete, his mouth crammed with Eggo waffles.

"Mom!" implored Jim.

"Pete!" said Mom sharply. "Don't talk with your mouth full!" She was looking at some slides with this black, boxy viewer.

On Mondays Pete got to drive Mom's beat-up Dodge Polara to school. He didn't understand why he couldn't just use the car every day. After all, Mom stayed home to work, and she had her bicycle if she really needed to get to town, but she said nothing doing. Mom had no intention of getting stranded at home. Only on Mondays did she let Pete use it, and on the way he dropped Jim off at the middle school.

"If I could drive, I'd leave you here and you'd walk to school," Jim said.

"But you can't, and so I guess you will have to wait, little bro," said Pete, scraping the last bit of syrup from his plate.

The telephone started ringing. Pete said, "Oh, I better answer this. It could be Stacy or Tricia. . . . Hello? Oh, yeah, he's here. . . ." Pete tossed the receiver to Jim, shrugging as if to say he didn't know who it was, nor did he care.

Jim had not told anyone that Mr. Mondini was supposed to call Sunday night. He had stayed up until ten o'clock and then decided to call Josh and see if he'd heard anything. The phone rang and rang, which meant someone at Josh's house was talking and ignoring the call waiting. Then Jim went to bed. He hadn't slept well.

"Jim, I'm glad I caught you," came Mr. Mondini's voice over the phone. "I was looking at my list this morning and realized I forgot to call you last night, and I didn't want you seeing everyone in school before I got to you."

This sounded like bad news. Jim turned away from the inquiring eyes of Mom and Pete. He stared at the calendar on the wall. It was some museum calendar Mom had bought for the new year. January's picture showed a circus scene, a white horse racing around the ring with a woman in yellow standing on his bare back on one toe. An acrobat did a flip in the background. He hung smiling in midair, on the verge of landing gracefully or collapsing in a heap.

"Are you there, Jim?" asked Mr. Mondini.

"Oh, yeah, yeah, I'm here," said Jim.

"Mr. O'Malley and I talked long and hard about you, Jim. We were a little undecided about taking you on the team. We both felt you ran hot and cold at the tryout. What do you think?"

What the heck does it matter what I think? thought Jim. "I dunno."

"But we've decided to give you a chance, Jim, because we both think you have potential. With some hard work you could become a very fine point guard."

Jim had the oddest feeling. Happy and relieved but also angry and resentful. Potential? What about all the other guys? Were they so much better? What about Mondini's squinty-eyed daughter?

"Don't you want to say anything, Jim?" asked Mr. Mondini.

"Uh, yeah, thanks a lot," said Jim finally.

"Our first practice is Wednesday night at Pigeon Hill, and we'll be scrimmaging Saturday there, too. Is your mother around? Can I talk to her?"

Jim turned to see Mom and Pete both staring at him with concerned looks. He handed Mom the phone, picked up his book bag, and walked out the back door.

Josh was waiting for him by his locker. "Did you hear about Kenny? He *made* the team. Do you believe that? What a joke!"

"Did you make it?" asked Jim.

"Of course I made it," said Josh. "You did, too."

"How do you know I made it?"

"I spoke to Lisa last night. She called me," Josh said a little too casually.

"Lisa Mondini?" said Jim incredulously. "She called you?"

"Well, yeah," said Josh with sudden embarrassment. Josh always said things without thinking. It was as if he had to say whatever popped into his head. Sometimes it drove Jim crazy, especially when he did things like tell Jim's parents about riding their bikes down Pigeon Hill without their helmets or about the hunting knife they had found in the woods. Sometimes Josh was just clueless.

"So why didn't you call me?" asked Jim.

Josh looked at his fingernails with great concentration. Finally he said, "By the time I got off the phone with her, it was almost eleven."

Eleven? What could they possibly have been yakking about? They hardly knew each other!

"Why did she call you?" Jim felt as if an icy breeze were blowing between them.

"I don't know," said Josh. "She wanted to talk about the team, who could play what position, about tournaments her dad is thinking about, you know, stuff like that."

"So what about *her*?" Jim asked, slamming his locker door a bit too hard.

"What about her?"

"Is she on the team or not?" demanded Jim.

"Yeah, she's on the team. Of course she's on the team. I mean, how could she not make the team?"

Of course she was on the team, Jim thought. It didn't matter how she had done in the tryout; she was going to be the only girl on a boys' basketball team because of her father. The whole season would be like that. She would always start, always be in during clutch moments, probably be a minicoach on the floor. Why did he feel so uneasy about this whole thing when just Saturday he had been obsessed with playing on the travel team? And what was the deal with Josh? Josh and Lisa? No girl had ever called Jim for anything.

He knew he was too scrawny and small to be of any interest to the girls. They were all swooning over Bobby Triazy and Gary Banks with their hairy legs and football muscles. Jim could see Lisa passing the ball to Josh in the scrimmage, how they slapped fives after every basket as Josh yelled, "Sweet!" Jim felt the utter chill of being left out by his best friend.

The first bell rang.

"Hey, I'll see you at lunch!" said Josh, and they walked down the hall in opposite directions.

For Jim, school was a chore. Actually he'd rather be doing chores at home than sit at a desk all day listening to boring teachers, trying to pay attention, writing his notes, praying not to be called on. When he heard his name, Jim knew his ears would grow red, his cheeks would start to burn, his palms would turn sweaty. Words would come tumbling out in a monotone until the teacher asked him to speak up, and he could feel all eyes on him. Something the teacher had just been talking about, like the way a prism broke light into its rainbow of colors or how the Confederates had stormed a certain city, something that had been totally clear in his mind a minute before would suddenly dissolve into a puddle of words. Jim never felt this way when he played basketball, no matter how many people were watching from the sidelines. But in school he felt so dumb, so slow, and so embarrassed.

What made matters worse was having a brother like Pete. He glided through school, year after year, bringing home the same report cards with a column of straight As except for his usual B in phys ed. Every now and then a teacher would recognize Jim's last name and ask if Pete was his brother. Oh, Pete Malone, he was quite a student! So hardworking, so curious, so well mannered. Yeah, but he never got an A in gym, Jim wanted to say. In September these teachers would look at Jim with great warmth, but as the year went on and they saw how he missed easy questions on quizzes and daydreamed in class and stammered when called on, the warmth would turn to tolerance and then to pity or, worse, to disdain.

Jim slid into his seat behind Mariah Jones. She was the smartest girl in the class. Every day she appeared with her hair tightly woven into a noisy mass of beaded braids. She sat very primly with her shoulders back and her head high. Mariah was a good shield for someone like Jim who did not want to be called on. First period was English with Ms. Durbin, a new teacher in the school. She was right out of college and looked like a teenager. She seemed to like the girls better than the boys. Well, why not? The girls would prance in and say things like "Oh, Ms. Durbin, that's a really cool necklace you're wearing," or "What a beautiful sweater, Ms. Durbin. I love it!" Such brownnoses.

Frankie was also in this class. He sat across the aisle from Jim. He gave Jim a thumbs-up sign. "Josh told me you made it," he said.

Ms. Durbin came sashaying in just as the second bell rang, an enormous brown leather briefcase hanging from her shoulder. She slung it with some effort onto her desk, put down her thermos, and let out a loud sigh. "Good morning, class. Let's get right down to business!" Business was always the same thing, a sentence to diagram. She scrawled the words in white chalk, speaking them as she wrote. Today's sentence was: "When it stopped raining, I played basketball with my brother."

Rare, thought Jim. A sentence about sports. He set to work copying the words in his notebook. He wrote the whole thing in capital letters. Jim was using a mechanical pencil he had found in the kitchen. He loved the way the lead was always so sharp, how each of his lines dug into the paper. He had just placed the period at the end of the sentence when he heard Ms. Durbin call his name.

"Jim, why don't you start us off? The subject, please."

Jim knew his ears were getting red. His mouth felt dry. The words on his page seemed to swim over and under the blue lines. The subject? Okay, he tried to concentrate, but the longer it took, the more kids seemed to be twisting around in their seats to look at him.

"Jim."

Was it *it* or was it *I*? Why had he written this all in capital letters? It would be so much more obvious in regular writing. "It?" he finally blurted out.

Mariah snickered and turned back to the teacher. She raised her hand, throwing it up like a victory flag. Her beads clacked triumphantly as she proclaimed the correct answer: "I."

Big deal, thought Jim. When will I ever have to do this in real life? Mariah, you couldn't run or jump your way out of a paper bag. All you know how to do is read books and give your smart-ass answers. I bet you've got little computer chips in all those beads that feed you the answers.

Jim drew a circle on the page below the sentence. He drew a face in the circle and added two big jug ears. Then he began drawing spokes of hair radiating from the head. He made tiny dark circles all along the spokes. This pencil was great. He could get really vivid blacks and grays. When he looked up, Ms. Durbin was erasing the sentence from the board. Jim realized he did not have the sentence diagrammed at all. He had missed the whole thing.

"Okay, you can close your notebooks," said Ms. Durbin, clapping the chalk dust from her hands. "I hope you all did your reading assignment this weekend because we are going to have a discussion now."

Reading assignment! Jim felt the panic in his legs first. He had forgotten all about the reading assignment. How could he have done it anyway? He had been too busy with the tryouts. That was what he would tell her if she called on him.

"Who wants to give us a synopsis of what has happened so far? Frankie?" said Ms. Durbin.

"Well, the sea captain just arrived on this island, and he checked into this tavern-inn kind of place with his trunk, which is very heavy and mysterious. Everyone wants to know what's in it."

How did Frankie get time to read? Well, there goes that excuse, thought Jim.

"Good," said Ms. Durbin. "What has the author done so well in this first chapter?" She whirled her body to the other side of the room. "Sean?"

Sean was a bony kid with skin the color of honey. He had wide, flat eyes that looked almost sleepy. He had tried out for the travel team, but Jim was sure he hadn't made it. "Foreshadowing," Sean answered without looking up.

"Excellent, Sean," said Ms. Durbin. "The author plants the seeds of what may happen next and makes the reader want to do what? Mariah?"

"Makes the reader want to read on!" said Mariah in this bright, happy voice like someone trying to sell cars on television. "In fact, Ms. Durbin, I couldn't put the book down. I read the next two chapters!"

Jim wanted to puke. Why doesn't Mariah just skip seventh grade altogether and leave us alone? He was holding the mechanical pencil in his hand, shooting the lead out longer and longer. He wanted to draw on something. He wanted to get up and stretch his legs. Jim felt his foot tapping on the floor, the way it did sometimes during dinner when it drove Mom crazy. Mariah shot him a dirty look. Jim checked the clock. He watched the second hand and tapped his foot in time to its jerky sweep. Three seconds seemed so long this way, but he thought about how easy it was to get caught in the paint for that three-second violation in basketball. He counted out twenty-four seconds, the time the shot clock gave you to get a shot off in the NBA. Whoa, that seemed like plenty of time here in this boring English class. He heard the discussion droning on around him. He heard the roar of a crowd in the stands during the last minute of a close game. Jim heard the announcer: "Malone brings the ball down the court. He's pacing it, trying to use all the time so the other team doesn't get the ball again this quarter. Now he's passing it to Gross on his right, and it's Gross to Bellini, who doesn't have a good shot, he's double-teamed over there, oh, no, but wait, there goes Malone, no one's with him, he's cutting to the basket, takes the short pass from Bellini, goes up left-handed, off the glass. It's goooood. . . ." *Rrrring.* The bell went off, and the class was over.

Jim pushed his notebook and pencil into his backpack and started to leave. As he was rounding the first desk in his row, he heard Ms. Durbin's voice behind him. "Jim. Jim Malone, could I talk to you for a minute before you go?"

Jim thought about pretending he hadn't heard her, but Mariah turned to him and said, in her talk show host voice, *"Jim, Ms. Durbin wants to see you!"*

Ms. Durbin was looking at a piece of paper in her hand. Even from a distance Jim could tell it was one of his assignments, just by the way the paper was all crinkly. Ms. Durbin glanced up at Jim and then looked past him at the kids who were leaving. Maybe she hadn't really called his name? Maybe she wanted to speak to someone else? But as soon as the last person disappeared into the hallway, Ms. Durbin turned her piercing eyes on Jim. She held out the paper for Jim to see. There, in traffic-light red, was a gigantic F.

"This essay you handed in was unacceptable, Jim," Ms. Durbin said in a parched, thin voice. She cleared her throat. She looked almost embarrassed to be showing Jim this piece of paper. He wanted to comfort her, to say, Look, it's okay. You're not the first teacher who ever gave me an F. I can take it. I'll hide it under my bed just like the others. By the end of the marking quarter Jim would always manage to bring his grades up to at least a C–. That way Mom and Dad never found out about the Fs.

"But I am willing to give you another chance," Ms Durbin said in a stronger voice. "You can write a new essay. I'll even let you choose something else to write about. But it has to be a work of art, a book, a painting, a film, a poem—"

"So I guess basketball is out?" said Jim.

"Jim, I let you write about basketball last time. And you did an excellent job. You made it exciting for the reader. That's one of the reasons I want to give you another chance on this. I know you *can* write if you want to."

"No, I can't write, Ms. Durbin. I hate to write. I know Pete is an awesome writer and won that junior book award last year, but I'm really kind of dumber than he is, even though we're brothers—"

"Who's Pete?" Ms. Durbin interrupted.

Suddenly Jim realized that Ms. Durbin didn't know Pete. She was a brand-new teacher. Pete had never been in her class.

"It doesn't matter," said Jim, feeling his ears get warm. "Pete's just my brother. No big deal." Jim reached out to take the essay, but Ms. Durbin snapped it back down to her desk.

"I'm going to hold on to this until you write a new one because if you don't do it, this will have to stand as your grade. It's your choice."

A girl with a big moon face and a pair of sunglasses stuck on top of her head walked into the classroom and cheerily sang out, "Hi, Ms. Durbin. I like your sweater!"

Jim turned to leave.

"Monday, Jim. Monday!" Ms. Durbin called over his shoulder. "You have to hand it in next Monday to get credit."

$\mathbf{J}$IM TOOK THE bus home because Pete had to stay after school for band. When he got off the bus, Jim saw Jake sleeping on a sunny patch of brown grass alongside the driveway.

"Hey, big fella!" Jim yelled out. Jake remained perfectly still. Jim came closer. "Jake!" Why didn't he even lift his head? *"Jake!"*

Jim stood over the big yellow dog, casting him in a shadow. Jake opened one eye and peered up at Jim. His look was more "What do you want?" than "Hey, I'm so glad you're home." Jim crouched down and patted Jake's belly. "What's going on, big fella? Are you okay?" Jake stretched, slowly pulling his head off the grass as though it was a heavy burden. His eyes looked cloudy, his nose was rubbed pink in one spot, and the fur under his chin was white, not tan.

Jim remembered the old days when Jake would spring to his feet at the sound of his name. Jake used to scramble for the door every morning, anxious to go out. He would run across the back porch, leap off the steps, and take off for the woods behind their house. He always entered at the exact same spot, north of the big ash tree, following his preferred route as though he were commuting to a job somewhere deep in the forest. Whenever he returned, usually just before noon, Jake looked very proud of himself. Sometimes he brought back a treasure he had found: the bone of an unknown animal, a live mouse dangling by its tail from his mouth, an old shoe.

Now Jake put his head back down on the grass and started to pant as though he had just raced down the driveway. Jim got up and went into the house. There was a note taped to the back door: "Jim, please do not disturb me. I'm in the studio printing."

"Mom!" Jim called up the stairs.

There was no answer. Jim dropped his book bag and trotted up the steps two at a time. "Mom!"

The door to Mom's studio was closed. "Jim, I can't talk right now," came her muffled voice. "I've just mixed my ink. I'm about to print. You'll have to wait."

"But, Mom, I think Jake is dying!" Jim was surprised at the words coming out of his mouth.

"No, honey, he's okay. He's just old and tired. Please go back downstairs, and leave me alone. See if he'll take some water. He's been very thirsty today."

Jim heard the squeak of the metal hinges that meant Mom was lowering her silk screen and getting ready to glop on the ink along the top edge and then pull the rubber squeegee across the silk. Jim loved to watch her print, and sometimes he helped by hanging up each printed sheet with clothespins on the line she had strung across the studio. But on certain projects, like this series she was doing for a calendar, Mom liked to work alone.

Jim went back downstairs. He filled the metal dish with cold water and walked out to offer it to Jake. Jake clumsily hoisted himself up. He dropped his snout to the water and lapped noisily. He drank every drop.

"Good boy!" said Jim. "Come on, let's go." Jim slapped his leg. Jake took slow, careful steps. His face seemed to grimace with pain. Jim helped him along, patting his neck with encouragement, until he had made it into the kitchen. Jake immediately dropped his body onto his bed. He panted furiously. Jim offered him more water, but Jake looked away and continued to pant.

Jim made himself a snack, some toast with peanut butter and a glass of root beer. Mom wouldn't approve of the soda, so he drank it down fast and threw the can into the recycling bag under the sink. He wanted to go outside and shoot, but he didn't want to leave Jake alone. When no one was around, Jim always talked to Jake. When Jim was small, he believed that Jake could understand every word and was trying to answer with small gestures, like yawns, or licks or even by scratching himself.

"So, Jake"—Jim lifted the edge of the tablecloth so he could see Jake's half-closed eyes and panting tongue—"you're not going to go and get all lame on me, are you? The basketball season is just beginning, and we're going to be outside practicing a lot, you and me. I saw that Lisa Mondini in the cafeteria today, and she looked at me like I was some kind of alien. She didn't smile or anything. She stopped at our table and talked to Josh in this low, quiet voice and then went over to sit with her dorky friends. I asked Josh what she said, and he just went, 'Aw, nothing, just see you at practice.' And I found out Sean Butler made the team, and this kid Damian. Damian's not real big, like me, so I wonder where he'll be playing. I can't wait to get to practice Wednesday night. Wouldn't it be cool if instead of school, we went to practice every day and then just had a couple of nights of school? I hate school, Jake. And now, listen to this, I've gotta write that stupid essay over again. Like I don't have enough work already!"

Jim opened his book bag. He looked at the textbooks covered in brown paper (Mom didn't believe in those college team covers), the ink spots and squiggles on the edges of the pages. Someone had printed the word *fart* in big block letters on his social studies book. Jim slid out the math textbook and his loose-leaf and began his homework. After doing two problems, he looked up and noticed a library book lying there on the table. There were always books from the library all over the house. Mom and Dad both liked to read. But this book caught Jim's eye.

"Hi, Jim," Mom said. She was still wearing her work shirt, and she smelled of her printing ink. Mom crouched down to pet Jake. His panting had slowed. Standing up, she said, "I'm just taking a quick break." She kissed the top of Jim's head. "Oh, you're looking at *Madama Butterfly*. Good. That's the opera Nana is taking you to on Saturday night."

"What are you talking about?" asked Jim.

"Remember, Nana invited you to stay overnight at her apartment?" said Mom as she opened the refrigerator. She pulled out a bottle of apple juice. "It was only yesterday we talked about it. She's so excited. You'll love the opera."

"But, Mom, this Saturday I have basketball practice. I can't miss the second practice!" Jim was horrified. Maybe they had talked about this stupid plan, but he didn't remember agreeing to it.

"What's one practice compared to the opportunity to see a real live opera? I'm sure your coach will understand."

"Mom, I want to get a starting position on this team! Mr. Mondini is going to think I'm some kind of slacker or something. Please. You've gotta tell Nana to make it some other time!"

"No, Jim," said Mom. "Nana already bought the tickets."

"How about if I go to my practice and *then* you drive me down to Nana's?"

"No," said Mom more emphatically. "Nana wants to spend the whole day with her grandson. She never gets to do that."

"So let Pete go! Why doesn't Pete go? He doesn't do anything on Saturday except hang out with his stupid friends. It's not fair!" Jim wanted to throw his books on the floor. He knew something bad was going to come out of his mouth any minute, something that would get him punished big time. Luckily the phone rang.

"Yes, this is Mrs. Malone," said Mom as she turned her back to Jim. He clicked and clicked and clicked until the lead from his pencil was three inches long and then he snapped it off.

"No, he didn't tell me. He just got home," said Mom, now turning back to fix her gaze on Jim. "Really? . . . I see. . . . Yes, I understand. . . . That's very nice of you. . . . As a matter of fact, he is going to an opera this weekend with his grandmother. Maybe he can write about that? . . . I think so, too. . . . Yes. . . . Well, thank you, Ms. Durbin. Good-bye."

Mom hung up the phone. She just stood there with her arms folded across her paint-spattered shirt and stared at Jim. Finally she spoke.

"An F! James W. Malone! An F is unacceptable!" It took a lot to get Mom this angry. Broken glasses, spilled orange juice, even burping contests at the dinner table didn't put this shrill, tinny sound in her voice or turn her usually smiling face into a mask of stone. Up until now Jim had been able to keep his Fs hidden away. But Ms.

Durbin's phone call meant trouble, big trouble. Mom and Dad were really into school. Dad was a high school teacher. Mom used to be an art teacher at a private school. Now she was working part-time as a consultant to a school in a nearby town. "Education first," Dad always said. "The other stuff comes second." Nana talked the same way. "You don't understand how precious education is until they take everything else away from you—everything!" Even Pete kept warning Jim, "You've gotta get your grades up, Jim. School just keeps getting harder."

Then Mom cut through his thoughts with words as sharp as the X-Acto knife she used to cut her silk screen stencils: "Maybe playing on this travel team isn't such a good idea."

"Mom!" Jim jumped up. "Mom, I'm sorry I messed up. I mean it, I'll do better from now on. I promise. I'll write that essay again. It will be so good, you'll see—"

"I think Nana is right," said Mom. "You're much too obsessed with sports. An opera at the Metropolitan Opera House will be good for you."

Nana and her stupid opera! Before Jim could say another word, Mom left the kitchen to return to her printing.

Jim had three pairs of true basketball shorts. There was the Villanova pair, mostly white with the giant maroon *V*; the UNC shorts, light blue with the tar heel in the corner of one leg; and the bright yellow Michigan shorts that Dad's brother had sent him from Ann Arbor, where he was a professor. Jim liked the name of that team, the Wolverines. What were wolverines anyway? Little wolves? He looked it up in the dictionary. "A stocky, ferocious, flesh-eating mammal." Now that was an awesome name for a basketball team. Could almost describe Jake back in the old days. "The Michigan Jakes!"

On Wednesday, for the first travel team practice, Jim chose his Michigan shorts. He wore the faded blue T-shirt from the Harry T. Young Basketball Camp he had attended last summer. Short black socks. His thick white sneakers.

When Jim walked downstairs, Dad looked him over and said, "What's with the socks?"

"You look like a traveling salesman who lost his pants!" said Pete.

"Don't you watch college hoops? This is what the cool players are wearing," said Jim.

"Oh, yeah," said Pete. "And I've seen Stockton, and it doesn't mean I'm going to wear dukers like him!"

"What are you talking about? You don't even play basketball!" said Jim.

"Fellas, fellas," said Dad, "why do you always have to get so personal with each other?"

"You started it, Dad," said Jim.

"I think you look fine," Mom chimed in from the living room, where she was on the floor cutting out pieces of fabric for a skirt she was making.

"How do you know?" asked Jim. "You can't even see me!"

"I just know."

Mom was back to her good self. If she had told Dad about the F, he wasn't letting on. Jim thought Dad knew. Something about the way he talked about the opera Jim was going to see with Nana. As if it were the most exciting thing Jim had ever done in his life. Well, that was fine with Jim. Leave me alone, he thought. If I can pull at least a C+, maybe they'll forget about my grades for a while. I'll go to that old opera with Nana, I won't complain, I'll tell Mondini tonight. Only I won't tell him it's for an opera. What if that got out? I'll tell him I have to go visit my sick grandmother. That's better.

The Pigeon Hill gym seemed enormous with only twelve players and the two coaches. Jim looked at the other players and started to group them in his mind by position. The two tallest—Kenny and Frankie—at center; Slade, this kid with the Afro like Kobe Bryant, was quick and fierce, so he looked like a shoo-in for the power forward spot, along with Danny probably; forward could be Matt or Corey; and the shooting guards, Sean and Lisa and probably Marco. That left the three smallest, Jim, Josh, and Damian, for the point guard.

"Congratulations to all of you on making the travel team," said Mr. Mondini. "We will be known as the Thunderbirds." His beady eyes swept the circle of kids. "I expect a lot from you, and I hope you expect a lot from yourselves. We are going to work on the fundamentals, and I want to see hard work during the drills and not just in the scrimmages."

Yeah, yeah, yeah, thought Jim, let's just start practice. He shifted his weight from one foot to the other and back again. He hated standing around like this.

"I am a strict coach," said Mondini in his slightly nasal voice. "But I am fair. However, I will not tolerate goofing around or talking or cursing during practice. Zero tolerance! Got it?" He paused and looked at them. "Got it?" he repeated. He reminded Jim of a marine sergeant he'd once seen in an old movie that Mom loved so much.

Frankie barked back, "Got it!" like one of the recruits. Then a couple of others chimed in. Jim was thinking about how funny it would be if they all had to have their heads shaved like those guys in the movie. Then he heard Mr. Mondini say, "How about you, Jim? Got it?"

"Yes, sir!" Jim shot back. He heard Josh stifling a laugh.

"Don't you mock me, Jim!" said Mr. Mondini.

Jim wondered if he'd heard right. That was exactly what the sergeant in the movie said! Now Jim realized that he had already messed up with the coach. How was it possible? One minute he was just one of the twelve players, all equal (except for maybe Lisa) in the eyes of the coaches, and the next he was singled out, branded as a troublemaker, a wise guy. If only they would start moving. This was becoming more like school and less like basketball.

They spread out and did some stretching and then a jog around the gym. Mr. O'Malley asked them to line up in size order. This was almost as bad as taking off his shirt. Jim knew he was taller than Damian, but Damian squeezed in between Sean and Jim, leaving Jim and Josh at the end of the line.

"Here you go," said Mr. O'Malley, walking along and handing out practice jerseys. By the time he got to Jim and Josh there were only two jerseys left, a medium and a small. Jim reached for the medium, but Mr. O'Malley said, "Wait, Jim, I think we'll give this one to Josh since he's a little huskier than you are." So Jim got stuck with the small, marked number 84.

So now I've gotta wear skintight, thought Jim, with some number that belongs on a football uniform. Could things get any worse?

Mr. O'Malley ran a few drills. He demonstrated, and it was obvious that despite his slight paunch and funny old-school shorts (he was clearly a Stockton wanna-be), Mr. O'Malley could play the game. "Come on, come on," he called encouragingly as they wove the ball back and forth and went up for layups. "Use your legs, Marco. . . . Better passes, Matt. . . . Right up, Kenny. . . . Keep the ball tight, Lisa. . . ." He had a slight Irish accent that made his words sound like a song. Meanwhile, Mr. Mondini stood to one side, watching and making notes on his clipboard.

When they took a water break, Jim noticed that Josh walked right over to Lisa. They looked funny standing side by side, Lisa so much taller, her long arms arced around her head as she adjusted her ponytail, and Josh looking up at her while he drank from his neon green water bottle. They were talking in quiet voices, a private conversation about what? Josh's new Jordan sneakers? Lisa's favorite Knick? The gross sloppy joes they had served for lunch in school today? It was bad enough having a girl on the team. Josh didn't have to go making friends with her!

Jim stopped himself from staring. He looked at Marco, who was standing next to him, and said, "How long does it take you to get your hair like that?" and immediately felt stupid for asking. Marco had a long, serious face, with large brown eyes.

"My aunt braids it for me," said Marco. "It takes her about three hours. I really hate sitting so long, but that's the price of looking cool." Suddenly Marco's long, serious face broke into a wide toothy smile.

Jim looked at the zigzaggy design. It was pretty cool. "You look like Iverson."

"Yeah, my aunt says that, too. Now if I could just do that crossover, I'd be unstoppable." Marco and Jim both laughed.

"Fellas"—Mr. Mondini's voice came from behind them—"let's get back to work."

As the practice went on, it became clear that Frankie, Slade, Matt, and Lisa were four of the starters. When they scrimmaged, Mondini left them in as a unit and kept switching the point guards. Damian was slow and deliberate bringing the ball down the court, as if he was afraid of making a mistake. Josh pushed the ball harder and grunted with exertion as he passed and moved, but his passes were off, and only Lisa was able to reach up or out with her long arms and save them. A couple of times she barely grabbed the ball.

Then it was Jim's turn. For some reason Mondini decided to switch Kenny for Frankie and Sean for Lisa at the same time. Why don't you make me play with one arm tied behind my back? thought Jim. On Jim's first trip down the floor he saw Kenny waving from under the basket, so he launched a neat hard pass to him, high enough so all Kenny had to do was tap the ball into the hoop. But of course Kenny brought the ball all the way down to his knees for a bounce as if he were looking for a bug to crush on the floor. This gave Corey from the opposing team time to steal it. Now Jim had to hustle back on defense. The next time down, Jim made a bounce pass over to Sean. Then Jim scooted across the paint, using Matt's pick to lose his defender. Jim clapped and called to Sean, "Come on," but Sean looked up with his sleepy eyes and threw the ball in the direction of Slade. It sailed out of bounds.

"Jeez," Jim muttered as he trotted back.

Dad always said the best players make the weaker players look good. Jim thought he was trying to do that, but what was he supposed to do when the other guys couldn't catch a pass? How do you force them to play faster? After a few minutes Jim's natural impatience caught up with him, and he snapped at Sean, "Wake up!"

Mr. Mondini ended the practice with his five apparent starters, now including Josh, scrimmaging against Kenny, Danny, Marco, Sean, and Jim. A few fathers filtered into the gym and leaned against the wall. Jim was happy to see Dad wasn't among them.

"Thirty seconds!" Mr. O'Malley announced, looking at his watch.

Jim stripped the ball from Josh and tore down the left-hand side of the court. He dribbled and then passed to Marco. Josh left Jim to double-team Marco along with Matt, so Marco flipped the ball back to Jim. Jim turned to avoid the lunging Lisa, then revolved back to face the basket. "Five, four, three . . ." Mr. O'Malley was counting down the time. Jim lifted off the ground and shot the ball, the fade-away jumper he had been practicing in the driveway. The ball touched the rim, balanced itself there for a moment, and then dropped into the basket. Mr. O'Malley made the sound of a buzzer.

Marco ran over to Jim and raised his hand to slap fives. "That was sweet!" he said. Then he turned to Lisa. "You sure you want to play with the big boys? You know this ain't no WNBA!"

Jim cracked up.

"Lisa, you can't take Squeak for granted," said Frankie. "He may be a toothpick, but he's crafty." Frankie gave Jim a light punch in the arm.

Ever since third grade the guys on the playground had called Jim Squeak or the Squeaker because he always managed to squeak past the bigger guys and take the ball to the hoop.

Now it was Lisa who cracked up. "Squeak?" she said. Her laugh was loud and almost musical. It was one of those laughs that make everyone else laugh. Now Frankie and Marco and even Josh were chortling right along with Lisa.

Jim felt the heat in his ears and neck. Their laughter was like a waterfall crashing all around him, making it hard to hear anything else. He should have said, "Shut up, Frankie! Don't you ever call me Squeak again," but he didn't have the nerve. Frankie could flatten him with one pinkie. And anyway, Jim had never really minded his nickname until five seconds ago, when Lisa Mondini had said it out loud.

What about his great move on Lisa? It was already forgotten.

Mr. Mondini called them in. He droned on about how he liked what he was seeing, keep it up, fellas, something like that. Jim wasn't really listening. He had seen Pete stroll into the gym. Pete with his end-of-the-day stubble, wearing that crusty Clemson hat backward, his hands thrust deep in the pockets of his baggy jeans. He made a face and pointed to his wristwatch. But Jim had to tell Mondini about Saturday. He wanted to wait until all the other kids had walked away.

"Okay, anyone who can't make it to the next practice?" Mondini asked.

The others all shook their heads and mumbled no, and Jim hadn't planned to speak but suddenly heard himself blurt out, "I can't." Everyone looked at Jim. He was glad his face was already flushed and sweaty.

"Why not?" asked Mondini icily.

"Well, uh, my grandmother is sick," said Jim. "We're going to visit her, uh, in the hospital." Why didn't he just stop talking? Why was he weaving this whole stupid explanation?

"Your grandmother's in the hospital?" said Josh. "I saw her on Sunday sitting in your car after tryouts. She looked okay. What happened?"

Leave it to Josh to open his big mouth and make things worse, thought Jim. "Well, I don't know exactly . . . she's sick, that's all," Jim said.

Mondini was staring at him with a questioning look, but all he said was "I hope she feels better."

Jim felt a knot in his stomach. This was all so ridiculous. He was angry at Nana and Mom for ruining his life, he was furious at Ms. Durbin for giving him that F, he was disgusted with Josh for being such a loudmouth, and he did not want to ride home with Pete. He took off his practice jersey and stuffed it in his bag. He could already hear Pete making fun of it. Jim slung the bag on his shoulder and turned to leave.

NANA WAS WAITING in her doorway at the end of the hall when Jim and Mom got off the elevator. There was a strong smell of fried onions.

"*Ach, du lieber Gott!*" Nana said in her deep voice. "That Mrs. Steinmetz is always cooking, always cooking. Who fries onions at one o'clock in the afternoon? It's disgusting! *Schrecklich*! My Jimmy! At last, my Jimmy comes to see his old nana!" She enfolded him in a hug. He felt her stiff hair brush his chin.

Jim could tell Nana had been to the beauty parlor that morning. Her dyed blond hair was teased and sprayed into a poofy bubble that looked like cotton candy. She was wearing a silver and black striped sweater over a black skirt. A collection of gold chains hung around her neck. Her lucky fish hung from the longest.

Nana lived in a studio apartment, which meant it was one big room with a tiny bathroom and an even tinier kitchen. There were tall windows, but they looked out on a dismal courtyard and the windows of other apartments. At home Mom had never bothered hanging curtains on any of the windows except for the bathrooms. She said, "Who's looking in, the squirrels and chipmunks?" But Nana had three kinds of window coverings: venetian blinds, sheer white curtains, and heavy blue velvet drapes.

Every bit of wall space was covered with pictures and paintings. A series of silk screens Mom had done in college were framed and hanging over the couch. There were collages of yellowing newspaper, metal screws, and painted ribbon glued onto rough pieces of wood. These were Mom's, too. A crayon drawing of a dinosaur that Jim had done in first grade was framed and displayed over Nana's bed. Hanging at pillow level along one side of the bed was a row of photographs of Mom, Dad, Pete, and Jim. There were certificates in other languages with fancy seals and right in the middle a framed medal that Nana said she had won in the war.

Jim had heard lots of Nana's war stories. He knew she had left her family in Germany to follow her boyfriend to Italy. He knew she had gone later to the mountains to hide with her husband and little son when the Fascists started rounding up the Jews in Rome. He knew that the night the Nazis came to take her husband, they had shot Nana in her leg. That leg still bothered her when she had to stand for a long time. But even though Nana had once showed him her scar, a deep fold of skin across her kneecap, Jim couldn't quite believe that his little grandmother, who always got her hair done and polished her nails and wore crimson lipstick and lots of jewelry, had ever been in any war.

"Mama, this is pretty," said Mom, picking up a cut-glass paperweight. "Is it new?"

"Oh, I got it from Henry, you know, that man I was telling you I met at the dance at the Jewish Center?" said Nana as she winked at Jim.

Jim didn't know anyone who had a grandmother like Nana. She was always talking about men she met and dates and parties. She had been married a few times, three or four . . . he didn't know for sure. Her second husband was Mom's father, but Jim had never even seen a picture of the man. Nobody ever talked about him. Jim wanted to know one thing about the guy: Was he tall? Because if he was a shrimp, too, like Nana and Mom, then Jim's chances of ever growing would be pretty bleak. But Mom and Nana both refused to talk about him.

"It doesn't make any difference anyway," said Mom. "He's dead now."

At home Mom had a whole wall filled with framed old-time photos of ladies in high-necked black dresses and men with curling mustaches, but they were all people from Dad's side of the family, the

Malones and Turners. There was only one picture of Mom's side. It was a black-and-white photograph of Nana as a young girl standing on a bridge carrying a small suitcase. On the back Nana had written, "12 years old going to gym w. suitcase (bathing suit etc. inside)." The girl stared out from that picture with serious brown eyes. If you looked hard at those eyes, you could see Nana's look, the one she gave Jim when she was really listening. Mom said all the other family pictures had been lost in the war.

"You see, Jimmy," said Nana, "I still like to have some fun, too. It's not so easy when you go to these dances. So few men and so many women! But the men always find me. My dance card is always full!"

Jim had no idea what Nana was talking about. What was a "dance card" anyway?

"Don't they have dances at your school?" asked Nana. "Didn't you tell me, Gabby?" she said to Mom.

There were once-a-month gatherings at the middle school for the seventh and eighth graders, where they had a DJ and dancing in the cafeteria and also an open gym for basketball and Ping-Pong in the hallway. Jim had gone to a couple of them, but he always headed straight for the gym. The cafeteria with its strobe lights and loud music was for the sophisticated eighth graders and some of the wanna-be-cool seventh graders, people like Mariah Jones. Jim liked to dance to his CDs at home, alone, when Pete wasn't around, but there was no way in a million years he would ever dance in public.

"Do you dance, my Jimmy?" asked Nana as she started to move like some drunken boxer. Why couldn't she act like a normal grandmother? Just sit down on an armchair and crochet stuff the way Josh's grandmother did. Nana abruptly stopped her crazy dance and fell heavily onto her green velvet armchair.

"Mama!" said Mom in an alarmed voice. "You'd better take it easy. Your heart!"

Nana seemed to be having trouble breathing, but she waved at Mom as if she were trying to get rid of a pesky housefly.

"Don't worry so much about me. My heart is strong," said Nana. "I'm not ready to die yet!"

Jim looked at the blackened screen of Nana's big television. His eye caught sight of the white numbers on the VCR clock: 1:05. The second travel team basketball practice had just begun in the Pigeon Hill gym without him. Everyone was probably still messing around, shooting at random, swatting balls away from one another, waiting for Mondini to call them in, while he was here, in this stuffy apartment, listening to his eighty-two-year-old grandmother talk about dances!

Jim knew he couldn't complain. He couldn't even make a bored face because he was treading on thin ice with both Mom and Dad. And it wasn't only because of the F. Mom had found out from Mrs. DeLonga, Josh's mom, that Jim had told the team his grandmother was in the hospital. If there was one thing that made Mom mad (besides Fs in English), it was lying.

"Now you're lying?" she had said to Jim. She had taken a deep breath and then exhaled, the breathing she used when she was doing her yoga exercises in the middle of the living room. "How could you make up a story like that? You know, Jim, lies always come back to haunt you."

Haunt, smaunt, Jim had thought. Mom and Nana would never understand anyway. They didn't know anything about team sports. You don't just go and miss your second practice with your travel basketball team because your old grandmother wants you to get some culture! Sometimes you just have to lie to save face.

But here he was in Nana's apartment instead of in the gym at Pigeon Hill where he belonged. It was like sitting through social studies or something. Jim was going to sleepwalk through this whole Nana-opera thing. He would be polite to Nana and agree to whatever she wanted to do, but that didn't mean he was going to enjoy it.

Nana was showing Mom a letter. "Look, I was asked to be a speaker at this conference down in Washington," Nana was saying. "My teacher recommended me."

Nana was taking classes in writing at the YMCA. Jim couldn't understand why anyone who was so old would choose to go to school. It was another example of how Nana didn't act the way a grandmother was supposed to act. Nana wrote something every week for her class. Every week!

"Do you need any help?" asked Mom. "With the English? The grammar?"

"Na, so was!" Nana said with a chuckle. "I don't need any help. I can tell my own story. My English is fine!" Then she looked at Jim. "Maybe my intelligent American grandson will correct me."

"You mean Pete," said Jim.

"I'm talking about you, my Jimmy," said Nana. "Don't be so negative. You're a very smart boy. Don't compare yourself to your brother."

Why not? thought Jim. It's hard not to when every night at dinner Pete announces another A plus plus plus or some special honor society they asked him to join in school. Mom and Dad were always so excited by Pete's academic news. They were positively glowing when he told them about the book award. How could Jim compete with that? What could he say: "Oh, yeah, I almost forgot to tell everybody, I did twenty-five push-ups today in gym, the most in my class!" That's why getting tall was so important. If he wanted to stand out in one thing when he got to high school, it was basketball, and for that he had to get taller. A few muscles wouldn't hurt either.

But Nana treated Pete and Jim exactly the same. "You are my handsome American grandsons, and you will both go far if you work hard," she said. Nana was probably the only person in the world who thought Jim was just as smart as Pete. Jim figured it was probably because she was so old and didn't know any better.

"Anyway," Nana said, "the main thing is that you all come to Washington to hear me speak. No excuses, no sports events! You'll have to shut down the House of Sports for a day!" She looked at Jim. "I'll write down the date for you, so you don't forget!" Nana began scrawling out some words in her tall, spidery handwriting. She ripped out the piece of paper and handed it to Mom. "Make sure you mark the date on your calendar," she said. "Make sure she doesn't forget," Nana said to Jim as if he were the grown-up and Mom his child.

Nana laid the pad down on the coffee table and stood up with some effort. "Okay, Gabby," she said, "it's time for you to go now and leave me with my handsome grandson."

Nana was never one to beat around the bush. She said life was too short and getting shorter, so you had to speak up. Nana always told Jim, "You can't be a nebbish in this life! No one can read your mind."

Nebbish was Nana's word for loser or weakling. She had all kinds of funny words, words that Jim never heard anyone else say except for Mom once in a while. Nana said they were Yiddish words that her family always used when she was a little girl.

"Is there anything you want me to do before I leave?" asked Mom. "Some laundry, food shopping—"

"No, no, no!" said Nana, making a face. "You think I'm so help-less, some old helpless woman." She made a clucking sound. "Don't be such a *nudzh*. I can take care of myself!"

Mom looked a little hurt. She walked over to the closet by the front door and pulled out her plaid wool jacket. "Okay, Mama," she said. "I'm leaving, then." She kissed Jim and hugged Nana.

After Mom had left, Nana folded her hands together in front of her as though she were about to pray and said, "Okay, my darling, what do you want to do before dinner?"

Jim couldn't say what he really wanted to do, which was snap his fingers and be immediately back at the Pigeon Hill gym, practicing free throws. "I don't care," he said.

"What kind of answer is that?" said Nana. "You must always care about what you do in your life!"

Why did Nana make such a big deal about everything? Why did she have to be so dramatic?

"How about a carriage ride in the park?"

"No," said Jim. "We always do that."

"I thought you liked the horses?" said Nana. "What about the merry-go-round?"

Merry-go-round? What did Nana think he was, three years old?

"Or the zoo? The polar bears! Such good swimmers! Did I ever tell you about my swimming when I was a young girl in Germany? I was a champion!"

Jim wasn't in the mood for one of Nana's olden days stories. He didn't understand how all these stories could be true anyway. How could Nana be a championship swimmer and a war hero, too?

Jim shook his head. Then he remembered something. "Isn't there a new store near here with all basketball stuff? I saw an ad for it in the newspaper."

"Basketball is verboten today, Jimmy," said Nana. "This is your nonsports weekend. You are not in the House of Sports!"

Well, then, Jim just didn't care what they did.

"We don't have to go out," said Nana. "How about a game of Scrabble?"

"Sure," said Jim. Whatever, he thought.

Nana kept a shelf full of games for whenever her grandsons came to visit, which she said was never often enough. She had Monopoly, checkers, Life, and Connect Four, but Scrabble was her favorite. When she opened the worn brown box, Jim saw a pile of old score sheets from long-forgotten games. Nana set up the board on her tiny dining table. The wooden tiles were in a worn paper bag. She shook the bag to mix them up. Then she sat down and took a long, deep breath.

Jim fished out seven tiles and arranged them on his rack: *K, B, Z,* blank, *T, A,* and *X.*

"You go first, Nana," he said.

Nana put on her glasses and studied her letters. She scrunched up her mouth until you couldn't see the lipstick.

Jim looked at the clock again. They must be scrimmaging, he thought gloomily.

Suddenly Nana exclaimed loudly, "Aha!" She carefully arranged four letters across the star in the middle of the board. Jim looked at her gnarled fingers, strangely bent, and thought her hand looked scary. Even with the red nail polish and wide gold rings, it looked like a claw. Jim saw Nana's word: *hero.*

Jim counted up the points: fourteen. "Not bad, Nana," he said.

Everyone always beat Jim at Scrabble except for Mom, and he thought she let him win. He rearranged the letters on his little rack. He looked at the board. At least there were a couple of free vowels.

He wanted to save the *Z* and *X* for a triple-letter square. Finally he placed the *T, A,* and blank around the *E* in *hero.*

"What's that?" asked Nana.

"*Team,*" said Jim.

"Always sports," Nana said with a laugh. "What's wrong with *meat*?"

"I like *team* better," said Jim.

With every turn Nana seemed to create longer and longer words—*gripe, pencil, tender*—until she used all her letters in one turn to form *animism*, which gave her a fifty-point bonus. On top of that, the last *M* sat next to Jim's previous word *old* to make *mold*, giving Nana even more points! Jim had never seen anybody do that before, not even Pete.

"That's not a word!" said Jim. "You're thinking of *animated*, like cartoons or something."

"It most certainly is a word! There's even a word in German like it," said Nana. "Look it up in the dictionary."

Jim found *animism* right above *animosity* in the Webster's. He reluctantly read the meaning out loud: "the doctrine that all life is produced by a spiritual force separate from matter." Jim read the next two listed meanings. Number three was: "a belief in the existence of spirits, demons, etc." No wonder Nana knew this word!

"You see, *animus* is Latin for your soul or your mind, not your body. It's what we can't see with our eyes. But it's more important than anything we can see or touch. It's our passion!" said Nana. "Don't they teach Latin in this country?" She was really getting into this.

Jim added the points and saw little hope of catching up to Nana.

"What's my score?" Nana asked eagerly. Jim saw a gleam in her eyes. She looked like a fierce basketball player shooting from the line. My grandmother actually wants to beat me, thought Jim. She wants to win!

After Jim told her she was way ahead, that he had virtually no chance of catching up, she smiled and said sweetly, "Go ahead, my darling. It's your turn."

Jim only had five letters left. It was like being down by ten with ten seconds left in a game. And he still had that stupid *Z* worth ten points, which would be deducted from his score if he didn't get it on the board *now*. Finally he saw an available *E*. He carefully squeezed in an *F* and the *Z* to spell *fez*.

"Do you know what that means?" asked Nana.

Jim couldn't remember even though he knew Mom had once told him.

"Old fizz?"

Nana started to laugh. "No, Jimmy, it is a type of hat that they wear in Turkey."

"I'm not very good at vocabulary," said Jim. "English is my worst subject."

"How can English be your worst subject?" said Nana. "I don't get it. You were born in this beautiful country and learned English as a baby."

"Did Mom tell you about the essay?"

"I think it's impossible for you to get an F," said Nana. "If you're lazy, well, then, there you are. But if you try, Jimmy, you will have success. Look at me, I take this writing class with all these young people, and me with my lousy English, I always get the best grades of everyone! Imagine!" Nana looked proud of herself like a little kid who had just learned to ride a two-wheeler.

Jim added up the points, and Nana won by ninety-eight.

"Without that bonus, we would have been very close," said Nana.

Jim took one last look at the board before clearing all the tiles. "How do you know so many words in English?" he asked. "Even Pete doesn't come up with words like these!"

"When I came to this country, I knew a little English," said Nana. "I studied in school. In Germany we all studied English. It's not like here, where you don't learn foreign languages until you're big and then it's too late! My first apartment in New York I shared with my sister, Sarah. She would always speak to me in German, but I stopped her. 'No!' I said. 'We're in America now. It is time to speak English, only English.' Every day I forced myself to talk to people even when they laughed at my accent. Every night, no matter how tired I was when I got home from work, I took out my dictionary and read the newspaper." Nana looked off into space. Then she looked at Jim, her old brown eyes wide and serious. "Remember this, my darling, you have to go after the things you want in this life. You can't be shy. You work hard for the things you want, you speak up for yourself . . . then you will have success. Anything is possible here in this country. You are lucky to be born here."

Uh-oh, here comes the national anthem, thought Jim. America was such a big deal to Nana. Gram and Pappy, Dad's parents, who had been born somewhere in upstate New York, never said anything to Jim about his being their "handsome American grandson." Everyone on their side was American. Nobody had an accent like Nana. Jim never thought about the United States's being this magical place, the way Nana described it. It was just where he had been born and where he lived and totally normal and regular like the telephone or the refrigerator or the NBA. But Nana said living in this free country was a blessing he needed to be thankful for. Sometimes she sounded like one of those guys running for president or Congress or something.

Nana looked at the clock. "It's getting late, my darling. You must be hungry?"

She went to the bathroom to fix her makeup. Jim got up and stretched hard. He jumped to see if he could touch Nana's ceiling, but he didn't come close. He picked up a pillow from the couch and tossed it up and caught it. Jim thought, I would go nuts if I lived in this tiny apartment.

By now the basketball practice was over, the Pigeon Hill gym dark and locked up for the night. Had they chosen a starting lineup? Had Josh blabbed to everyone that Jim had not gone to any hospital but was really going to an opera? Mondini seemed like the type who would blow his stack if he found out you had lied.

By the time Nana and Jim had eaten dinner at an Italian restaurant where Nana seemed to know all the waiters and begun walking the two blocks to the opera house, the weather had turned sharply colder, and the wind was blowing. Nana held on to Jim's arm. She stopped every few steps, looking back as if she were measuring how far they had come. Suddenly she said, "Jimmy, let's stop here in this doorway." It was the entrance to a closed shoe repair shop. Nana opened her purse and pulled out a small amber vial with a white cap. She dropped two pills into her hand and swallowed them. "For my heart," she said with a weak smile. "Don't get old, my sweetheart. It's no fun."

Jim was getting impatient with Nana's turtle pace. When they finally reached the corner of Broadway, he felt like picking her up and running across the many lanes of traffic. As the white WALK light turned to a flashing red DON'T WALK, Nana muttered, "Idiotic! How do they expect anyone to cross this street so fast?"

Inside the lobby under the brightly lit chandeliers, Jim could see Nana's face glowing with sweat. A bright red stripe ran down her forehead. She had a wild look in her eyes, and she was panting.

"Nana, are you okay?" Jim asked.

"Of course, my darling," Nana said as she caressed Jim's cheek with the back of her hand. "Isn't this fantastic?"

Their seats were in the seventh row. Jim helped Nana take off her coat. When she sat down, she laid the coat over her knees. There was a little screen attached to the back of every seat.

"What are these for?" asked Jim.

"The words to the opera will appear in English, so you can understand what is going on," said Nana, opening her program. "My Jimmy, do you know anything about this opera?"

"Yeah, I know the whole story."

Jim had read the synopsis of *Madama Butterfly*. Basically it went like this: Some American soldier hooks up with a Japanese geisha, then leaves her to go back to the United States. He doesn't tell the geisha he won't be returning. She waits and waits, then has this baby, a little boy. One day the soldier comes sailing in with his American wife. The geisha loses it and kills herself with a dagger. Except for the dagger part it sounded like a girl's story, all that romance and love and babies, and Jim knew he was going to hate it. He was already getting a headache just thinking about the hours of singing in a language he couldn't understand. Why did they have to sing every line in opera anyway?

Jim could hear the tumbling notes of a trumpet warming up. It sounded like Dad. He could see the orchestra pit, the musicians adjusting themselves, chatting with one another, arranging their sheets of music. He looked up to the ceiling and turned to see the back of the opera house. This place was gigantic. Nana was reading the program, her glasses slipping down her long nose.

Once, when Jim was little, Mom had taken him to see *The Nutcracker* at a local junior college. The only thing he remembered was the girl sitting next to him. She was wearing a fancy pink party dress and a little crown, as if she thought she was one of the ballerinas. All of a sudden, during the Dance of the Sugarplum Fairies, she began to throw up all over the pink party dress and onto the floor, where the puke spattered on Jim's shoes before he could leap into Mom's lap. Jim could still remember the awful smell.

He glanced to his left. An old lady with about three chins and a wide pearl choker was looking at the orchestra through some miniature binoculars. She didn't look like the type to puke during an opera.

The lights dimmed. There was a final burst of talking from the

56

audience, and then everyone grew silent. The orchestra began to play, the heavy red curtains swept apart, and there on the stage was a terrace ringed with flowers, a harbor with ships anchored in the distance, and a navy lieutenant.

When the man in the uniform began to sing, his voice filled the theater like a tall crashing wave, dragging the audience onto the stage. Jim looked over at Nana. Her eyes were wide, and her mouth was open as if she were about to speak. For a moment, here in the dim light, Nana looked like a young woman with no bags under her eyes, no wrinkles. She seemed to be in a trance.

Jim couldn't understand what they all were singing about. For a while he followed along by reading the words in English on the screen. But then he got tired of looking down and up and down again. Jim kept his eyes on the stage. He started making up words to go along with the music. Why did all these people have to stand around on the stage singing and waving their arms and making faces? Why wasn't there more action? Too bad Nana hadn't just taken him to see that new football movie, the one with Keanu Reeves.

What if people sang all the time instead of talked? How weird would that be? Jim imagined Mr. Mondini singing to the team, "Okay now, brea-a-a-k yourselves into fooooouuur groups." How about Ms. Durbin leading a class discussion? "Wha-ha-at can we tell about this cha-a-aracter?" He was sure Mariah would be thrilled to sing her answers, holding her hands to her neck and bowing after each solo.

Jim tried to focus on the opera again. He squirmed around in his seat and knocked his elbow into the arm of the lady sitting on his left. She cleared her throat but refused to look at him.

Here was the wedding scene where the bride's uncle bursts in to curse the wedding because it isn't a Buddhist ceremony. Now the navy lieutenant curses back, although it didn't sound so bad in this opera lingo. What was the geisha's name? Suddenly Jim remembered: Cio-Cio-San. He was surprised how much he remembered. After the guests leave, the lieutenant and the geisha sing to each other under the moonlight. How cornball, thought Jim.

When the lights came on for the first intermission, Nana placed her hand on Jim's arm and brought her face close to his. "So what do you think, my darling?" she said loudly. "More interesting than another basketball game?"

Jim looked at Nana's hopeful eyes and felt sad that he couldn't jump up and down and get excited about her old opera. What could he say to her? It is way cool, Nana. Totally awesome! She'd know he was lying. But if he was honest and said, I bet if we leave now, we could still catch the fourth quarter of the Knicks game, it would break her heart. And Nana's heart was weak to begin with. He'd seen her pop those pills. Finally he just said, "Nana, it's really good," and hoped she believed him.

"So let's get some air. I need to walk a little," said Nana.

Nana took Jim's arm as they made their way slowly up the aisle. Jim could hear her panting. Why did she get so out of breath after only a few steps? As they entered the lobby, Jim heard a voice in the crowd say, "Ah, there you are, Erna!"

A short woman wearing a beaded sweater and glasses hanging from a chain approached Nana. "Why didn't you call us? We could have shared a taxi."

"Ruth, come here. I want you to meet my grandson."

Ruth, whose hair was black and puffy, had long, deep wrinkles radiating from the corners of her eyes. A woman with silver hair and a cane walked beside her.

"Who is this handsome young man?" said Ruth. "No wonder you don't want to come to the opera with two old hags like us!"

"Ruth, Frieda, this is my grandson Jim," said Nana, taking his hand and squeezing it.

"Very nice to meet you, Jim," said Frieda. "Your grandmother has talked so much about you. She is very proud. Have you decided which college you want to apply to?"

"No, no, no," said Nana. "That's my other grandson, Pete. Jim is only in the seventh grade."

"Oh, you're the one who loves sports so much," said Ruth.

"Yes, he made the big basketball team in his school, and he is one of the best players," said Nana proudly.

What was Nana talking about? Where did she get this stuff? Nana loved to exaggerate. Like when she told Jim and Pete stories about Mom as a little girl. "Your mother, such a ballerina! I can't believe she gave it up! Her ballet school did *Peter Pan* once. Your mother wore this fantastic costume, all green with sequins and little chiffon scarves hanging from her wrists." Nana went on and on until Mom finally interrupted.

"Mama! I was not a graceful dancer! Don't you remember how chubby I was? I played a tree in *Peter Pan*. A very quiet tree. I mostly stood like scenery with my arms over my head! Madame Kornichka didn't know what else to do with me!"

That was one of the reasons Jim wasn't sure he could always believe Nana's stories. Champion swimmer? Top student in her writing class? War hero?

"Tell me, Erna," said Ruth, "have you heard from Henry yet?"

"Yes, the man you stole from me," said Frieda with a chuckle.

"I can't help it if I have so much sex appeal!" Nana chortled.

"Erna! Your grandson," said Ruth, trying to suppress her laughter. Then she looked at Jim. "Your grandmother is quite a character. I guess you know that."

The three old women continued to joke around with one another and laugh. Jim had never thought about old people like Nana having friends, the way he and Pete did. But these women were acting like a bunch of seventh-grade girls, all giggly and silly.

The lights flashed on and off.

"Time to go back to our seats," said Nana. "I'll talk to you this week," she said to her friends.

"Don't keep your grandson out too late, Erna!" said Frieda. "No dancing at the Rainbow Room!"

When Jim and Nana had settled into their seats again, Nana said, "Now comes the good part. I'd better get my tissues ready."

The music began, the curtains opened, and they were back in Japan with Cio-Cio-San waiting for her navy lieutenant to return. There was singing and more singing, and Jim closed his eyes for a minute. He suddenly remembered that he was going to have to write about this opera for Ms. Durbin. He couldn't exactly write that he had slept through the last part. Jim opened his eyes. There was the crashing boom of a cannon. He remembered that meant Pinkerton was returning. Good. The end was in sight. The dagger scene was coming. Then the red curtains closed again, and the houselights came on. Another intermission? thought Jim. This had to be the longest opera ever written. He looked at Nana. She was holding a tissue to her nose, blowing softly. Why was she getting so emotional about this? What could Nana possibly have in common with a geisha and a navy lieutenant? Girls, and that included Nana, could be such wimps!

Luckily the opera ended with the third act. After Cio-Cio-San killed herself with the dagger, the lieutenant sang his last aria. At the final note the audience broke into a frenzy of clapping and shouts of "Bravo!" People started to stand, and Nana struggled to her feet, her fur coat sliding to the floor. Jim bent over to pick it up. He stood, happy to stretch his legs. Well, he'd survived. He had made it through an opera, his first and hopefully his last. He thought about the crowds cheering at a basketball game, jumping to their feet to applaud a buzzer beater, some fans pumping their fists, others slapping fives. How funny it would be if Nana did that. But Nana was clapping her hands and wiping her cheeks, oblivious of Jim.

As soon as the applause died down, Nana pulled Jim to sit again. "Let's wait for the crowds to thin out," she said. She was blowing her nose. "So, Jim, wasn't it breathtaking? So magnificent! Those voices. Those costumes."

"Why are you crying, Nana?" asked Jim.

Nana look embarrassed.

"I guess I never told you about my father? He was a dashing soldier in World War One, before I was born. I adored him. He got me started on swimming lessons, and he pushed me, always pushed me to do well in swimming. But as I was growing up, I noticed he was getting unhappy and always had a gloomy face. I swam harder, practiced all the time, hoping it would make him happy again. The Nazis were coming into power. Suddenly they closed all the pools to the Jewish people. Every club . . . *kaput*! And I had nowhere to practice." Nana took a deep breath. Jim didn't understand how this had anything to do with *Madama Butterfly*. "One evening—it was a Friday and we were all sitting in the dining room—all of a sudden my father stood up and announced to us that he was leaving. Leaving! I thought he meant he was going out for a walk! But he never came back! I was thirteen years old, and I thought it was all my fault because of my swimming. I cried myself to sleep every night." Nana looked at the stage and the closed curtains. She folded and unfolded her hands. "Many years later, when I came to this country and saw my sister, Sarah, again, she told me a great secret she had discovered. Our father left us because he fell in love with another woman! It had nothing to do with my swimming! And there I had blamed myself for all those years! Life is funny, my darling, now, isn't it?"

Nana took a deep breath. She seemed very tired. "Enough with the reminiscing! The past is over and done. Now I am sitting here with my handsome American grandson, far from all those miserable times. It is a blessing!" Nana put her handkerchief back in her purse and sat up straighter. "You give me *naches*, my darling, more *naches* than you'll ever know. I'm a lucky grandma!"

Naches was another one of Nana's funny words. She used it only when she spoke about Pete or Jim. It meant something like joy or happiness. Jim had never heard anyone else say the word.

"Look, the crowd is thinning out. Come, my darling, let's go home."

As they stepped outside into the cold night air, Nana gasped and linked arms with Jim. "Make sure you are zipped up, Jimmy."

The wind was funneling scraps of paper into the air around the fountain. People were striding purposefully toward the lights of Broadway, their heads bowed against the gusts. Nana and Jim took baby steps while the people ahead all disappeared into taxicabs.

Jim woke up to the sound of Nana's radio. A voice fuzzy with static was saying, "I would certainly advise you to diversify your portfolio using a certificate of deposit as the centerpiece." Jim rolled over to face the back of the couch. He hadn't slept well. Nana snored almost as much as Pete.

"Jimmy, are you awake?" Jim did not answer.

Jim just wanted to go home. He had had a bad dream about Jake.

In the dream it was a hot summer day, and Jim was walking with his dog along a beach. Jake stopped to sniff at a sand crab. As the crab disappeared under the wet sand, Jake burrowed his nose deeper and deeper until his snout was buried. When Jim tried to pull him out, Jake just continued to sink, pulled faster and faster by the sand until he completely disappeared. Jim cried, "Jake!" but no sound emerged from his throat. He tried over and over to scream until he heard a cannon's boom off in the distance. Then Jim exploded out of sleep to find himself sweaty and tangled in his blanket.

"Jimmy?" Nana's slippers made loud, slapping noises on the floor. "I'm making some toast for you."

Jim rolled back to see Nana's purple-and-red bathrobe. Her head was wrapped in a turban of toilet paper.

"What's on your head?" asked Jim.

"Oh, that's to keep my hair nice while I sleep," said Nana. "I just had it done yesterday."

Nana looked older now in the morning light. She was pale and wrinkly. A bluish smudge under each eye made her look like she'd been in a fight.

"What time is my mom coming to get me?" Jim asked.

"Not until three or four," said Nana. "We have plenty of time!"

Three or four? That wasn't the deal. Jim had agreed to go to the opera with Nana and stay over, not to spend all Sunday with her, too. "Nana, can I call her?" he said. "I have to get home and write this essay for school."

"I know, my darling. She told me," said Nana. "I have plenty of paper for you to use. I can even type it up for you if you like."

"Is it okay if I call my mom?" said Jim.

"Of course," said Nana. A shadow seemed to cross her face, but then she quickly added, "Honey or jelly?"

"Jelly," said Jim, reaching for the phone. "Please."

The line was busy. Jim looked at the digital clock: 9:37. Too early for Pete to be up on a Sunday. Who was on the phone? Jim tried again. Still busy.

Nana had set out breakfast on the tiny table in her kitchen: a bowl of cottage cheese, a basket of toast and rye crackers, small jars of jellies with funny German names, and a plate of sliced melon.

"Do you have any cereal?" asked Jim. Cottage cheese made him gag.

"I might have some cornflakes," said Nana, rummaging in a cabinet. She pulled out a crushed-looking box and shook it. "Sounds like there's enough for one bowl."

"No, thanks," said Jim.

Nana switched off the radio. "So eat, my darling," she said as she squeezed into her tiny chair.

Jim was hungry. He put a mound of purple jelly on a piece of toast and bit into it. Nana heaped a spoonful of cottage cheese onto a rye cracker and took a bite. The cottage cheese stuck to the corners of her mouth. Jim looked down at his plate. He didn't want to see Nana like this, her face all saggy and tired, her hair covered by toilet paper, hunched over her little table, eating gross cottage cheese. Jim and Pete had slept over at Nana's before, but Jim didn't remember her looking so nasty in the morning.

Nana had been Jim's favorite person in the world when he was little. Maybe she had always looked really old, but he just hadn't noticed. Whenever she came to visit, Jim was the first person to run to the door to greet her. He loved the perfume on her clothes, the softness of her cheek, the bear hug she wrapped him in. Her perfume reminded him of the yellow roses Mom grew in her flower garden. When Nana said, "How *are* you, my darling?" Jim felt like the most important person in the world. He couldn't wait to see what surprises she had in her magic shopping bag. He always had something to give her, too, like a torn page from his coloring book or a picture frame made of Popsicle sticks. "This is fantastic!" she would say as if she were holding a precious piece of jewelry in her hands.

Sometimes Nana took Jim on her lap and said, "Don't tell anyone, my Jimmy, but your nana is a witch! A good witch, the kind who helps people and sees the future." He absolutely believed her. He didn't care if Pete made fun of him or Mom and Dad both laughed.

Of course, now that Jim was older, he knew there was no such thing as witches. Sometimes stuff Nana predicted would come true, but he figured those had to be coincidences. Nana wasn't some character out of a fairy tale who could cast spells or break them. She was just this regular old lady, his grandmother. Still, a part of him wanted to believe that Nana had magical powers. Jim wanted her predictions to come true. Like the one about his getting as tall as Dad. But with his thirteenth birthday only a few months away, it didn't seem likely. He was still the same scrawny kid he had been in elementary school. Every day he checked his height against a little pencil mark inside the door to his closet. He would put a ruler on his head, carefully flatten his hair, and hold one end as steadily as he could next to the doorframe. But in the six months since he had started, he hadn't grown even one-sixteenth of an inch. Some days he seemed to have shrunk!

Meanwhile, all around him things were changing at an alarming rate. Pete was getting bigger and stronger and more obnoxious. Jake was going downhill fast. Dad was losing his hair, and Mom was getting a streak of gray across the top of hers. And Nana, she was getting slower and more feeble and wrinkly by the minute! Look at her now, this creaky, ancient lady with gross cottage cheese lips!

After breakfast, while Nana was in the shower, Jim tried calling home again. There was no answer. Pete was probably still sleeping, but where were Mom and Dad? Jim left a message. "Mom, when are you coming to pick me up? I'm ready to go home."

Nana got dressed and took off the paper hair wrap and put on some lipstick. She emerged from the bathroom looking a million percent better.

"So now we will have our writing time," said Nana. "I can work on my speech, and you can do your homework." She handed Jim a long pad of yellow paper and a pencil. "I have a surprise to show you. Can you keep a secret?"

"Sure, Nana," Jim said.

"You must promise not to tell your mother."

"I promise," said Jim, making an X over his chest.

Nana loved surprises. She told Jim to close his eyes. He heard a door open and then a sliding sound, like the sound of his basketball bag when he dragged it on the kitchen floor.

"Okay, you can look!" said Nana.

She was carrying a small black nylon briefcase. She placed it on her dining table by the window. When she unzipped it, Jim saw a flat rectangular box. It was a laptop computer.

"Cool," said Jim.

"I didn't want to tell your mother because she would have called it extravagant," said Nana, opening the computer and switching it on. "It was rather expensive, but I'm trying to write more, and my old typewriter is slow and heavy . . . just like me!" She let out one of her rumbling laughs. "But this is a pleasure. Look!" Nana pressed one of the keys with a gnarled finger. A menu of choices appeared.

Jim couldn't believe it. Here his eighty-two-year-old grand-mother, who was born practically before the telephone was even invented, had a brand-new laptop computer while his parents were stuck in the Stone Age, using manual typewriters and Wite-Out.

"Wow!" said Jim. "I'm jealous! Pete and I have been trying to convince Mom and Dad to get a computer, but they are so stubborn. They just don't get it."

"Don't worry, Jimmy, you can inherit this when I die." Lately Nana had been saying stuff like that a lot: "Pete, you can have my television when I die," or, "Gabby, all my jewelry is yours when I die. I hope you'll wear it and enjoy it."

Nana showed Jim some of the programs and then opened a new folder. She typed in "My Journey to America: How I Survived the War by Erna Wallach."

"There," said Nana. "A title for my speech in Washington."

Nana began typing. Her fingers flew, and the tapping sounded like a motor. Her eyes never looked at the keys. Jim read over her shoulder. "I was born a very long time ago in a medium-sized city in Germany. We lived across the street from a beautiful park. When I was a little girl, I thought I would live in Germany forever. But things changed."

Nana abruptly stopped typing and looked up at Jim. "It's not polite to read over someone's shoulder, Jimmy," she said, swatting him gently on his stomach. "I thought you had work to do!"

Jim moved away from the table and threw himself down on the couch. Nana resumed her typing, and it sounded as if the words were just pouring out of her. How could Nana, little ancient Nana, own a computer?

Jim stared at the yellow pad on his lap. Blank. He put the pencil point on the first blue line, hoping it would miraculously begin to spell out words, like a Ouija board. The pencil did begin to move, but before Jim could stop himself, he had drawn Nana's profile, her long, pointy nose, her big glasses, her deflated blond hair, the rounded shape of her back. He drew the black laptop and the lace tablecloth. Beneath the drawing he wrote in neat block letters, "Nana and her brand-new, supercool laptop."

"How are you doing, my darling?" asked Nana, peering at him over the top of her glasses.

"Oh, fine, Nana," said Jim, turning the pad so Nana couldn't see it.

On Wednesday Ms. Durbin asked Jim to stay after school.

"I have basketball practice, Ms. Durbin," he protested.

"What time?"

"Well, it's at, uh, seven-thirty, but I want to get all my homework done before dinner," said Jim, confident that the homework angle would get him off the hook.

"It won't take long, Jim. Be in my office right at two-forty, and I promise you'll be out of there by three."

Jim wondered what Ms. Durbin wanted from his life anyway. He had handed in the essay on Monday. If he had failed again, why didn't she just tell him?

In the cafeteria Jim always sat at the same table back in the corner near the soda machine. After the first few weeks of school you had to choose a table and then eat lunch there for the rest of the year. It was one of the principal's dumb ideas. Aside from Josh, the only other kids from the travel team were Frankie and Matt. Then there were kids who played soccer in the fall and kids who played baseball in the spring. It was known as the jock table.

Josh never brought lunch from home. He ate the school lunches, finishing every bite whether it was fish sticks or spaghetti. His parents were divorced, and his mother was a nurse, so she worked at all hours of the day and night. He had a sister, but she was away at some college in Ohio. Jim thought maybe that was why Josh talked so much in school; he didn't have anyone at home to talk to.

"Hey, Jim, sit here," said Josh, patting the empty chair next to him. His cheeks were puffed out like a chipmunk's, stuffed with today's special, tacos.

Lately Jim had been growing impatient with Josh's eternal chatter. Today he was in no mood for it. He was still trying to figure out what Ms. Durbin wanted to tell him. He knew his basketball career was hanging by a thread. Mom had made it clear: no travel team unless his grade in English improved.

"So my mom told me your grandmother wasn't even in the hospital," said Josh. He had a speck of tomato sauce on his chin. The other bad thing about Josh's blabbering was that it was loud enough for anyone within ten feet to hear.

"Whoa there, Squeak, you lyin' to Coach M?" said Frankie. "That could mean some nasty splinters in your butt!"

Jim could see that everyone at his end of the table was waiting for his reply. Now what? Another lie to cover the first lie? No, Mom had already told Josh's mother about the stupid opera. There was no use.

"My mom made me do it," said Jim. "My grandmother is so old that no matter what she wants, they always say yes. It was really dumb."

"Grandmothers can be so annoying," said Matt. "Mine sends me these handkerchiefs every Christmas with my initials embroidered on them. Like, what am I supposed to do with those?"

"Wipe your nose, dork! What do you think?" said Frankie.

"So what did your granny make you do?" asked Matt.

Before Jim could open his mouth, Josh blurted out, "She took him to the opera!"

"Me-me-me-me!" sang Frankie in a fake deep voice.

Jim wanted to take the rest of Josh's taco and plaster his face with it. "What did I miss at practice?" Jim asked, trying to change the subject.

"Not much," said Matt. "Some new drills, some scrimmaging. Mr. O'Malley ran most of it. Mondini was busy chewing out Lisa."

"Yeah, that was weird," said Frankie. "She made a bad pass, and he went ballistic on her and yanked her out and just kept right on wailing on her."

"I think she was crying," said Josh.

"I wish Mr. O was the head coach," said Frankie. "That old dude knows what he's doing."

"Mondini's a loose cannon, that's what my dad says," said Matt. "My dad went to high school with him. Says he was always crazy for basketball, went out for the team every year but was too small."

"Yeah, he is kinda runty," said Frankie.

"Then he went and married the tallest girl in their class," continued Matt.

"You mean tall like Rebecca Lobo?"

"Oh, yeah, big like that," said Matt. "She was voted the best girl athlete in their class."

"No wonder Lisa is so tall," said Frankie.

"My dad says Mondini is just pissed off because he never had any sons. He's got four daughters! Four of 'em, and only Lisa likes sports."

"So what's he trying to do? Make Lisa into a friggin' boy?" said Frankie.

"Yeah, what's she doing on a boys' travel team anyway?" said Jim.

"I think she's pretty good," said Josh. He was scraping the ice cream out of his Dixie cup.

They all stared at him. Actually, Jim had to admit Lisa was good, even better than some of the guys on the team, but he wasn't about to go public with that information. So he stared at Josh, too.

"What?" said Josh.

"You got a thing for Lisa Mondini?" said Frankie.

"Want to get hooked up with Lisa M?" said Matt.

"Hey, you guys, knock it off," said Josh. "I think she's a good player, that's all."

"Oooh, sounds serious to me," said Frankie, getting up to clear his tray.

"Young love," said Matt, putting a hand to his chest as if he were pledging allegiance to the flag.

Frankie and Matt left the table. Brad, who had been listening to the whole thing, said, "They'd never let a girl play on our baseball team. Softball is for girls. You guys should tell Lisa to go play tetherball!" He got up to follow Frankie and Matt out to the blacktop.

Josh muttered something under his breath. Then he looked at Jim. "Why are they such losers?"

Jim didn't know what to say. This was all part of what was getting more complicated here in seventh grade, part of how everything around Jim (except for him!) was changing. Girls. Girls you used to hang out with at the vacant lot down on Colonial Street were now becoming these mysterious beings who smelled different and giggled all the time about their little secrets. They were getting tall. They were getting boobs. Jim felt shy around most of them.

Lisa Mondini was different. Sure, in school she tried to glam herself up with blue eye shadow and dangly earrings like the other girls. But then she went and played basketball with the boys! Not tennis or volleyball. Basketball! She got all sweaty and jabbed her elbows in their ribs and jumped as high as any of them. Lisa Mondini wasn't normal. How could anybody have a crush on her? Plus she was the coach's daughter. Josh was crazy to have a crush on a girl like that.

Josh sat there with that speck of sauce still on his chin and some chocolate ice cream now on his Lakers T-shirt, looking forlornly at Jim. Like a lovesick puppy, Jim thought.

"Hey, no big deal, Josh," said Jim. "Lisa's a cool girl. Just don't go talking about her so much."

"But all I said was—"

"Yeah, she is a pretty good player," Jim interrupted. Even though I totally skinned her last week and she laughed at my nickname. "But you've gotta admit it's weird that she wants to play on a boys' team."

Jim got up to throw away his brown paper bag of lunch trash. He suddenly realized how smoothly he had avoided talking about the opera mess. He also felt relieved that he wasn't the one with the crush on Lisa.

"Come on, Josh," said Jim. "Let's go play some hoops."

When Jim got to room 119 at exactly two-forty, Ms. Durbin was sitting at her desk, grading papers.

70

She gestured for Jim to sit down while she finished writing a comment in red ink on the page before her. Jim didn't even have to read the name scrawled across the second line. He knew the big loopy handwriting, all the *i*'s dotted with circles the size of Red Hots. It had to be Mariah's. Ms. Durbin wrote a big red A.

"Jim, I finally had a chance to read your essay last night," Ms. Durbin said. She reached for a pile of paper pinned down by a heavy gray stapler. "It was very interesting."

"Thanks," Jim said. Did "interesting" mean good or bad?

"You typed this yourself?"

Jim thought about lying, just saying yeah so he wouldn't have to get into a long explanation, but instead he said, "No, my grandmother did. She's a really fast typist."

"Did she change any of it when she typed it?" asked Ms. Durbin as her eyes scanned the essay. "I mean, did she correct or add words?"

"No way," said Jim. "My grandmother doesn't really speak much English. She's from Germany and has this serious accent. You can hardly understand her." Now Jim was treading on shaky ground. Nana *had* made a few suggestions. In fact, the whole part about the costumes was Nana's idea. But why did Durbin have to know anyway?

"Well, it's very well written," said Ms. Durbin. "I especially liked the first part about visiting with your grandmother at her apartment before the opera. You did a nice job of describing everything."

"Thanks," said Jim. He had written that part all by himself.

"You know, we'll be doing interviews with older members of our families at the end of the year, as part of our Roots project," said Ms. Durbin. "You should use your grandmother. She sounds like a very interesting lady."

Ms. Durbin continued to read Jim's essay silently. He wondered how much longer this would take. "I like this part a lot: 'My grandmother is very slow in her arms and legs. She can't move fast, but her mind is faster than most people I know. She notices everything. My grandmother is a modern lady.'" Ms. Durbin put the essay down in front of Jim. He saw the grade. An A. Jim couldn't tell Ms. Durbin, but this was the first A he'd gotten in English since that poem about baseball he had written in the third grade.

"Cool," Jim said. "Thanks."

"Don't thank me. You did it, Jim." Ms. Durbin pushed up her sleeves as though she were about to wash dishes. She plunged her hands into a big pile of papers on her desk. "There's something I want to talk to you about," she said.

Ms. Durbin pulled out a piece of paper. Across the top, in bold letters, were the words *Essay Contest.*

Why had he ever let Nana help him, even a little bit? Now Ms. Durbin thought he was a some kind of writing genius. This was getting out of control!

"I want you to read your essay in the county public speaking contest in April. I think you have a good chance of winning."

Had Ms. Durbin gone off the deep end? Didn't she remember how hard it was for Jim even to answer questions in class? She expected him to get up on a stage in front of a hundred people? "I can't do that," said Jim. "I really can't."

"Why not?" said Ms. Durbin. She leaned closer to Jim until he could see this chicken pox scar she had over her upper lip. "You just need to practice a little. It's not as scary as it looks. I'll tell you a little secret. When I started student teaching, I was terrified!"

"I—uh, I don't know," Jim stammered, trying to find the right words. He didn't want to sound like a wimp. *Terrified* was the word that came to mind when he pictured a sea of faces all looking at him and waiting for him to speak, but instead he said, "Ms. Durbin, I don't have a very loud voice."

"You'll have a microphone."

"My ears turn red."

"You'll be up on a stage, behind a lectern. No one will be able to see that."

"I start sweating like a pig," said Jim. He didn't know if pigs really sweat or not, but Pete always used this expression.

"Well, if worse comes to worst, you can always designate one of your classmates to read it for you—maybe Mariah? She has a wonderful loud voice, and we all know she isn't shy."

Mariah read his essay? No way!

"Here, take your essay. Think about it," said Ms. Durbin. Then she added, "By the way, there are prizes. First prize is a computer, second is a CD player, and third is a calculator. Here's a copy of the contest rules. Think about it. Show your folks and your grandmother."

Jim stuffed everything into his book bag. "I really better go," he said. "The late bus will leave without me if I'm not out front when it gets here." As Jim stood up, his chair made a loud, scraping noise.

"You know, Jim, it's amazing to me that your grandmother, who speaks so little English, could beat you in Scrabble!"

"Just lucky, I guess," said Jim as he turned to leave before Ms. Durbin could see his reddening ears and maybe reconsider the A.

Jim made sure he got to the gym early for the practice. The school custodian was just unlocking the doors and turning on the lights.

"Hey, young fella," he said. "You must be one of those hotshot basketball players. Saw you fellas practicing on Saturday. Nice team you got there, some real talent." He was an older man with a grooved red face and sparse gray hair. His jeans were held up by suspenders. He had been the janitor at Pigeon Hill since Pete went to school there. Jim remembered his name. Mr. McSorley.

Jim had brought his own basketball and bounced it once on the gym floor.

"You're a wee fella for a basketball player, ain'tcha?" continued Mr. McSorley. "Ever consider switching to soccer or something?"

Jim didn't answer. He dribbled furiously in the direction of one of the baskets. Wee fella this, old man, Jim thought as he sprang to the basket to make a layup.

"Hey, not bad!" Mr. McSorley's voice echoed through the gym.

Jim dribbled around the arc, enjoying the rhythm of the basketball thuds, the intense gleam of the polished floor, the vast emptiness of the gym. He remembered last fall, when they had driven through the pouring rain to look at colleges for Pete in Philadelphia. At every stop Jim had insisted that they visit the field house and see the basketball court. He had seen most of these courts on TV, the stands filled with crazed fans, college kids with painted faces, pep bands swinging their horns from side to side. But it was different when he walked into the middle of the empty arena or climbed to a seat up by the broadcasters' booth. Jim could imagine himself in a college game, where all the players were huge and strong and fast and he was the starting point guard.

"You think you'll ever play D-one ball, little kid?" Pete had said in his most sarcastic voice. "Dream on!"

"Villanova!" came Marco's voice from the doorway. "Come on, Malone, Villanova hasn't been a true contender for years!"

"I got these when we visited Villanova last fall with my brother," said Jim, practicing a jump shot. "He's looking at colleges."

"Well, don't tell me you went beggin' your mama for a pair of those sorry old 'Nova shorts," said Marco with a laugh. "That's pathetic." Marco knocked the ball away from Jim. "Missed you Saturday."

"I hear I didn't miss anything."

"Oh, you missed something, my friend," said Marco. "Mondini was in a ripe mood. From now on I'm calling him Mondo Mondini!"

More players arrived. Lisa threw down the bag of basketballs she was carrying and started to unzip her warm-up suit. She was frowning. Josh and Mr. Mondini followed her.

Jim was chasing a ball rolling off the court and happened to hear Mr. Mondini say, "Look, Josh, you have to be honest with me. If your hamstring is bothering you, you should take it easy. I want you to be ready for Saturday's scrimmage."

"Well, I really want to play in the scrimmage. Maybe I'll sit out tonight's practice," said Josh.

As Jim jogged back out to Marco, Sean, and Frankie, he tried not to smile, but Marco said, "What's so funny, man?"

"Nothing," Jim said. He was thinking that maybe he'd get a chance to prove himself with the starters tonight.

"Mondini in a bad mood again?" said Marco.

"No, he seems okay," said Jim. "Lisa's in a funk, but she always is."

"Don't be harsh," said Marco, grinning widely as he took a long floating jump shot. "She's a woman, and you know how women can get!" Then his expression changed. "Heck, she has no business trying to hang with the big boys anyway. She's playing *my* position. I worked my butt off all fall down at the playground with the high school dudes, but now, just because her daddy is the coach, she skates right into the starting lineup!"

"Hey, Marco, it's only week two," said Jim. "Me and you, we'll both crack the starting lineup. You'll see."

Again, Mr. O'Malley ran all the drills while Mr. Mondini made notes on his clipboard. Jim wondered what the man could be writing, a novel? Mr. O, as he had instructed them to call him, had some new drills, weaves, and shooting, stuff Jim had never done before. He felt good, moving easily around the other players, making good passes, just "getting the job done," as Dad liked to say. "The coach always wants the guys who can get the job done. No fancy dribbling moves, no between-the-legs stuff, just good solid basketball." Dad told the story about Arnie Harmon, a high school teammate who was skinny and geeky but started every basketball game. "When the whistle blew, Arnie just went to work. Everybody forgot about his old beat-up sneakers and Coke bottle glasses. He couldn't slam dunk or get above the rim. But Arnie always found the open man and made the thoughtful pass. He got the job done."

When they finally got down to scrimmaging, Mr. Mondini called Lisa, Frankie, Slade, and Matt and then hesitated before he called Jim to join them. Josh was sitting on the floor, making a big show of stretching his legs.

The first few times down the floor Jim pushed the ball hard and sprinted. He made a quick, clean jump shot. On his team's second possession Jim made a good pass to Frankie, who missed his shot. The third trip down the court Jim made a bounce pass to Lisa, who gave a bad pass to Slade, letting Marco steal the ball for a breakaway.

"Lisa, you have to make eye contact on these passes," bellowed Mr. Mondini. "How many times do I have to tell you these things?" He shook his head as if he had just seen something really pathetic. "And, Jim, you don't always have to rush so fast down the court!" Mr Mondini called out. "Work with your teammates. Call some plays. Try Carolina."

"Carolina" was one of the three plays Mr. Mondini had dia- grammed out for them. Jim thought it was dumb because it relied on passing the ball around the perimeter until someone could break free. To Jim it felt like basketball in slow motion, a party game for kindergarten kids.

"Carolina!" Jim yelled the next time he brought the ball down. He passed to Matt, who passed back to him. He passed to Lisa, who passed to Slade and over to Frankie. This is fun, thought Jim, trying not to yawn. Even Nana could do this! When the ball got back to him, he made a good fake and shot over Damian. *Swish.*

"Attaboy!" said Mr. Mondini. "See what a little patience will get you!"

"Mr. Mondini, I think I could play," said Josh the next time Matt took the ball out of bounds.

"No, Josh, you take it easy tonight," said Mr. Mondini. "Save yourself for Saturday. We're going to need you."

You're not going to need him at all, thought Jim as he caught Matt's pass. I'm your point guard, Mr. Mondini. I may not be big and flashy, but I get the job done.

J IM DID NOT want anyone in his family to come to the first Thunderbirds scrimmage. All week he had been careful not to mention it to Mom, Dad, and especially Pete. Nobody on the team had said anything about their parents' coming. He sure didn't want Mom and Dad to be the only ones. Jim was also getting anxious about who was going to start the game. Mondini had made no promises at the end of practice, but Jim had heard him say to Josh, "I'm counting on you to be ready on Saturday!" Jim tried to convince himself it was no big deal, it was just a stupid scrimmage. But they were going to wear their brand-new, Carolina blue game jerseys and have two official referees and a scoreboard, and Jim did not want to be sitting on the bench.

On Saturday morning, as Jim was standing in the kitchen filling a bowl with Cheerios, Mom said, "Did I hear something about a basketball scrimmage today?"

How had Mom found out? Mrs. DeLonga, no doubt.

Jim shrugged.

"What time does it start?" asked Mom.

"Look, Mom, it's just a scrimmage. It'll be more like a practice. Nobody has to come. They probably won't even have chairs," said Jim.

He could see Dad's big feet sticking out from under the table. Dad was measuring a piece of molding that ran along the floor in the kitchen.

"Jim, write this down: fifty-two inches long, two and one half inches tall," said Dad.

"So you won't come, right?" Jim said to Dad's feet.

"Come where, little Jimmy?" said Pete, walking into the kitchen.

"Nowhere," said Jim.

"Come on, tell your big brother. Are we talking about . . . mmm . . . basketball?"

"It's nothing," insisted Jim.

"Oh, but it is! And you know, little bro, how I wish I could come, but alas, I have to play in the pep band at the high school game today," said Pete. "Oh, the disappointment of it all!"

Dad crawled out from under the table with tufts of dog fur clinging to the elbows of his flannel shirt. "Now, what were you saying, Jim?"

"My scrimmage today, you don't have to come."

"I might get over there a little late," said Dad. "I really want to finish replacing this molding and get it painted. You won't be disappointed if I miss it? I promise I'll get to the first real game."

"No, Dad," said Jim. "No big deal."

"Don't worry, Jim," said Mom. "Nana and I will be there to cheer you on."

Nana? Again? She had to be kidding. Who did Nana think she was, the president of the Jim Malone Fan Club?

"Aw, come on, Mom, no!" said Jim. He was not going to become the laughingstock of his team with his old grandmother in her fur coat like some little bear mascot sitting there cheering him on. "I don't want anyone to come. Nobody else's parents are coming!"

"But, Jim, she loves to see you play your sports. I know you guys don't believe it, but Nana was really into sports as a young girl. She was quite a swimmer!"

"Yeah, right," said Jim. "Big deal. She still doesn't know anything about basketball. She'll probably be rooting for the wrong team!"

"Last fall she came to almost all your soccer games."

"That was different," said Jim. It was one thing to be outdoors on a gigantic field where the fans yelled and screamed but seemed very far away. In the gym the fans sat on folding chairs right up along the sidelines.

"Well, it's too late," said Mom. "She's already on her way."

"Mom, how can you do this to me? It's not fair!" Jim made a fist and, before he could stop himself, pounded on the table, causing Dad's box of nails to fall over.

Pete let out a long, ominous whistle and walked away, carrying his bowl of cereal.

"James, please pick up those nails, every last one, and then go to your room," said Dad stonily.

Mom remained silent. She walked over to the cabinet and got out her travel mug and filled it with hot coffee. She stirred in some sugar. Now the only sounds were the spoon in the mug, the nails falling back into their box, the tags on Jake's collar as he scratched himself under the table. Then Mom said, "I'm going down to the station to pick up Nana," and left.

Jim went up to his room. He had all his basketball stuff laid out on his bed, the jersey, the shorts, some black socks, and a white T-shirt to wear under the jersey to hide his bony arms. His sneakers were lined up under the bed. On his desk a copy of *Sports Illustrated* lay open to a full-page picture of Tim Duncan. There were pictures of other players in a pile next to the magazine, pictures Jim was cutting out to use in a collage to hang over his bed. He sat down at the desk and picked up the scissors.

It *wasn't* fair! It was *his* life! Nobody ever bothered to ask him. They were always just assuming and planning. Why couldn't *he* decide if he wanted Nana there? Why did Nana have to come up here all the time anyway? Why couldn't she be like Pappy and Gram, Dad's parents, who only came for Thanksgiving and Christmas? Actually it wouldn't even be so bad if Pappy came because at least he knew something about basketball! And Gram, she was quieter than Nana; she didn't stand out as much. She wore plain clothes and didn't talk with that annoying German accent. Gram would just sit there almost invisible, not like Nana, who had to talk to everyone and would probably go right up to Mondini and say something crazy like "My Jimmy is the best player on the team!"

"Have you calmed down?" asked Dad from the doorway.

"Yeah . . . but, Dad, I still don't see why Nana has to come to my scrimmage. She doesn't even like sports," said Jim, snipping the edge of the magazine cover until it looked like fringe. "I mean, she doesn't know the difference between a layup and a floater, a forward and a guard. She's clueless when it comes to basketball."

"That's not the point," said Dad. "She comes to see you play because she loves you very much. It wouldn't matter if it were sumo wrestling! You and Pete are her only grandchildren. You can't understand how deeply she loves you guys." Dad paused. Jim knew what was coming next. "Nana came to this country with only one relative left in the world, her sister. That was it."

Jim knew the whole story about how Nana had lost every member of her family in the Holocaust except for Tante Sarah. It was a story Nana told every Thanksgiving just before they blessed their food and Dad carved the turkey. When Jim was little, he would take Nana's hand and say, "Don't be sad, Nana. You have us now." And Nana would always answer the same way: "Such a lucky woman, I am, my darling. I am blessed."

"You should listen to the stories your nana tells you," said Dad. "You can learn a lot from her."

Yeah, sure, thought Jim. Maybe if I wanted to learn German or opera history or something useful like that.

"She certainly has taught me a lot about what really matters in life," said Dad.

Well, what really matters in my life right now is Nana not coming to my scrimmage, thought Jim. She can love me and tell me her stories some other time. Why does my basketball have to be a family affair? Jim knew he should just back off and say, "Fine, Dad, you're right," but he couldn't bring himself to say anything.

"Maybe I shouldn't even let you go to the scrimmage because of your little outburst," said Dad, eyeing the uniform on Jim's bed.

Jim sucked in his breath hard and held it.

"What do you think?" said Dad.

"Look, Dad, I'm really, really sorry. I swear," said Jim.

"Glad to hear it."

Dad looked down at the pictures on Jim's desk. "You sure love this game, don't you, Jim?"

Jim smiled his fakest smile. That's it, Dad, he thought, let's move away from punishment right into quality father-son time.

"When I was your age, I thought about only two things: basketball and the trumpet."

Yeah, yeah, yeah. Blah, blah, blah. Jim had heard these stories a million times, but hey, he'd be very happy to hear them for the million and first time if it could distract Dad from punishing him. Jim looked right at Dad to show him he was eager to hear the classic tales of Mitch Malone, high school superstar.

Dad had been cut from his basketball team when he was a sophomore because he was too small, so he had turned to his trumpet and played with a jazz band to fill his spare time. "Then I shot up five inches, and the next year Coach Briggs begged me to come out for the team again." Jim was starting to fade out. ". . . high school's all-time leading scorer in just two years . . . then college ball . . . hulking forward . . . biggest rival . . . a jump shot, a buzzer beater . . . then the next year . . . conference title . . . two-hundred-twenty-pound mountain of a guy . . . on my right foot . . . crushed my anklebone . . . end of my basketball career." Jim shook his head sympathetically. "But I still have my trumpet!" Dad said as if Jim hadn't known that already.

"Well, I'd better get going." Dad looked at his watch. He started to leave but then turned back and said, "Have fun today. And don't forget, arch your wrists on release." Dad raised one of his long arms and demonstrated. "Got it?"

There were only twenty minutes until Jim was due at the Pigeon Hill gym. Mondini had told them to all be there forty-five minutes before tip-off and not one minute later. Jim paced the kitchen anxiously and looked at the clock on the stove. He was ready to go, had been for half an hour, with his warm-up jacket zipped to his chin, his fat sneakers laced, his bag over his shoulder.

"Where are they?" he asked Jake, who was watching him cross the kitchen over and over. Mom and Nana still had not gotten back from the station. "It's all Nana's fault. If I get there late, I can forget about starting the game. No chance of that. I may as well stay home."

Pete walked into the kitchen in his bright red band T-shirt. "Hey, punk, don't you have to be over at the gym now? What happened to Mom and Nana?"

"Who knows?" said Jim. "At the rate Nana moves, she's probably still coming down the stairs at the station."

"Yo, shrimp! Ease up on your grandmother," said Pete. "I mean, she is almost seven times older than you! I'd like to see you sprint down those stairs when you're eighty-two!"

"Well, maybe if Mom and Dad would get into this century and buy a cell phone, we could call Mom and find out where she is," said Jim.

"Dream on, little Jimmy," said Pete. "In case you haven't noticed, our parents are stuck in a seventies time warp."

There was the sound of a motor in the driveway and a couple of honks.

"It's Tricia," said Pete, grabbing his jacket off the chair. "Come on, we'll drop you off."

Tricia was Pete's latest girlfriend and his most glamorous yet. She was a cheerleader, had long, straight hair the color of maple syrup, and drove a red Miata. Jim got nervous around her. When she walked into their house, the whole place started to smell like lilacs. It was as if some MTV girl had stepped out of the television set. She didn't seem real.

"Hi, cutie," she said to Jim as he squeezed into the backseat.

Pete changed completely around Tricia. "Hey, Trish," he said cheerily. "Do you mind if we take a detour by Pigeon Hill? Jim's got a basketball scrimmage." Pete said this with such concern as if he were the most wonderful big brother on the planet.

"No problema," said Tricia. She looked over her shoulder as she backed up, and Jim leaned to one side so he wouldn't be staring into her face. Jim could not figure out why she wanted to date crusty Pete. He had those ugly zits on his forehead and those bushy eyebrows and that floppy ear. Jim wondered if they had ever made out, maybe here in this car? Jim had kissed a girl only once, at Gillian Dunphy's birthday party in September, the one where they played flashlight tag in the backyard. During the second round he had found himself behind the rhododendron bush by the garage with Liz Bertini, this girl with Brillo-y blond hair and red-framed glasses. As they crouched down, the branches poking their backs, she had suddenly leaned over and

planted a wet one right on his lips! Jim had stared at her in surprise. Even in the dark he could clearly see her demented bug eyes staring back at him. As she pushed against him, they both lost their balance and fell into the bush. Then someone's flashlight scanned their knees, and Jim heard giggling. He scrambled to his feet, trying to find out who was laughing, but all he saw was a fluttering shadow and all he heard was the crackling of leaves. Seventh-grade girls were such losers.

But kissing Tricia . . . now, that would be cool.

"So Katie tells me that Andrea, you know Andrea Mondini, she like makes up this whole story about how I was flirting with Jay during the fire drill and how I'm such a slut and can't be trusted, and I was like, whoa, lady, take a chill pill. I've never said two words to Jay." Tricia talked the way she drove, very fast.

Pete did not seem to be listening. He just nodded.

"I know what's up with Andrea," Tricia continued. "She's mad because I was picked to be the captain of the cheerleaders. I know that's it. She thinks just because her big sister Jen was captain a couple of years ago, it's like her right to be captain this year. Give me a break! Those Mondinis are the most stuck-up girls I ever saw."

Mondinis? Lisa's sisters? Jim wondered if he had heard that right. He wanted to ask, but when he saw Tricia's eyes looking at him in the rearview mirror, he couldn't bring himself to speak.

"Don't worry, little Malone, we're almost there!" she said.

Tricia and Pete dropped Jim at the outside gym doors and sped off. He pulled on the door handles, but they wouldn't budge. Now Jim had to run around the entire building to the front doors of the school, down the first-grade hall, past the library to the gym. He looked through the little square window before entering and saw Mr. Mondini and Mr. O setting up a giant clock on wheels. Lisa, Josh, and Frankie were stretching on the floor next to some folding chairs. Slade was tying his shoelaces. Good, thought Jim, at least I'm not late. The other team wasn't even there yet.

"Hey, Jim!" said Frankie.

Josh gave him a funny little salute, something he had picked up from a movie and now did all the time because he thought it was cool.

Lisa said, "Hi," but in an uninterested way. She looked as if she'd rather be anywhere but here.

Mr. McSorley came in carrying two armloads of gray metal folding chairs, which he took to the other side of the gym. There were a couple of parents talking. "Sorry, sir, but you'll have to take that coffee outside," Mr. McSorley bellowed. "No drinking in the gym. Gotta keep these floors clean as a whistle for these hotshot basketball players!"

After the rest of the team had gotten there, they took a group jog around the perimeter of the court. A few of the Kings were just coming in, wearing matching warm-ups, dark green with yellow lettering. One of them was almost Pete's size.

"These guys look serious," said Marco.

Jim noticed the folding chairs filling with parents. Scrimmage or no scrimmage, people were coming to watch. One woman was bouncing a baby on her lap.

"Hey, Mama!" called Marco as they passed her.

Jim felt a surge of relief. Other parents, other fans, meant Nana and Mom wouldn't stand out. If they ever got there.

Jim listened to Mr. O announce the starting lineup: Frankie, check; Lisa, check; Slade, check; Matt, check; and Josh—what? Jim couldn't believe his ears. Josh hadn't even practiced with them!

"Jeez," Jim muttered under his breath.

"Okay, hands in," said Mr. Mondini, looking right at Jim. "One, two, three, *together*!" Everyone bellowed it out except for Jim who said "together" in a quiet monotone.

He collapsed onto one of the chairs and sat slouched forward, looking down at the floor between his feet.

"If you expect to play, Mr. Malone, I suggest you get rid of the attitude," said Mr. Mondini as he took the chair next to Jim.

Jim sat up and folded his arms across his chest. He looked out at the tip-off and watched Frankie win it and pass the ball to Josh, who called, "Georgetown," in his bossiest voice.

Jim knew this bossy voice. It was the one Josh used when he played goalie on the soccer team and screamed, "Mark up!" to the defenders. It was the one Josh used when he told Jim to hurry up and make his move during Monopoly games. This bossy voice usually made Jim laugh but not today. He kept reminding himself it was only the first scrimmage, but if things kept going this way, it was going to be awfully hard to remain best friends with Josh DeLonga.

Josh passed to Matt, and the team began an in-and-out pattern, like a square dance they had done in third-grade gym class. Everyone moved smoothly and comfortably. The passes were all good. "That's what we want to see," said Mr. Mondini. "Nice work, guys."

Out of the corner of his eye Jim saw some rustling on the other side of the gym. It was Nana! A man was getting up to give her his seat, and she was thanking him in a loud voice. Mom was standing behind them, and she caught Jim's eye and waved to him. Jim looked away quickly.

He watched the ball go up and down the court, a basket, a miss, a rebound; the score stayed close. Frankie and Slade were doing most of the scoring, Matt was working hard, rebounding with fury, and Lisa was basically passing the ball a lot. Her passes were good but it seemed as if she were afraid to hold on to the ball for too long. It reminded Jim of someone playing Hot Potato. Josh didn't seem to be doing anything much except bringing the ball down and calling out plays. A couple of times the point guard for the Kings, a wiry little guy with goggles strapped across his face, snatched the ball right out of Josh's dribble, but even though he had an open net, the wiry guy missed both layups.

"Josh should be toasting that little string bean," said Marco. "That's pathetic!"

Mr. Mondini looked across Jim to Marco. "What is it, Coach?" said Marco. "I'm just saying what I see."

"Sean and Kenny, get ready to go in," Mr. Mondini called out.

Jim glanced at the clock and wondered if he would get in this half at all.

The Kings called a time-out. When the Thunderbirds came off the floor, Jim and Marco and the others stood up to let them sit down. Josh was drenched in sweat and grabbed his towel before noisily taking Jim's chair.

"Okay, fellas," said Mr. Mondini. "You're holding your own out there. Maybe a little slow to make the transitions, but you're doing a nice job with the zone defense—once you get there. Lisa, I want you to tighten up on number five. He's a dangerous player." The referee blew his whistle. "Okay, one, two, three . . . *together*!"

Jim imagined he was out on the floor, how he'd slice and dice that little googly-eyed guard and make his head spin. He pictured himself peeling away from the kid, moving past that number 22 with a dazzling stutter step, and making the fadeaway jumper. He looked across the floor and saw Nana talking to the woman next to her, Marco's mother. Nana was waving her hands around as if she were describing the shape and size of an elephant, and then he saw her point right in his direction. Jim looked away before she started waving and calling his name.

"Jim!" It was Mr. Mondini. "Come on, I want you to go in."

Jim trotted over to the table where Kenny's father was running the clock and crouched down. Of course, now it seemed that the ball never went out of bounds. Jim watched the seconds ticking away. There were less than two minutes left in the half. Finally a ball came rolling off the court, and the ref blew his whistle.

Well, it wasn't exactly a Duke-UNC game, but it felt good to be running out to the center of the court. Some of the parents clapped. Jim knew they were clapping for Josh, who was leaving the game, but then he heard Nana's voice above the clapping: "Go, Jimmy!" Lisa grinned at him.

The google-eyed kid immediately threw his arms up in front of Jim's face. They were even skinnier and bonier than Jim's own arms. This kid was one of those annoying pesky players who jump and flail like moths around a flashlight. There was only one way to handle this kid: Burn him!

On his first trip down the court Jim turned on his jets and streaked past the flapping arms of the other point guard. Come on, kid, Jim thought, let's see how fast you are anyway. Jim called, "Kentucky," a play they had learned at the end of the last practice. He had gone over all the plays again this morning and felt confident he could complete this one. But he wasn't so sure about the other players, especially Kenny, who was going to have to be aggressive to the hoop. Well, Jim was ready to dive in if necessary, so he started the play, passing to

Lisa. Sean began to slide across the paint, as he was supposed to, Matt executed a perfect pick, and Jim rolled by two defenders to receive Lisa's pass, which he then passed to Kenny, who was positioned under the basket. Come on, Kenny, nice and easy, catch the ball and just shoot it, Jim thought as he watched his pass sail over the last defender's outstretched hands. Kenny jumped, his arms fully extended above his head, found the ball, and for once didn't bobble it. Jim knew he was thinking about taking a dribble, just one, to be sure he had the ball, so Jim yelled out, "Shoot the ball, Kenny! *Shoot!*" Like a remote-control car under Jim's direction, Kenny immediately shot the basketball. It dropped. Jim could hear Mondini and Mr. O clapping loudly.

Before he knew it, in what seemed seconds, the buzzer sounded, marking halftime.

"Okay, guys, you're really holding your own against a very tough opponent," said Mr. Mondini. "We're down by only two. Now we'll start the second half the way we started the game."

"What the . . ." Marco muttered.

"Do you have something to say, Marco?" asked Mr. Mondini, his eyes narrower than ever, a vague sneer crossing his face.

"Yeah, as a matter of fact, I do, Coach," said Marco, jutting out his chin and folding his arms across his chest. "What about some of us who haven't played yet? I mean, I thought this was a scrimmage, not the NBA finals!"

Jim could not believe Marco's nerve. He spoke as though he and Mr. Mondini were equals. Jim knew if he had tried to utter these words, it would have sounded like a tantrum or whining or both.

Mr. Mondini found a little more space around his eyes to narrow. "Marco Brooks, don't ever question a coach's decision. Ever! Not if you expect to play."

"Oh, I expect to play," said Marco. "I just want to know when."

"You are using up team time here," said Mr. Mondini. "I'll speak to you after the game."

As Mr. Mondini continued his halftime pep talk, Jim stopped listening altogether. What was the point if he was going to be riding the bench again? When Dad asked him how the scrimmage had gone, what would he say: "Oh, yeah, Dad, the bench was real comfy, just like a sofa." With Mom and Nana there as witnesses, the whole thing would be discussed at dinner, and Pete would have lots of new ammunition for future mocking.

Marco and Jim took the end seats, the farthest from the coaches. Dad had always told Jim that when you're a sub, you want to stay "in the coach's face, so he doesn't forget about you." But Jim could not bring himself to sit next to Mondini.

"This whole thing is whack, man," said Marco. "My mama has to sit over there with the baby to watch me on the bench? I'm growing friggin' roots here. And all because Mondo Mondini doesn't know a dog's eyelash about the game of basketball."

Jim dismissed what Dad had said about showing the same intensity even if you're sitting on the bench. He started to laugh at what Marco said. Why shouldn't we yuck it up a little? he thought. We're not doing anything else!

Jim looked over and saw Nana and Marco's mother still engrossed in conversation, only now Nana had the baby on her lap! That's how Nana always was. She'd start talking to someone and next thing you knew they were best friends. "Hey, look," said Marco. "Your grandma is holding Cherise, my sister!"

Damian was the first sub in. He lost the ball three times in a row, so Mr. O called him out again and put Josh back in.

Finally, with about three minutes left in the fourth quarter, Marco and Jim went in.

"Well, hallelujah. Come on, Malone, let's kick some butt!" said Marco.

The Kings were ahead by six. Their big guy had fouled out, but the rest of their starters were in. As soon as Jim began playing, he forgot everything that was bothering him: riding the bench, Nana visiting again, Josh being the starter. In fact, everything outside the court disappeared. It didn't matter if one person or a hundred were watching him. As long as Jim didn't have to speak, the way he did in front of his classes at school, he could do anything. He knew with every cell in his body that he was good at this game. When he held a basketball in his hands, something happened to him. He suddenly felt two things he never felt any other time: confident and smart.

This was a good team on the floor: Frankie, Slade, Lisa, Marco, and him. Jim felt sure of himself calling out the plays. Also, the google-eyed kid seemed to be getting tired. His arms were drooping and not flapping as much. "Georgetown!" "Kentucky!" "Purdue!" The ball was moving quickly from hand to hand, and the Thunderbirds were shooting well.

When there were seventeen seconds left, Jim glanced at the scoreboard. His team was up by two. They had to keep possession and eat the clock. He dribbled slowly and called, "Carolina!"—the nice, outside passing play. Just an easygoing game of catch. Suddenly Google-Eyes leaped in and stole a bounce pass going from Marco to Lisa. He took off down the court. Where had this burst of energy come from? Jim tore off after him, and as the kid started to jump up for a shot, Jim tried desperately to slap the ball away but caught the kid's bony arm instead. The referee's whistle shrieked, and he signaled a foul. Then Jim realized they were outside the arc and the kid was going to get three foul shots. He could win the game for the Kings!

As they lined up for the foul shots, Jim felt his eyes sting. No way this kid would make all three. No way!

The kid bounced the ball five times, then heaved it up as though it were incredibly heavy. *Swish*. Then he bounced the ball five times again, brought the ball up, and, with a smoother, stronger motion, shot the ball right through the hoop. Jim felt shooting pains running down both legs. He hated this, not being able to do anything but watch. The kid took his lucky five bounces again and with a groan pushed the ball up and out toward the basket. It seemed to hang in the air. Then with a boingy sound it hit the rim and fell in. Six seconds later the final buzzer sounded.

Jim tried to jog off the court, but his legs felt like lead.

"Why'd you have to foul him?" said Slade with a pained expression.

"Yeah, man, that was foolish!" Frankie chimed in.

"Fellas, we'll discuss the game after we line up and shake hands with the other team," said Mr. Mondini.

Josh looked at Jim and said, "Sorry."

"Yeah, right, sure you are," said Jim bitterly.

Mr. Mondini told them they had played a good game and except for a few mistakes, "meltdowns" he called them, they could have easily beaten the Kings. He never looked at Jim or said anything about the foul. "I'll see you guys at practice Wednesday night, right here, at seven-thirty."

Jim put on his warm-up jacket and stuffed the pants in his bag. He saw Nana and Mom waiting for him by the gym doors. Nana! He had forgotten all about her being there.

"Good game," said Mom as he approached them. "Sorry we were so late. Nana was confused about the train schedule. She took the eleven-oh-five instead of the ten-oh-five."

"I'm such a *dummkopf* sometimes!" said Nana with a laugh.

"Tough luck at the end there, but you played well, honey," said Mom.

"You played fantastic," said Nana. "Not 'well,' fantastic!"

Stop, Nana. Please stop. Jim was not in the mood for Nana's expert analysis. Or Mom's, for that matter.

"And you!" Nana said with enthusiasm to someone behind Jim. "Josh, you were wonderful, too. So fast!"

"Hi, Nana," said Josh. "Thanks a lot." Nana had known Josh since he and Jim were in kindergarten. Josh had always called her Nana. He called his own grandmother Grandma. Jim called Josh's grandmother Grandma, too. But all of a sudden it annoyed Jim to hear Josh say "Nana." She's my grandmother, not yours, thought Jim.

"Do you need a ride home?" asked Mom.

"Uh, no, thanks, Mrs. Malone. Coach said he'd drop me off," said Josh.

Isn't that nice and cozy? thought Jim.

"I'll go get the car," said Mom. "Jim, you help Nana walk to the door."

Jim wanted to run, no, sprint out of this school away from the phony calls of "Good game!" by the exiting Kings and the grudging responses of his fellow Thunderbirds. But no, he had to slow down for Nana and listen to her labored breathing as everyone passed them.

"Nice game," said Lisa as she came up alongside Jim. Instead of passing Jim and Nana, she fell into step with them.

"Ah, the very brave young lady!" said Nana, smiling at Lisa. "You play just as good as those boys. What is your name?"

"Lisa."

"I'm Jim's grandmother. It is very nice to meet you." Nana came to a complete stop and faced Lisa. She put out one of her old hands to shake Lisa's. "What a pretty girl you are! Isn't she pretty?" Nana said to Jim. He knew his face was red.

"I hope you can make it to some of our other games," said Lisa.

She doesn't need season tickets, Jim wanted to say.

"Well, since Jimmy is going to be so busy with this basketball business, I will have to come if I want to see him!" Nana continued to hold Lisa's hand and now patted it. "You be careful out there with those big boys. Don't let them break any of your teeth or your pretty nose."

Lisa seemed delighted. "Don't worry. I can handle them!"

"Let's go, Lisa," said Mr. Mondini. "We have to get to the supermarket."

"Oh, here is the coach," said Nana as if she were the hostess at some party and Mr. Mondini a newly arrived guest. "Congratulations!"

Jim wanted to duck into one of the first-grade classrooms. Hadn't Nana even been watching the game? Could she really be that clueless? Lisa giggled.

"Ma'am?" Mr. Mondini said.

"Oh, I'm Jim's grandmother," she said, offering her gnarled old hand again. "I enjoyed the game. Such players you have!"

"Yeah, well, thanks," said Mr. Mondini, casting a dry glance at Jim. "They need some work, but I guess they do have potential."

"It's not easy to be a coach. You need to be strict, yes, I know, but your boys . . . and this beautiful girl . . . are so good!" Nana stroked Lisa's cheek! Jim thought fouling Google-Eyes had been the low point of the day, but this moment was quickly eclipsing that.

Mr. Mondini seemed to lose a bit of his scowl. "This girl is my daughter," he said proudly. "She is good, isn't she? Could be great if she worked a little more."

"Don't be so hard with her," said Nana. "There is more to life than sports!"

Mr. Mondini and Lisa moved on ahead down the hall. Josh was waiting for them by the front doors.

"My father was a lot like that man," said Nana. "Never satisfied. Bitter. But my grandfather! Ah, he was a prince! He understood life. He studied and he prayed and he always was proud of me."

Jim stopped listening to Nana. He thought about what he could have done to stop that google-eyed kid. How had he let that kid get a jump on him anyway? Was it because Jim thought they had the game in the bag? Maybe if he had run a little faster. Just a little faster . . .

"Jimmy! My darling." He heard Nana's deep voice. "Slow down. I can't walk so fast. You know, I think I stayed up too late last night. I was writing more of my speech on my . . . laptop." Nana winked at Jim. "I've got twenty pages already."

Nana stopped by a bulletin board covered with crayon drawings and pretended she was fascinated by them. Jim knew she only wanted to rest. "By the way, Jimmy, how did you do on your essay?"

"I got an A."

"*Na, so was!* I told you you'd get an A! I knew it!" Nana said. "My Jimmy! We are a good team, you and me. Congratulations!"

"Don't tell Mom or Dad, but my teacher wants me to read it in this contest," said Jim.

"*Wunderbar!*" said Nana.

"No, Nana, I can't get up in front of hundreds of people and speak."

"You'll be reading, my darling. That's easy. I have to do the same thing in Washington," said Nana. "You think I'm not nervous? Me with my ugly accent and deep voice in front of all these big shots! But we'll practice together, Jimmy. We are a good team."

"I don't know, Nana," said Jim.

"My friend Ruth, she's a very smart woman, she told me to pretend the audience is sitting there in their underwear!"

Even though Jim had heard this somewhere before, it sounded funny coming from Nana. Jim's laughter echoed down the empty hallway. Mr. McSorley was whistling in the distance. A car outside was honking.

"You will do this, my darling," said Nana, squeezing his arm. "All you need is some confidence. Don't worry. I will help you."

ONE OF MOM and Dad's crazy, old-fashioned ideas was to heat the house with a woodstove. Dad's biggest hobby besides playing music and running was organizing his wood. He chain-sawed and split and stacked piles and piles of wood. He took down dead trees with his buddy Phil. He split the thick hunks of wood with a heavy metal awl. Then he stacked the pieces by size all along the stone wall behind the house. Pete and Jim took turns helping Dad stack.

"Wouldn't it be easier if we just turned up the thermostat?" said Pete whenever it was his turn to stack. "I mean, this is the twenty-first century. Last time I looked, we did have a functioning oil burner in the basement."

Thursday night the temperature dropped to near zero. Mom was cooking a pot of pasta and frying chicken cutlets in her heavy black skillet. Jake was lying on his bed under the table. Lately he had been refusing to come out for anything, including biscuits. They had taken him to the vet, but she had said there was nothing she could do. Jim was crouched down next to Jake, patting his belly, trying to talk him into eating his dog food, which was waiting in his bowl by the back door.

"Come on, Pete," said Dad as he laced up his work boots. "I need some help bringing in the wood."

"Not tonight, Dad," called Pete from the living room, his voice all trembly and weak. "I'm not feeling so good. My throat is killing me."

"What a faker!" said Jim.

"Okay, Jim, guess you've got to pinch-hit for your brother," said Dad.

"Pete always has some lame excuse," said Jim. "Look at him just relaxing on the couch, all cozy with his blanket. Why do I always have to help with the wood?"

"It will build up your muscles," said Pete. "You'd better work on that upper body strength if you want to make it in the NBA!"

"Shut up!" said Jim. "I thought you were sooo sick."

"Okay, fellas, that's enough," said Dad.

It was very still outside. The air was so cold it felt as if Jim were in a tub full of ice cubes. He tried to blow circles with his billowing smoky breaths. It had snowed that morning, and there was a thin crust of sparkling white on the tarp covering the woodpile, on the bushes, and even on the basketball rim.

Dad pulled back the tarp and shook off the snow. Then he hoisted a couple of medium-size pieces of wood and placed them onto Jim's extended arms. "Is that too heavy?" asked Dad.

Jim didn't want Dad to think he was a total weakling, so he said, "No, it's fine," even though his shoulders were curling with pain.

Dad picked up a couple of stout pieces, and they headed back to the house. Even though they had been outside only a few minutes, as soon as Jim walked into the kitchen he knew something was wrong. Mom was standing there with the phone cradled between her ear and her shoulder, flipping a cutlet and saying, "What do you mean, she's confused?" Jim had no idea who Mom was talking about, but there was a strange gray color to her skin and a crazy, scared look in her eyes that made him stop and stare at her.

Dad didn't notice it or hadn't heard Mom. He gave Jim a little push and said, "Yo, come on, big guy, what's the holdup?" Jim went out to the living room and laid the wood in the metal tub by the stove.

"Hey, Pete, who's Mom talking to?" Jim asked.

"How should I know? I'm watching a movie."

"What's the matter?" said Dad. His wood made loud thuds as he dropped it on top of Jim's.

"Mitch!" Mom's voice sounded shrill. "Mitch! Come here, please."

Jim followed Dad to the kitchen. Mom was standing there holding the telephone receiver down by her hip and staring at the frying cutlets. When she turned to Dad, Jim could see tears in her eyes.

"My mother's in the hospital," Mom said. "They think she had a stroke."

Jim had no idea what a stroke was, but it had to be bad if Nana was in the hospital. And it had to be really bad because Dad walked over and hugged Mom long and hard. He took the receiver out of her hand and hung it back on the wall phone. "What else did they say? Which hospital?"

Mom didn't answer. She flipped the cutlets and then flipped them again. She looked like some kind of zombie who couldn't stop flipping chicken.

Dad took the tongs from her and said, "Gabby, sit down and tell me what they said."

Jim pulled out a chair for Mom. She sat down in slow motion.

"I can't believe it! The nurse in the emergency room said that Nana was coming home from shopping and she fainted on the sidewalk, right there in front of her apartment building. The doorman called the ambulance. When she got to the hospital, her right side was numb, and she wasn't speaking clearly, kept mixing up words, so they admitted her right away."

Nana mixes up words all the time, thought Jim. She has a wicked German accent. He remembered the cabbie who couldn't understand her. Maybe that was why the nurses didn't think Nana was speaking clearly.

Mom stood up and began pacing back and forth. "They said she's resting comfortably and I don't need to rush down there, but maybe I should go. I mean, they said she's okay and Dr. Mazer has already seen her and they started her on blood thinner, but—I don't know what to do. Oh, my God, a stroke! What if she's paralyzed?"

Jim had never seen Mom like this before. Mom never let an emergency freak her out. Even when Jim threw up all night or Pete sliced open his finger with the bread knife, Mom never got flustered. She always knew what to do.

"Look, honey, she's in a hospital with round-the-clock care, her own doctor has seen her, and she's resting," said Dad. He was lifting the cutlets out of the frying pan and laying them on a double layer of paper towels. "I think everything is under control."

Jim tried to imagine Nana paralyzed. He knew that as slow as she was, it would drive her nuts to be forced to sit in a wheelchair. Look at how she plodded her way up and down the stairs at the train station.

"She seemed fine on Saturday, didn't she, Jim?" said Mom.

"I dunno. I guess," said Jim. If fine meant huffing and puffing and walking like a turtle, then Nana was certainly fine.

"Actually, she was kind of forgetful," said Mom, still pacing.

Jake seemed to sense something was wrong because he got up and began loping after Mom. "Jake, what's the matter? You don't have to follow me around," said Mom. "Yes, you're a good dog. A very good dog." Mom stopped to pet Jake, and he looked at her adoringly, panting as if he had just run a mile.

Mom went upstairs to call Pappy and Gram and Nana's sister, Tante Sarah, who lived in Florida. Dad finished cooking the rest of the cutlets and drained the spaghetti. Mom had already made a salad.

"What's the matter?" Pete called from the other room. "Who's in the hospital?"

Jim went out to tell him.

"Man, a stroke? Wow," said Pete. "That's really major. My math teacher's husband had one last fall and he came to school and he can't walk or talk or even feed himself. And he's not even as old as Nana!"

What if Nana couldn't talk or feed herself anymore? Jim tried to imagine a silent, frozen Nana staring at him. In his mind Nana looked like a dead person. He shook his head, trying to get rid of the image of a dead Nana.

Jim and Dad ate dinner silently by themselves. Pete said he was too weak to eat or get up, and Mom said she wasn't hungry. They could hear her voice coming from upstairs, where she was on the phone again.

"Do you think Nana's going to be okay?" said Jim finally.

Dad hesitated. He finished chewing and swallowed. He wiped his mouth with a napkin. He took a sip of his water. "I think so, Jim," he said. "Your nana is a fighter. She never gives up at anything or on anyone. She won't give up on herself."

Dad was right, thought Jim. Nana would never give up on herself. But how would she be able to fight anything if she couldn't walk or talk or feed herself?

The next morning Mom drove Jim to school. She had her small suit-case on the backseat.

"Now, you're going to have to take the bus home after school," Mom was saying. "I'll take a taxi to the train station and leave the car for Pete to use, but I think he's still too sick to drive. Make sure you take Jake out as soon as you get home. You've got to help him down those stairs. He's having a hard time. There's some turkey and cheese in the refrigerator and a bag of pretzels—"

"Mom, I know, I know," Jim interrupted. "You told me all this stuff at breakfast."

"Oh, I guess I did," Mom said quietly. She stared ahead, frowning at the road. "Well, I'll call and make sure you guys are—"

"Mom! Stop worrying about us. We'll be fine."

They pulled up in front of the middle school. Jim reached for the door handle, but Mom leaned over and kissed him on the cheek.

"Hey, at least you can give me a small kiss good-bye. I probably won't see you until tomorrow or Sunday!" said Mom.

This was humiliating. A seventh grader kissing his mommy good-bye right in front of the middle school. What had gotten into Mom? She never did anything this embarrassing.

"Come on, Mom," Jim said, trying to pull away. But when he looked at her eyes, he saw they were red and wet with tears. He pecked her cheek and yanked down hard on the door handle. "Bye, Mom," Jim said as he sprang out of the car. He looked around and realized with some relief that the other kids coming to school were so bundled up against the cold, heads bowed against the bitter wind, that no one was looking at him. As Mom pulled away from the curb, she honked the horn twice.

When Jim got to his locker, Josh was standing there waiting for him. "Hey, what's up?" Josh said, giving his little salute.

"Nothin'," said Jim. He wasn't about to start telling Josh, the blabbermouth, about Nana.

"What are you doing after school?"

"Nothin'."

"You wanna come over to my house?"

"I don't know," said Jim.

"I just got this new game for the computer, NBA on Fire. You should check it out."

Jim was cramming his fat down jacket and his book bag into his locker. He'd heard that NBA on Fire was a really cool game. It would probably be more fun than dealing with "sick" Pete all afternoon without Mom around. Had Mom told Mrs. DeLonga about Nana? No, she had been on the phone with the hospital at ten and then called Tante Sarah again. Well, it was Friday, and he'd have all weekend to worry about homework. It wouldn't hurt to go play a few games with Josh.

The first bell rang.

"So what do you think?" said Josh.

"Yeah, sure," said Jim. "I'll meet you at your bus after school."

Jim knew every corner of Josh's house. He knew where Josh kept his basketball cards (under his dresser), where Josh's dog, Molly, hid her toys (behind the giant begonia plant in the living room), and even where they stored the extra rolls of toilet paper (in a cabinet down in the basement). Mrs. DeLonga was home when they got there. Sometimes she was sleeping in the afternoon if she had the night shift; sometimes she wasn't home at all. Today she was dressed in a matching shirt and pants, with a design of yellow flowers. They looked like pajamas, but Jim knew they were her nurse's clothes. She had just come home from work.

"Hi, Jim!" she said cheerily. "Long time no see!"

Before he could resist, Mrs. DeLonga had folded him into a bear hug. She was short and stout and very strong.

"Can you believe this weather," Mrs. DeLonga continued after releasing Jim. "I came out of the hospital, and I couldn't even start my car! Had to call the security guys to give me a jump. Lucky I had my cables in the trunk 'cause they sure didn't have any. But then the lock to the trunk was frozen, so we had to blow on it to warm it up. What a mess!"

Mrs. DeLonga was a lot like Josh. She had the same springy black hair, the same square shoulders, and she loved to talk. Jim stood there politely while his eyes glazed over until Josh pulled his sleeve and said, "Come on, let's get something to eat."

Unlike Mom and Dad, who were health food fanatics, Josh's mom kept their kitchen stocked with boxes of doughnuts, bags of chips, and sugary cereal. Jim didn't even wait for Josh to say anything; he tore open the new box of chocolate-glazed doughnuts and put two on a plate. Josh took a doughnut and poured two glasses of milk. They sat at the table and ate silently. It was a comfortable silence. A "best-friends-on-a-Friday-afternoon-with-the-whole-weekend-before-them" kind of silence. Josh was solid. A blabbermouth, yes. Clueless sometimes, yes. Bossy every now and then, definitely. But also loyal. And honest. Sometimes a little too honest.

Jim looked at the pictures stuck on the refrigerator with magnets that looked like pieces of fruit: a picture of Josh's sister, Jessica, who was in college; a postcard from Las Vegas; a picture of twin babies both wearing tiny pink headbands, Josh's cousins who lived in Tennessee. Jim knew Josh's whole family, had met them at a big barbecue they had had to celebrate Jessica's high school graduation.

At the party Jim had even seen Mr. DeLonga, who lived down south with his girlfriend and hardly ever came to visit. He didn't look anything like Josh. He was real tall and skinny. Instead of black, curly hair, Mr. DeLonga had almost no hair, and what little he had was shaved down to a millimeter. He wore these wraparound black sunglasses that made him look like some kind of secret agent. And an earring in one ear. The DeLongas had been divorced for as long as Jim had known Josh. Josh used to talk about how great his dad was—about the new sports car he was driving, the speedboat he was going to buy, the business trips he took all over the world. Every summer Josh went on a camping trip with his father. When he got back, it was all he talked about for weeks and weeks until Jim finally had to tell him to put a cork in it. Jim and Pete and Dad went camping in the summer, too, but he didn't go describing every nanosecond of it to Josh. Who cared what kind of campfire Mr. DeLonga had built in five minutes flat? Who cared if Mr. DeLonga had this tackle box with forty-five types of flies?

But lately Josh seemed to be losing interest in his father. Or maybe it was the other way around. Josh told Jim that his dad had got married to his girlfriend and they had just had a baby. "My dad says he has to take care of his new wife, so we won't be going camping this summer," Josh had told him the other day. "No big deal. I never liked camping that much anyway."

They dropped their plates in the sink and ran down to the basement family room. Now this was a real family room, not some little winterized porch with a ratty old couch, a BarcaLounger, and a TV like Jim's. This was an entertainment center with a humongous TV, a Foosball table, a stereo system, and a computer in the corner. The couch was covered in black leather. A kid could spend days down here and never come up except for maybe a pizza delivery.

"Are you mad at me?" Josh asked as he got the NBA on Fire game out of its box.

"What do you mean?" said Jim. Josh could read Jim like a book. Maybe it was because they had spent so much time together, but Josh was always alert to even the slightest wrinkle in their friendship.

"I don't know. You seemed a little ticked off at me. Is it about basketball?"

Jim didn't want to admit it, but yeah, he was jealous of the way Mr. Mondini fawned over Josh all the time. It was as if Josh were this little angel. Teacher's pet. Sure, Josh was very attentive whenever Mondini addressed the team as a group. Jim could get distracted by one of Marco's whispered wisecracks or Frankie's goofy faces, but he was trying harder than ever to pay attention to Mondini, no matter how boring he was. Josh always had a polite response or a serious question. Marco called him the little Boy Scout behind his back.

"Nah, I'm just pissed off at Mondini," said Jim. "He has his favorites, and I'm not one of them. I don't know why, but I don't think he likes me, and after what happened at the game . . . he'll never play me. I really blew it!"

"No way, Jim," said Josh. "You definitely did the right thing when you fouled that kid last Saturday. I mean, I was watching, and he had a real clear shot. That ball was going in!"

"Yeah, well, I've pretty much forgotten the whole thing," Jim lied. "Anyway, it doesn't matter what I do. You're the man! Mondini's first-round pick for point guard. I'm just some second-string string bean to him. Maybe if I'd finally grow . . ." Jim looked down at his skinny arms in disgust.

But Jim knew that wasn't it. Even if he woke up tomorrow bigger and beefier, Mondo Mondini wouldn't care. Mondini seemed to have this grudge against him, maybe because Jim could beat his dumb daughter one on one. Then why had he taken him on the team? What had he said on the phone that day he called to invite Jim onto the team? "We both think you have potential. . . . You ran hot and cold. . . . With some hard work you could become a very fine point guard." Jim should have seen the handwriting on the wall. That was basketball code for "We need another body sitting on the bench!"

Josh didn't answer. He got the video game set up and silently handed Jim one of the control pads. He didn't even look Jim in the eye.

"The guy has favorites. It's so friggin' obvious!" said Jim, trying to get a response out of Josh.

"Speaking of favorites, my dad called last night and said he wants to come up and see me play basketball," said Josh, trying to change the subject. "He's coming for the Pineville Tournament."

"You sound thrilled," said Jim.

Josh shrugged. "Whatever. He never calls me up just to talk or ask me what's new. He yaps on and on about the baby. The baby this, the baby that. Do I care?"

"You should just blow him off," said Jim. "Give him the cold shoulder."

"I can't do that, he's my dad!"

"And you're his kid!" said Jim. He knew that Josh would never give up hope. His dad could forget his birthday or send him a roll of Scotch tape for Christmas, and Josh would find some way to justify it. It was all part of Josh being the most loyal person Jim had ever met. And it also drove Jim nuts sometimes.

"You don't understand, Jim," said Josh, shaking his head.

Jim decided it was time for him to change the subject. "Did you tell Lisa you like her?"

"I don't like her!"

"Come on, Josh. This is me, Jim Malone, your best buddy in the whole world. You can tell me."

"Up yours!" said Josh.

"Listen, how about if you tell me how you really feel about Lisa Mondini, I'll tell you who I've been checking out?"

Josh bit his pinkie nail again. Then he said, "Okay. I do think Lisa is pretty, and she's a really good basketball player, but she likes someone else on the team. She told me."

"Interesting," said Jim, mulling over the possibilities. "I bet it's Frankie." Ever since the Squeak incident, he'd noticed that Lisa always laughed at whatever Frankie said.

"Sorry, I'm sworn to secrecy," said Josh. "Okay, go ahead. It's your turn."

Jim had to think a minute before he answered. He flipped through the girls he knew. It was easy to eliminate most of them like Mariah or Liz. Kim, the girl in math, was pretty, but she had just gotten braces. Why did Lisa come to his mind? Lisa, not all sweaty and ferocious the way she looked in practice but Lisa the way she had looked today, when he had passed her in the hall, with her hair smooth and shiny around her face, her brown eyes wide and friendly, her teeth very white as she smiled and said, "Hey, Jim!" Lisa? All he had to do was remind himself that her last name was Mondini, and her face melted, replaced by Mr. Mondini's shifty, slinty-eyed grin. Gross.

"Tricia Van Huff. Definitely," said Jim. "You know, the cheerleader? My brother goes out with her."

"Yeah, but she's in high school! Way out of your league."

"Doesn't mean I can't check her out," said Jim. "She's hot!"

Josh said, "And you're nuts!" and clicked Start on his control pad. They chose their teams.

"Let the games begin!" roared Josh, as he always did.

"Look out!"

"You're toast!"

"Oh, yeah? Eat my dust."

"This kid can play."

"You're mine."

"Not gonna happen!"

"Hey, how do you get the turnaround jump shot on this thing?"

This game was awesome, and all thoughts of Mr. Mondini and Lisa disappeared. They played six straight games. Jim won three, and Josh won three.

"Okay, tiebreaker," said Josh, setting them up for another game.

"Jim!" called Mrs. DeLonga from the top of the stairs. "Phone's for you."

Jim picked up the extension on the desk.

"Where the hell are you?" said Pete.

"Duh, you're calling me at Josh's house," said Jim. "You obviously know where I am."

"You were supposed to come straight home from school! Why didn't you call, you little maggot?" said Pete. He sounded pretty healthy. "Mom's worried sick about you."

"But she went to see Nana," said Jim. He suddenly remembered how he had told her not to worry about anything.

"She called here a little while ago and woke me up," said Pete. "I didn't know where you were, it's getting dark, Jake pissed all over the kitchen floor. Mom told me to try Josh's house—Jesus Christ, he took a dump, too! I just stepped in it! Wait till I get my hands on you, Jim! You're dead meat."

Jim didn't like the sound of any of this. He prayed that Dad was the one coming to pick him up. Then he heard Pete say, "I'll be there in ten minutes. You better be waiting in the driveway."

Pete did not say one word to Jim the entire ride home from Josh's house. It was eerie. Jim knew that Pete's silent treatment meant something was wrong, terribly wrong. It had to be more than Jake's messing in the kitchen. The car radio wasn't even switched on. Pete never drove without music blasting. Just as Pete swung the car into their driveway, he finally spoke.

"Nana's much worse than Mom thought. It sounds like my math

teacher's husband. Nana can't speak or walk or even swallow her food. The doctor says she might die," said Pete. "Not that you care or anything."

Jim wanted to shout, "I do, too, care!" but his voice got stuck somewhere deep in his throat.

O<small>N</small> S<small>ATURDAY</small> <small>MORNING</small> there were no pancakes or waffles or any of the special weekend breakfasts that Mom usually cooked, just bowls of cereal with cold milk. Mom had decided to stay overnight in the hospital, sleeping on a chair in Nana's room.

Dad was sitting at the kitchen table, drinking a cup of coffee and staring into space. Pete was still sleeping. Jake had moved from his bed over to the doormat, and he was nudging the bell that hung from the doorknob.

"Jim," said Dad, "better take him out again."

Jim had already walked Jake in the yard twice this morning. The dog had sniffed the snow but refused to go to the bathroom.

"Okay, old fella, wanna try again?" said Jim. He thought maybe Jake was giving him a hard time because of yesterday.

They walked out onto the back porch. Jim ran down the steps clapping his gloves together, calling, "Let's go, Jake! Good dog!" Instead of carefully stepping down the stairs the way he had before, Jake stood on the edge of the porch and stared at Jim.

"What's the matter? I know you want to go out," said Jim. "Look, I'm sorry about yesterday. Come on, old fella!"

All of a sudden Jake launched himself off the porch. He didn't slip on the steps. He flew from the porch directly to the slate path below. Jim froze and held his breath. Jake landed on the ground with a grunt, his body like an old sack of potatoes.

"Jake!" said Jim, crouching down beside the dog. He didn't see any blood or bones sticking out. Jake was trying to hoist himself up, but his back legs kept crumpling beneath him. Jim felt queasy. He remembered what Mom had told him before she dropped him off at school: "Help Jake down the stairs."

"Dad!" Jim yelled as loud as he could. "Dad, come here quick!"

Dad threw open the back door and ran out onto the porch in his socks. "Oh, my God, what happened?"

"I don't know," said Jim. "Jake just jumped off like he thought he could fly!"

"Don't try to move him," said Dad. "I'll get a blanket."

Dad and Jim carried Jake to the car, using the blanket like a stretcher.

When they got to the veterinarian's office, Dr. Hamilton was waiting by the door and shepherded them into the examining room in the back. In the old days Jake would have been growling at Dr. Hamilton. He had never been a good patient. In fact, Mom usually gave Jake a pill to calm him down before he had to go to the vet. But lately Jake seemed too tired to growl, and today he barely lifted his head when he heard Dr. Hamilton's voice saying, "Now this will only hurt for a second," as she stuck a needle in his thigh.

After taking an X ray, Dr. Hamilton said, "Looks as if we've got a broken leg here. How old is Jake now?"

"Fourteen," said Jim.

"Hmm." Dr. Hamilton bit her lip. "You may want to consider euthanasia," she said, looking at Dad. "There's really not much we can do for this."

"Eutha-what?" said Jim.

"Put him to sleep, Jim," said Dad softly.

"So you can fix his leg?" said Jim. But he thought that was called anesthesia.

"No, put him to sleep, so . . . he wouldn't wake up."

"You mean, kill him?" Jim said. "Kill him because he has a broken leg?" Were they nuts? Jim had always thought Dr. Hamilton looked like a pretty cool lady, with her long, wavy hair pulled back and her funny animal earrings, but now all he saw was this diabolical, mad scientist who wanted to kill his dog. And Dad seemed to be going along with her! "No way," said Jim, wrapping his arms around Jake's neck. "No way!"

"We don't set this kind of break," said Dr. Hamilton. "Dogs usually heal on their own. But because of Jake's age, it may not heal, and he's going to need a lot of care. You'll have to carry him in and out of the house. You'll have to hold up his rear in a sling so he can go to the bathroom." Dr. Hamilton shook her head. "I'm not sure he'll ever be able to walk again."

"I'll take care of him," said Jim. "You're not killing Jake. No way!"

"It's your decision," said Dr. Hamilton, looking only at Dad. "I'll leave you alone so you can talk about it."

"That's not necessary," said Dad. "Get him as comfortable as you can. We'll take him home."

In the car Jim sat in the back with Jake, who put his head on Jim's lap. Jim stroked the soft fur under Jake's chin, and Jake looked up at Jim. Jake's eyes were cloudy and distant. Please don't die on me, Jake, thought Jim. Nana always said that bad luck came in threes. If Nana's stroke was one, and Jake's broken leg was two, what could three possibly be?

Mom finally came back from the hospital on Saturday night long after Jim's basketball game, long after they had eaten a large pizza, and well into the third quarter of the Knicks-Hornets game. She walked into the family room in her stockinged feet but still wearing her hat and coat and dropped heavily onto the couch. When she pulled off her fleece cap, her hair fell in strings around her face as if she hadn't combed it in days.

"What a day!" She sighed. "I think today was the worst day of my life."

"It's not over yet, Mom," said Pete. "Wait till you hear what happened to Jake!" He looked at Jim.

"It's not my fault, you loser," said Jim. As if he didn't feel a churning sense of guilt right now in the pit of his stomach all mixed up with that mushroom pizza.

"Fellas, fellas," Dad said sharply. "Your mother has just spent a long, difficult day in the hospital with your grandmother. Let's show a little consideration!" He turned to Mom and said, "Jake fell off the porch. His leg is broken, and Dr. Hamilton . . ." Dad's voice trailed off as if he was about to say something else.

Strangely Mom didn't bat an eyelash. Instead she stared at the television screen like a zombie.

"Well, it looks like that will be number six on Camby," bellowed the announcer. "What a shame. He was really pouring it on this quarter."

"You bum!" said Pete.

"Aw, come on, that was no foul," said Dad.

Jim looked at Mom and saw tears running down her cheeks. No way she was that upset about Camby's foul.

"Mom, are you okay?" Jim asked softly.

Mom just kept right on staring at the TV. Her jacket was still zipped up to her neck.

"Mom?"

Dad pointed the remote control at the set and clicked the Off button.

"Yo, Dad! The game isn't over!" said Pete.

"Don't you want to talk to Mom?" said Dad. It was more a statement than a question. "I mean, she hasn't been home since yesterday morning!"

The three of them looked at Mom, who was still staring at the blackened screen.

It did feel as if Mom had been gone for a very long time, Jim thought. Last night, after the car ride home, he had convinced himself that Pete was exaggerating. How could Nana be in such bad shape? After all, Mom was with her: Mom, who could take care of anything, Mom, who had nursed all of them back from flu and strep throat and chicken pox. Nana was probably sitting up in her hospital bed watching an opera program on one of those cool little TVs that hang down from the ceiling. Jim remembered the one in his hospital room when he had had his appendix out in the third grade. That was another time Mom had come to the rescue, sleeping on a chair in the corner of the room, helping him walk to the bathroom, and holding his hand whenever that big, unfriendly nurse came in with the needle to give him a shot.

All that stroke stuff was probably clearing up, Jim had told himself all day. Hadn't Dr. Mazer told Mom that 60 percent of the people with this type of stroke recover? Nana was a tough little lady, even with all her huffing and puffing and vials of pills. Hadn't she scared off a couple of muggers just a few short weeks ago?

"I don't care what Dr. Mazer says," Mom suddenly blurted out as if she were in the middle of a conversation. "Nana's in very bad shape. Her whole right side is limp, and she can say only a couple of words."

"But there's rehab," said Dad.

Jim had heard of rehab for drug addicts. He couldn't imagine Nana in one of those places.

"Yeah, there's therapy, I guess," said Mom listlessly. "But, Mitch, guys, I have to be honest with you. She may not even make it."

The room fell into complete silence except for Jake's snoring wafting in from the kitchen.

"What if we all go down and see her tomorrow?" said Pete in his perfect-son voice. "Maybe she'll snap out of it. Like shock therapy!"

Why did Pete have to open his big mouth? Jim couldn't go to the hospital tomorrow.

"That would be great," said Mom. Her face perked up. "Can you guys go? No basketball, Jim?"

Mondini had called a practice for Sunday, but Jim knew he was going to have to miss it.

"Nope," said Jim. "No basketball."

On Sunday morning Mom packed a shopping bag with treats for Nana. "You know how she always comes up here loaded down with all those bags of useless stuff for us."

"I don't consider Tootsie Rolls useless stuff," said Pete.

"I'm trying to bring things she might respond to," said Mom. "You know, like nice-smelling lotion, some family pictures, a pretty scarf to drape over her blanket."

"How about my old cassette player and some opera tapes?" said Dad.

"Perfect," said Mom.

Jim packed some things in his book bag: the essay with the big red A, a sketchpad Mom had given him, and the mechanical pencil. Then he suddenly remembered that he had to call Mr. Mondini. He ran upstairs to use the phone in Mom and Dad's room.

Jim picked up the receiver and hesitated. He couldn't exactly tell Mondini his grandmother was in the hospital again.

When Mr. Mondini answered, Jim just blurted out the first thing that came into his head. "Hi, Mr. Mondini, this is Jim Malone. I won't be able to make practice today because my family has to go down and help my grandmother move some furniture in her apartment." It sounded stupid the minute it came out of his mouth.

For a moment Mr. Mondini was silent on the other end, and Jim thought they had been disconnected. "Mr. Mondini, are you there?" he said.

"You know, Jim, when you accepted a position on this team, you were making a commitment," said Mr. Mondini in a clipped, angry voice. "I understand there are family emergencies, but I don't think going to the opera or moving furniture is more important than basketball practice."

Jim should have figured that by now Mondini had heard about the opera. And he would probably find out about this lie, too. That was what Mom meant about lies messing things up.

"I know you think you deserve a starting place on this team," Mr. Mondini continued, "and I want you to know I have been impressed by some of your play. Yesterday you were putting on your own little shooting clinic."

Yeah, emphasis on *little*. Jim had only played in the fourth quarter.

"But if you continue to miss practices," said Mr. Mondini, "then I'm afraid you're going to continue to sit on the bench. It's not fair to the guys who show up every time."

Okay, so this was the second practice he would be missing, thought Jim. What about Josh's sitting out that practice with his hamstring injury? Didn't he get to start the next game? And this *is* an emergency! he wanted to scream. My grandmother might die today! But the only words that came out were "I understand."

"At practice, we'll be going over some new stuff," said Mr. Mondini. "I'll have Josh explain it to you on Wednesday."

Whatever, thought Jim. "Okay," he said.

"Jim?"

"Yeah."

"If you miss another practice over the next two weeks, I may ask you to step off the team," said Mr. Mondini. "I'm from the old school, and I demand one hundred percent from my players, and being at practices is part of that. Understood?"

"Yeah, I understand."

Jim hung up. There on Mom's dresser was a framed picture of Nana holding him as a baby. He looked angrily at Nana's face in the picture. "It's all your fault," he said out loud. "My whole basketball season is getting messed up because of you, Nana! You're ruining my life!"

The hall leading to Nana's room was wide, and the floors were polished to a glossy shine like the cafeteria floor at school. There were posters of teddy bears holding valentine hearts hanging on the walls. It reminded Jim of the first-grade hall near the the gym at Pigeon Hill. Their shoes made loud, squeaky noises.

"I'll go in first," said Mom. "You guys wait here a minute."

"Hi, Mama!" They could hear Mom's cheery, louder than normal voice. "It's me, Gabby. How are you feeling today?"

"Ohhh, ohhh," Nana's voice answered. "Stupid, stupid."

Was that really Nana's voice? Jim peeked into the room. There were two beds, but no one was in the one close to the door. It was neatly made. He saw Mom standing over the far bed. He couldn't see Nana, but he could see all kinds of tubes and a bleeping machine and a long neon light.

Mom turned around and motioned for him to come in. For some reason he tiptoed. Pete gave him a little push from behind. As he neared the bed, Jim felt a chill on his neck like the one he had felt when he saw Jake lying on the slate. Even the memory of Nana in her toilet paper turban with no makeup and cottage cheese stuck in the corners of her mouth had not prepared him for what she looked like now, staring up at him from this hospital bed. Her head looked shrunken, maybe because her hair was so flat and limp. In the middle of her chalky face, her red nose was harnessed to a long plastic tube. There were other tubes running from her nostrils and from the inside of her right arm, and there were wires. Nana looked like a marionette waiting to perform.

"Hi, Nana," Jim whispered hoarsely.

"Nana, how are ya doin'?" said Pete as though Nana had just walked into their kitchen. He touched her closer arm, the one without any tubes, but she didn't reach out for him, to stroke his cheek, the way she usually did.

Dad walked around to stand at the foot of the bed.

Nana stared at them with a crazed, hollow look.

"Ohhhh!"

Her voice was an eerie, rumbling growl. Jim felt himself moving back a step.

Then more sounds emerged from between her parched lips. "Riskling, reez-ling, drub-bish, drubble." It sounded like a magic spell. Maybe Nana really was a witch? She closed her eyes in exasperation and heaved a giant sigh. She shook her head angrily from side to side.

Jim had never been frightened by Nana, even when she burned her finger while cooking grilled cheese and started cursing loudly in German or when she punished Pete and him for fighting by making them taste vinegar. But right this minute he felt a growing knot of terror in his stomach. Why didn't she stop? Maybe this was just an act? Jim remembered when they used to set up talent shows in their living room after Thanksgiving dinner, how Nana would tell stories of trolls and billygoats and make all the voices sound so real.

"Mama, look, the boys came to see you!" said Mom in a forced happy voice. "And Mitch, too."

Nana opened her eyes again. She looked fiercely at Mom. "Stupid, so stupid," she said in disgust.

"Oh, Mrs. Wallach, I see you have some company!" A nurse came in carrying a Dixie cup. "Are you thirsty?"

Mom, Jim, and Pete stepped back to let the nurse pass through. She held the cup near Nana's chin and pulled out something that looked like a pink lollipop. It was a small sponge at the end of a stick. The nurse gently pushed the sponge into Nana's mouth and began rubbing her teeth with it. Nana let out a deep sigh of relief. She looked adoringly at the nurse.

"We've got to keep doing this because she's not allowed to drink yet," the nurse said to them over her shoulder. "We're not sure she can swallow. Poor thing, she gets so dry and thirsty."

"I'm her daughter," said Mom. "And this is my husband and our two sons."

"Mrs. Wallach, you have a lovely family," said the nurse in a loud voice.

Nana grimaced and tried to roll over on her side. "I need it! I need it!" She groaned.

"Now, darlin', come on, don't go pulling all your tubes out," said the nurse. "Dr. Mazer'll be in shortly to see you."

Nana closed her eyes and said, "Stupid, so stupid."

When the nurse left the room, Pete said, "This is mondo bizarro. It's like all her brain waves are crisscrossed. Do you think she understands us at all?"

"I haven't seen the CAT scan yet, but Dr. Mazer said a large area of her brain was affected," said Mom.

"It is possible for some of the uninjured portions of the brain to pick up the duties of the dead tissue," said Dad as if he were reading out loud from a medical textbook. "I asked Phil about it. You know, his father had a stroke last fall. But he said only time would tell. There's no way to predict."

Jim didn't say anything. He just stared at Nana, who seemed to be sleeping. Here they were standing around her, talking as if she were some big science experiment, this monster of Frankenstein they were trying to bring to life.

The night they came home from the opera, Nana had made Jim some hot chocolate and they had sat in the kitchen eating her favorite cookies, called lebkuchen. She had told Jim one of her war stories. It was about the night she had been tracked down by the Nazis while she was in a hospital trying to recover from a bad fever. She was sure they would take her away in the morning to the firing range or a concentration camp, and she believed it was her "last night on earth."

"All night I lay there with my eyes open, trying to remember everything around me, the way the cold white metal bars on the bed felt when I held on to them, the way the moonlight fell on the bedsheets, the shape of the leaves hanging from a branch just outside my window. I thought, *Unmöglich!* I never appreciated how beautiful the world is. I was too busy, too foolish. And I had a long talk with God. 'I'm not ready to leave the world yet, God. Please let me stay a little longer, so I can see my son grow up and maybe meet my grandchildren. I promise to teach them what you have taught me here tonight.' And you know what happened, my Jimmy? When the Nazi guarding me left for a moment to check on a commotion down the hall, the nurses picked me up and hid me in the basement of the hospital, in a laundry room with no windows. A month later came the liberation! That's when I found out my son had died of tuberculosis in the children's ward. I was lost. I was furious with God. Why did He let me live and take my husband and my only child? What good was my promise now? Of course I didn't know someday I would have another baby, your darling mother, and then such handsome American grandsons. How do they say? God works in mysterious ways? Well, I had made a promise, and I try to keep it and teach you something every time we are together."

Jim thought of that story now as he stared at Nana's closed eyes. Was she trying to make another deal with God? From the angry stares and outbursts, it didn't seem like she was appreciating the color of the walls or the bleeping of the machine next to her head. Maybe she couldn't remember that story anymore?

Jim felt suddenly guilty as he thought about yelling at Nana's picture.

"Good afternoon," came a voice from the doorway. It was Dr. Mazer. Mom, Dad, and Pete turned to greet him, but Jim kept staring at Nana.

Suddenly she opened her eyes and looked right back at him. Her eyes were no longer angry. They seemed to be pleading with Jim.

She was begging him to do something. What was she trying to tell him? Maybe there was one more thing she wanted to teach him? He started to say, "What is it, Nana?" but then she closed her eyes again.

Before driving home, they stopped by Nana's apartment building. Dad waited in the double-parked car while Mom, Pete, and Jim went up. The doorman bowed and nodded sadly at them.

It felt strange to be in Nana's apartment without her. There was her bathrobe in a heap on the bed, a coffee cup and plate in the sink, a vase of wilting roses on top of the television. It seemed as if Nana must be in the bathroom and would come out to greet them at any minute.

Pete slumped down on the couch. "Is it okay if I turn on the TV?"

"Sure," said Mom. "I just want to pick up a few things for Nana and get rid of these flowers and dishes."

Jim sat down next to Pete. Pete flipped on a college basketball game.

"Could one of you guys go into Nana's closet and grab a couple of sweaters?" called Mom from the kitchen.

"Get moving, little Jimmy," said Pete without taking his eyes off the TV.

"Why me?" said Jim.

"Because you have such excellent taste," said Pete.

Nana's clothes closet was in a narrow hall that led to the bathroom. When Jim opened the door, a light went on inside the closet. There were Nana's dresses: purple, yellow, hot pink, aqua, pumpkin, every possible color. Jim had never realized that Nana had so many clothes. The closet smelled like Nana's perfume, a bouquet of roses. A long plastic bag with cardboard shelves hung to one side with all her sweaters. Jim unzipped the bag and grabbed the top two sweaters. Why did Mom want these anyway? It wasn't like Nana was about to go dancing at one of those old-timer parties at the Jewish Center. As Jim started to close the door, something caught his eye. On the wooden shelf above the dresses right next to her pocketbooks was a black nylon case. Nana's laptop computer!

"Jim, did you find them?" Mom called.

"Yeah, I got 'em," Jim called back. He reached up and grabbed the computer. He stared at the case with its tiny rainbow apple in the corner. It's not like I want to keep it forever, thought Jim. Maybe that's what Nana was trying to tell me? I'll just take care of it for her while she's in the hospital. If I leave it here, who knows, it might even get stolen.

"Jim! Come on!" Mom's voice seemed to be coming toward the hall. "I don't want Dad to get a ticket."

How could he sneak the computer out of there? After all, it was Nana's big secret. Then Jim realized he still had his book bag on his back. He quickly dropped it off his shoulders, unzipped the bag, and slipped the black case inside.

Ms. Durbin had not forgotten about the essay contest. She announced a meeting in the cafeteria after school for the students who were entered. "You know who you are," she said, staring right at Jim.

There was no way around it. He had to go to the meeting. Even though Jim had squirreled away the sheet from Ms. Durbin inside the black case with Nana's laptop under his bed behind a stack of *Sports Illustrated*s, Pete had somehow managed to find out about the contest. One evening while Jim was in the kitchen, struggling to lift Jake, he heard Pete saying, "Listen to this, they're sending six contestants from the middle school to that county public speaking contest, and guess what! Our little Jimmy is one of 'em! I don't know about you, Mom and Dad, but that definitely rocks my world!"

Jim gently put Jake back on the floor and marched into the family room to demand, "How did you know about that?"

"I have my ways," said Pete, raising his eyebrows. He was grinning like a magician who had just sawed his assistant in half.

"I think it's wonderful!" said Dad.

"I'm so proud of you," said Mom, looking up from some of Nana's mail that she was sorting.

"And listen to this," said Pete. "The top prize is a PC! With a printer! Jim, you've gotta go for the gold, little bro. The future of this family is at stake! Think of how much time I could save on my final English Honors project."

Jim was silent. He looked at the three hopeful faces staring at him and knew he was doomed.

Jim had no idea who the other five contestants were, but when he got to the cafeteria, he wasn't surprised to see Mariah sitting there. She gave him a once-over, and said icily, "This is the essay contest meeting. Are you sure you're in the right place?"

Jim ignored her and took a seat at the other end of the table. There were two dorky-looking eighth graders and another seventh grader named Malcolm something, whom Jim knew from gym class. He was the kid who always came in last in the mile run, the one who wore the goofy terry-cloth sun visor. As soon as Jim was seated, Malcolm turned and said in a loud voice, "Hi, Jim. How's it going?" as though they were best friends.

One of the eighth graders, a dark-skinned boy wearing thick black-framed eyeglasses, pulled out a fancy calculator and started showing the other eighth grader, a chalky-faced girl with freckles and a double chin, "a really cool proof" he had just figured out. What am I doing here with these first-rate geeks? thought Jim.

Ms. Durbin arrived with the sixth contestant. Jim rubbed his eyes. It was Lisa Mondini! Lisa came over and sat next to him. "Hey, Jim," she said softly.

Jim noticed right away a perfumey smell, something he had smelled somewhere before. Then he remembered. It was Tricia's lilac stuff.

Ms. Durbin put her briefcase on a nearby table and sat down with them. "You are the six students who will be representing the Hollow Hill Middle School in the seventh annual countywide public speaking contest. No matter who wins, you all should feel great pride in having been chosen!" Ms. Durbin herself looked as if she were bursting with pride. "In my opinion, at least one of the top three winners will be from our school! I feel certain!" Then she went around the table and had each person introduce himself or herself and say a few words about his or her essay.

Malcolm just said one sentence: "It's about why I want to become an entomologist."

The boy eighth grader, whose name was Vishnu, said his was

about moving to America from India when he was nine, and the girl, whose name was Frederika, said hers was about going up in a hot-air balloon last summer. Vishnu said, "I hope your essay isn't full of hot air!" and they both cracked up as if that were the funniest thing they had ever heard.

Mariah said in her superior way, "I wrote about my greatest love, the theater. You know, I plan to be a great classical actress someday."

Jim figured there was no need to jazz up his essay subject for this bunch of losers, so he said simply, "Mine is about my grandmother and going to an opera with her." Malcolm nodded approvingly and said, "Good one!"

Finally it was Lisa's turn. She said, "My essay is about when my mother died." There was an uncomfortable silence. Jim was stunned. He remembered Matt's talking about Lisa's mother that day in the cafeteria. Didn't he say she was really tall and an amazing basketball player? How could she be dead?

"When did she die?" asked Jim. He immediately felt stupid for asking.

"Two years ago," Lisa answered. She looked down at her lap.

"Okay, thanks, boys and girls," said Ms. Durbin in a brisk, let's-keep-moving kind of voice. "Now I'd like to talk to you about some of the techniques of public speaking that might help you with your presentations. I know some of you are pretty nervous."

"I'm not nervous," Mariah chipped in. "My daddy says I inherited his talent for public speaking! He's a preacher."

Jim noticed that Lisa was now looking around as if she was back to normal again. She was pulling her hair away from her face and braiding it absentmindedly. He looked at her profile and realized that from this angle she didn't look anything like her father. Mondini had a beaky, birdlike face that Jim had memorized from sitting on the bench. Lisa had a pretty nose that kind of sloped up and down and really long black eyelashes. There was a gold basketball hanging from her earlobe and a small diamond stud farther up. All of a sudden he felt embarrassed to be sitting next to her.

"Jim!" Ms. Durbin was calling his name. "Jim! Everyone is taking notes here," she said. "I think it would help if you did, too."

He looked around and noticed that all the other kids had note-books and pencils out. Lisa had written three lines already. He felt the heat in his ears and knew they must be crimson. He bent down to get his notebook out of his book bag and to hide from the stares of all the essay contestants. Especially Lisa's.

Mom was hardly home anymore. She took the train down to the city almost every day to go to the hospital. She got home late, after they had finished eating dinner on tray tables in front of the TV while watching sports. The dining room table was now covered with Nana's mail, sorted into various piles.

The house seemed gloomy to Jim when he got home from school. He missed the sound of Mom's clogs on the stairs and the music coming out of her studio. He didn't even have the sound of Jake's tail happily thumping against the wall to welcome him anymore. The house was quiet except for Jake's uneven snoring and the ticking of the clock on the fireplace mantel.

Jim was still waiting for the third bad thing to happen. Nana's stroke, Jake's fall, and . . . ? Only one thing could burn off the haze of dread Jim felt each afternoon as he turned his key in the kitchen door lock and entered the quiet house: basketball.

So every afternoon Jim went outside to practice his shooting. He kept the driveway clear of snow and ice. He cut the fingertips off an old pair of gloves so he could get a good grip on the ball. Even when the sky turned dark and tiny white flurries began to fall, he continued his shooting. Fifty left-handed layups, fifty right-handed layups, fifty turnaround jump shots, fifty fadeaway jump shots, and fifty foul shots. He practiced hard because it took some of the tightness out of his arms and legs. He practiced hard because it gave his mind a chance to shut out the dread. But surprisingly, all this practice was beginning to pay off with the travel team. At the last league game Mr. Mondini had let him play the whole second half, and he had scored fourteen points. Maybe Mondini didn't really hate him after all. Or maybe Lisa had told him that Jim was a really smart kid, because he was going to be in the essay contest. Whatever the reason, Jim was focused at practice and determined to attend every single basketball event. No more missed practices.

Out on the driveway, with the cold ball rolling off his fingertips, all the clutter of the day disappeared. It didn't matter if Jim had failed the last social studies test (he could easily forge Mom's signature and return it to Mr. Ford tomorrow) or if he had seen Lisa and Frankie laughing together outside the nurse's office (what difference should that make anyway? That was Josh's problem). For a little while Jim stopped being the skinniest kid on the travel team. Jumping around on the blacktop of the rutted driveway, he became big and powerful, scoring winning baskets before frenzied crowds of adoring fans. His name was lighting up the scoreboard. No one cared if he had failed a social studies test in the seventh grade. There were Mom and Dad—and was that his brother, Pete?—all clapping for him. Even Mr. Mondini couldn't control himself. He was jumping up and down in the bleachers, yelling, "I used to coach that guy!"

One gray Thursday afternoon, just as Jim shot his forty-seventh foul shot, out of nowhere, he heard Nana's voice loud and clear: "Jimmy, take care of my stories. Don't forget."

Jim caught the ball and held it near his chest. He looked around in the fading light, at the icicles hanging from the garage roof, at the blue shadows cast by the hemlock trees. There was nothing, not even the sound of the chipmunk that lived in the woodpile.

Jim had not touched the laptop since hiding it under his bed. He still wasn't sure why he had taken it in the first place. It wouldn't do him any good to write school papers on it since he didn't have a printer. He was hoping to borrow a couple of Josh's games to play on the computer, but he didn't know how to ask without telling Josh about the laptop. So it sat on the rug hidden behind a stack of *Sports Illustrated*s.

After he made his fiftieth foul shot, Jim rolled the ball into the garage and blew on his numbing fingers. He went into the house and ate a bowl of cereal. Then he headed up the silent stairs to his room to get started on his homework.

When he had all his books spread out on his desk, Jim stared at the posters over his bed the way he did every day. How did those guys get up so high off the ground? He walked over to the closet and opened the door. He stood with his back up against the door frame and held a green plastic ruler on his head. Then he slipped out from under the ruler, holding one end securely to the frame. He looked carefully. Nothing. The ruler was even with the last penciled measurement. He hadn't grown at all.

Jim walked past his desk and his waiting homework. He sat on his bed and bent down to pull out the black nylon case from behind the stack of magazines. He unzipped the case and opened the laptop. He stared at the screen, remembering how proud Nana had been when she showed it to him. He remembered how fast her fingers, her old, gnarly fingers, had flown over the keys, the words just rushing out, as if she were in a race. Maybe she had seen the stroke coming up behind her, gaining on her, so she typed even faster. Everything about Nana was so unbearably slow except for those fingers. Jim touched a key so that the screen lit up. He clicked the File icon, and a list of titles appeared: "My Grandfather and Me," "Why I Loved to Swim," "My Dream Ends," "Leaving Home for Good," "Another Miracle," and finally "How I Survived the War, My Speech."

Jim tapped the edge of the keyboard nervously. He looked at the clock. Four-thirty. Pete would be home by five. It couldn't hurt to read one folder. The speech? After all, Nana was planning to make this speech in front of hundreds of people in Washington, wasn't she? Jim opened the folder. He read the entire speech, all twenty pages, from the first sentences—"I was born a very long time ago in a medium-sized city in Germany. We lived across the street from a beautiful park. When I was a little girl, I thought I would live in Germany forever. But things changed"—to the last—"And so I gathered up my old cardboard suitcase and boarded the ship to America. The future was waiting for me there. I had no idea how wonderful it would be."

Jim heard a car pull into the driveway. He shut down the computer and put it back under his bed.

The Saturday league game was scheduled for ten.

For the first time Mom, Dad, and Pete all were coming to see Jim play with the travel team. Another family affair. Jim knew better than to protest because the plan was to head straight down to the hospital after the game. Today was Nana's birthday. Mom wanted to get there early in the afternoon before Nana started having one of her "sundown" episodes. She told Jim there was something about the late afternoon, when the sun started to set, that made people who had strokes get very nervous. The nurses at the hospital called it sundowning.

Sundowning? To Jim it sounded like something that happened to werewolves.

"Do I have to go to Jim's stupid game?" said Pete. "Why can't I just meet you at the gym when it's over? Tricia will give me a ride."

"Yeah, that's a good idea," said Jim. He didn't want Pete watching his basketball game and making fun of it for days after.

"You haven't been to a single game," said Dad. "And neither have I. Jim hasn't had any fans in weeks!"

"But, Dad . . ." grumbled Pete.

"Case closed," said Dad, grabbing the car keys off the hook next to the back door.

Lisa didn't warm up with the team. She was dressed to play, but she sat on one of the metal folding chairs hunched over with her knees pulled up to her chest. As they jogged around the edge of the court, Jim asked Marco what was wrong with Lisa.

"Oh, I think it's that time of month. You know, that womanly problem," said Marco. He smiled widely as he said this. "Looks like it's showtime for Marco 'Cool Breeze' Brooks. Mondini gave me the nod. I'm starting!"

"That's cool," said Jim, slapping low fives with him. He had to admire Marco. Even with his flip remarks and swagger, he could talk his way out of a paper bag. He knew how to charm Mondini and Mr. O with his wide knowledge of basketball trivia. He seemed a little older than the rest of the guys.

"Of course, this has to happen on the one day my mama can't come. She had to take Cherise to the doctor," said Marco. "Hey, isn't that your brother over there?"

"Don't remind me," said Jim. "My whole friggin' family is here to watch me polish the bench."

As they jogged by, Pete called out, "Run, Squeak, run!"

Mr. Mondini announced the starting lineup, and Jim took a seat next to Lisa. She looked pale.

"What's up?" Jim said.

"Nothin'," said Lisa into her knees.

"Are you sick?"

"I feel fine!" she said indignantly. Color began to spread across her cheeks, and her eyes were blazing. "Sometimes I just hate my father."

Jim shifted uncomfortably in his seat. He felt as if he had walked into the girls' room at school. He was somewhere he shouldn't be. Jim looked sideways along the bench to see if Mr. Mondini was watching, but he was waving his clipboard in the air, yelling, "How many times do I have to tell you, Marco, to keep your hands up?"

"He thinks he's Mr. Basketball!" Lisa continued. Jim kept his eyes on the floor just in case Mondini happened to glance this way after he was done chewing out Marco. Sure, Jim agreed with Lisa that her father was obsessed and wacko when it came to the game of basketball. All the guys had started calling him Mondo Mondini behind his back. But Jim had worked hard to earn his minutes on the floor. He wasn't about to throw it all away by saying something stupid to the coach's daughter. Jim also knew how Mondini felt about Lisa, how hard he pushed her. No way Jim wanted his coach to think he was getting in the middle of a family squabble. He wished he hadn't sat down next to Lisa.

"You're so lucky. You don't have to ride home with him after every practice and game. He just drones on and on about what I didn't do right, how I'm never going to play for a D-one program with my work ethic, how I'm just wasting all this talent. . . ." Lisa rubbed her reddening nose on her knees. "Like basketball is so important! It may be his whole life, but it sure isn't mine!"

Jim thought about how Mom and Dad and even Nana were always trying to make him realize that basketball wasn't everything, that school was more important, and here was Lisa saying pretty much the same thing. Lisa was the only girl on this travel team, and she played just as hard as any of the guys, but it wasn't that important to her? Maybe if Mondini were his father, Jim would feel the same way. He'd probably be playing baseball or something Mondini didn't know how to coach, not that Mondo was exactly Jackson or Van Gundy.

"Didn't your mom play basketball?" said Jim.

Lisa looked at him as if he had just used a four-letter word.

"What difference does that make?" she shot back. "I'm not my mother!" Lisa's nose was bright red, and she seemed ready to explode.

Jim wanted to open a little hatch door in the floor and disappear. What was wrong with the connection between his brain and his mouth? Why did he say such stupid things?

"That's what my father doesn't seem to understand," said Lisa. "I'm never going to be my mother. Not in a million years."

For some reason Jim took his left hand and patted Lisa's shoulder. "You're a really great player, Lisa, better than a lot of these guys," he said.

The air horn honked noisily for a substitution. Jim was startled by the sound. In disbelief he saw his hand on Lisa's shoulder. What was he doing? He clumsily yanked his hand away. Had anyone noticed? He looked along the faces on the bench, but they all were engrossed in the game. Mr. Mondini was now on his feet, doing his Bobby Knight imitation. Jim looked across the floor and to his horror saw Pete staring right at him, smiling an evil smile.

"Thanks, Jim," said Lisa.

Jim was confused. What was she thanking him for? He couldn't even remember what he had just said to her.

"Anyway," said Lisa as if she were finishing up a long story, "I wish I could play on a girls' team with a different coach. Someone who had actually played the game."

Jim wanted to switch seats with someone closer to the coaches. He wanted to get on the floor and start playing. He needed to get away from Lisa Mondini as quickly as possible before he did something crazy like pat her on the shoulder again.

"My mother would have been an awesome coach," said Lisa.

"That's it," said Mr. Mondini, "I've had it with Josh. He can't make a pass to save his life today. Malone, get ready to go in."

Jim practically sprinted to the scorekeepers' table. He had a strange tingling in his arms. His heart was racing even as he waited in his crouching position. Was it Lisa's voice or Pete's smile or just the fact that he was about to play?

At the air horn, Jim exploded onto the court as though he were starting a foot race around the track. His left hand, his shooting hand, still felt hot from touching Lisa's shoulder. He heard Dad's voice coming from the fans: "Okay, Malone, let's get this game under control!" Under control? Jim had not even been watching the game. He had no idea what was going on. He didn't even know what the score was.

"Let's get ready to rumble!" Marco said in Jim's right ear.

Whatever had happened on the bench didn't seem to matter anymore. Jim played with a crazy intensity now, calling the plays with authority, running the floor, making the passes work, and even scrambling for rebounds. He remembered what Dad always told him before every game: "Don't be afraid to shoot!" Dad said you'd never know if you could score if you didn't take the shots and even if you missed, there was always the chance of a rebound. "Follow your shots!" was Dad's other basketball commandment. That way you might get a second chance. Much as Jim hated to admit it, Dad was right. If you wanted to play basketball, you couldn't be afraid. You had to go for it!

"Man, you are possessed," said Marco at halftime.

"Excellent hustle," said Mr. Mondini.

"Give the Squeak some respect," said Frankie. "He is the *man*!"

Mr. Mondini let Jim play the rest of the game. Jim felt really light today as if he could jump and touch the rim if he wanted to. The ball didn't seem as big as it usually did. His mind was clear of everything except basketball.

The Thunderbirds won by ten points. After the game Mr. O said, "We just beat the only undefeated team in the league! Congratulations, fellas!"

"Jim, I've never seen you so focused and confident. Excellent work!" said Mr. Mondini. "You have earned a starting place at the Pineville Tournament next weekend." Pineville was the first of two big tournaments the team was going to.

Marco was clapping Jim hard on the back, and Frankie was saying, "Squeak for president!" Slade and Matt gave Jim high fives.

"Mr. Mondini, I'm terribly sorry to interrupt." It was Mom. "But we really have to rush off. We're going to see Jim's grandmother in the hospital."

Mr. Mondini raised his eyebrows. Jim wanted to push Mom away from his team. How could she barge in like this and ruin his moment of glory? Nana could wait five minutes! Then he thought: Nana again! She's always messing up my basketball career. Even though she's lying in a bed and can't really speak, she's getting in the way. Nana!

"You sure you're not going to some opera again?" said Matt. A couple of the guys laughed.

Mom's smile faded, and she looked stone-faced at Matt. "Jim's grandmother had a stroke a few weeks ago," she said. "Today's her birthday. We're going down to try to celebrate."

Mr. Mondini cleared his throat. "I'm very sorry, Mrs. Malone. Jim, go ahead. Get your stuff. Don't keep your grandmother waiting."

It started the minute they got in the car.

"So what's the deal with you and that Mondini chick?" said Pete.

"What deal?" said Jim. "Leave me alone,"

"Oh, come on, I saw you put your arm around her."

Jim wanted to sock Pete right in the nose. "Get a life," said Jim. He stared out at the passing traffic.

"Hey, nothing wrong with having a cute little girlfriend. I had one, too, in the seventh grade," said Pete. "And what a bonus! Lisa even plays b-ball! Only wish you'd told me about it. You know, so I could give you some brotherly advice. I do have vast experience in the love department, as you know."

"What are you babbling about now, Pete?" said Dad. "Jim just played the game of his life, and you're talking about some girl?"

"I think Lisa is very pretty and very brave to be playing with all you big, aggressive boys!" said Mom, clueless as ever. "And I'm glad to see you're interested in something besides basketball!"

Nana was sitting in a wheelchair when they arrived in her room. She looked like a doll who had been propped up. When she saw them, her eyes widened, and she said, "Wow," over and over. Only one side of her mouth moved.

"Don't you look pretty, Mama," said Mom.

Jim knew Mom was lying to make Nana feel better. After all, Nana's hair was combed up and tied in a weird-looking topknot like the baby in *The Flintstones*, and she was wearing another one of the hospital gowns. He also knew that Nana could see right through this phony compliment. She was glaring at Mom.

Dad was busy tying a bunch of purple balloons to the foot of Nana's bed, Pete was taking the birthday cake Mom had baked out of a box, and Mom was unwrapping the bouquet of roses. Only Jim seemed to notice Nana rolling her eyes and shaking her head ever so slightly.

Jim leaned over to kiss Nana's left cheek, and suddenly her left arm shot up and she grabbed his basketball jersey. Jim was surprised at how strong she was. She began to grunt and tug at his jersey.

Jim tried to stand up without letting Nana rip his shirt. "Yeah, Nana," he said. "I had a basketball game today. We won! I scored eighteen points."

Nana released her grip but kept on staring at Jim. It was as if she wanted to hear more.

"I got to play a lot, Nana," Jim said. "We beat a really good team."

"Yeah, and Jimmy got himself a girlfriend, too!" said Pete in his most sarcastic voice.

Without any warning Nana's voice erupted from her contorted mouth. "Shut up!"

They all stopped what they were doing and looked at Nana. She was staring angrily at Pete.

Jim couldn't believe his ears. To Nana "shut up" was as forbidden as a curse. She would always punish him or Pete when they said it to each other.

"She's never said that in her life," said Mom, shaking her head. "But you know, all her wires are scrambled." Mom put her arm around Pete as if to comfort him. "She doesn't know what she's saying."

"So, so stupid," said Nana.

Nana started to lean over the left side of her wheelchair as if she wanted to get out. "Please," she said. "Shrumpf, butter."

"Mama, you can't go back to bed yet!" said Mom. "We want to sing 'Happy Birthday.' Look, I made you a cake."

Nana stared angrily at Mom. It was clear to Jim that Nana wanted only one thing, to get out of the wheelchair. She looked at the cake and starting making a clucking sound.

"Maybe she needs that pillow behind her back adjusted," said Dad.

"Her right arm looks all scrunched up," said Pete.

"I know she ate at twelve-thirty, and they like her to stay in the wheelchair for a while after lunch. She can't spend all day in bed or her lungs get congested," said Mom.

Jim hated the way they all were talking about Nana as if she weren't even there. She wasn't deaf! She knew what was going on. She wasn't stupid.

They weren't allowed to light the candles because of being in the hospital, but they sang "Happy Birthday." About halfway through, a tall, skinny nurse with a zillion tiny braids pulled back in a ponytail walked into the room. She joined them in the song. Nana closed her eyes and bobbed her head in time to the music.

"Happy birthday, Ms. Wallach," said the nurse. A black tag pinned to her shirt read "T. Nelson, R. N." "It's me, Tamara! Remember me from yesterday?"

Nana opened her eyes at the sound of the nurse's voice and looked adoringly at her. Jim noticed that Nana seemed much happier to see the nurses in this hospital than she was to see her family. Nana smiled this strange, forced half-smile as if she was having trouble curving her lips.

"Remember, I told you I'd be by to fix your hair today and get some lotion on those dry legs!" Tamara said. She had a bright, positive voice, a lot like Ms. Durbin's. "But I can come back later."

When Tamara leaned over Nana's wheelchair, Nana used her strong left arm again to pin the nurse in this bent position. Nana began to grunt and bob her head.

"What is it, honey?" asked Tamara.

"I think she wants to get back in bed," said Mom.

"Stupid," said Nana.

"Maybe something hurts," said Pete.

Jim couldn't believe them. Why was he the only one who seemed to understand Nana? It was so obvious. She wanted Tamara to eat some cake with them.

"Would you like a piece of cake?" Jim said to the nurse.

The cake, Mom's chocolate fudge layer cake, tasted like paper to Jim. He kept looking at Nana's angry face and shriveled body. He wanted to tell her he had read her speech. He wanted to ask her if it was all true. He wanted to tell her about the tips Ms. Durbin had given them about public speaking. He wanted to practice with Nana the way they had planned. But what good would it do? How would he know if she understood?

After they finished eating cake and cleaned up the party plates, everyone stepped out into the hall while Tamara and a nurse's aide moved Nana back into her bed. Dad said he wanted to get a cup of coffee, and Pete said he'd go to the cafeteria with him. They seemed anxious to go.

"Jim, you stay here with Nana, okay?" said Mom. "I have to run upstairs to the physical therapy department and talk to Nana's doctor."

Suddenly Jim found himself all alone outside the wide door to Nana's room.

"You can go back in to your grandma," said Tamara as she came out of the room. "She's looking pretty tired, but I know she'd love the company. Where is the rest of the family?"

"They had stuff to do," said Jim.

"I see," said the nurse with a smile. "Well, you keep on talking to her in that nice normal way, honey. I can tell you two have a special bond." With that she turned and walked briskly down the hall, her white shoes squeaking away.

Nana appeared to be sleeping. The purple balloons were waving softly over her bed. They had put the pale blue tubes back in her nose, and she was breathing deeply. Jim sat on the chair and watched her.

"Nana," he whispered. She didn't open her eyes.

"Nana, I just want you to know, your computer is safe and sound under my bed. And I didn't tell anyone about it," Jim said as though they were having a conversation on the phone. "I hope you won't be mad, but I read your speech. It's awesome! Mom wants to call the museum in Washington and tell them you won't be able to give your speech. I told her to wait and see what happens. I mean, it's still a few weeks away. But you've gotta hurry up and get better so we can practice together."

Nana wagged her head back and forth on the pillow as if she were saying no. Then she opened her eyes and looked right at Jim. She moved her lips as if she wanted to speak, but only a deep, ratchety sound emerged.

"I'm sorry I never believed all that stuff about your swimming," Jim continued. "I mean, it wasn't your fault that they closed all the pools and sports clubs because you were Jewish."

Nana's eyes were shiny, and then Jim realized she was crying.

"Let's talk about something else," said Jim. "How about your favorite subject, basketball? I bet you really miss the House of Sports!"

Nana pointed to her mouth. Maybe she was thirsty? There was a can of ginger ale with a straw on the nightstand. Jim picked it up and brought the straw near Nana's lips. Like a little bird, she opened her mouth. She gripped the straw with one side of her mouth and began drinking. Some soda dribbled down her chin. When Jim moved the can away, Nana sighed deeply and said, "Thank you." He saw a box of tissues near the phone. He gently wiped her chin.

Nana's eyes were closed again. Jim looked at her arms, as skinny as his own. There were black-and-blue marks inside her elbows. Her hands were balled into tight fists as if she were ready to fight. Nana the little fighter. She had fought off the Nazis, she had fought off the muggers, and now she was fighting off her stroke.

For the first time since her stroke Jim didn't feel scared of this strange new Nana with her contorted mouth and Martian language. The old Nana, the one who rubbed his cheek and told him he was very handsome and very smart, was in there somewhere. Just the way she was inside the picture of the little girl standing on the bridge with her suitcase.

"Nana," said Jim, "can you hear me?" Jim swallowed hard. "You have to get better." The room felt warm. Nana's breaths were short and fluttery.

Jim knew he was going to have to match Nana's strength if he wanted to help her. And it had nothing to do with muscles, which neither of them had anyway. He thought again about her lying in a bed in a hospital in Italy, praying for a longer life so she could meet her grandchildren. Was Nana trying to pray now? What if God didn't understand this strange stroke language of hers? Maybe Jim would have to do the praying for her.

Ms. Durbin called two more meetings of the essay contestants. At the second one she broke them into pairs. Practice teams she called them.

"I want you to meet with your partner at least once over the next week to practice giving your readings," said Ms. Durbin. "I know it will be an audience of only one person, but it will help to have a partner give you some constructive criticism." Ms. Durbin was really getting into this contest. She was even trying to rev up the entire student body of Hollow Hill Middle School by making posters to advertise the event, inviting them to "Come out and show your support!" Jim was humiliated when he saw his name in blazing gothic letters right there on the poster. This isn't a rock concert, Ms. Durbin, he wanted to tell her.

The guys at lunch had started teasing him. "Who knew?" said Matt. "The Squeak speaks!" "Brains and brawn! A regular scholar-athlete!" said Frankie. Josh, who had been quieter than usual since the last basketball game, didn't say a word.

Luckily they didn't know that Ms. Durbin had paired Jim with Lisa. Of course it was better than getting stuck with one of those eighth-grade eggheads or dweeby Malcolm or, God forbid, Mariah. But how would he explain Lisa's coming over to his house if anyone found out? And what about Pete? He would be fueled for the next six months.

The only possible day was Thursday. Pete had a band rehearsal after school, Dad had a meeting at his school, and Mom would be at the hospital. But there was no way Lisa and Jim could ride the school bus to his house, not if Jim wanted to keep this a secret. Lisa said her sister Andrea would be able to give them a ride home. Jim suggested she meet them at the other side of the faculty parking lot behind the giant fir tree. Lisa laughed, but she agreed.

Andrea pulled up in a rusty blue Toyota with colorful Grateful Dead bears dancing across the rear window. She had short brown hair tied off her face with a bandanna. There was an enormous hoop earring attached to each ear.

"Hey, Jim," Andrea said. "Lisa's told me all about you!"

Jim was surprised. He didn't think Lisa Mondini ever thought about him outside of basketball.

"Isn't your brother Pete Malone?" Andrea asked.

"Yeah."

"Let me tell you, that boy is a hottie!" said Andrea. "Too bad he goes out with that airhead Tricia Van Huff. What a waste!"

"Andie!" said Lisa. "Cut it out!"

Andrea popped a tape in the cassette player, and this old-time music, like the stuff Mom and Dad always listened to, came blasting out of the speakers behind Jim's head. The car slowly rolled out of the parking lot and stopped at the traffic light. It was a warm day, so Andrea and Lisa both had their windows rolled down. Suddenly Jim saw a red Miata come careering around the corner in front of them.

"Speak of the devil," said Andrea.

Jim ducked down in the backseat.

"And there's your brother giving her his puppy-dog look," said Andrea. "That boy is blinded by love!"

Andrea let them out at the end of Jim's driveway. "I'll pick you up on my way home from cheerleading practice, Lees," she said. "Bye, Jim! You know, you're almost as cute as your brother!"

As they walked along the driveway, Lisa said, "Sorry she's such a loser."

"You obviously don't know my brother!" said Jim. He thought Andrea was nice, and she kind of reminded him of Mom, the way she drove so leisurely and sang along with the music.

Lisa leaped up to try to touch the rim of Jim's basketball hoop. The sun was melting the snow from the tarps covering the wood, making the blacktop wet. "How about when we're done, we play a little one-on-one?" said Lisa.

Jim unlocked the kitchen door. Jake surprisingly tried to get up to greet them. He furiously sniffed Lisa's jeans.

"How are you doing, big yellow dog!" she said, bending down to scratch his ears. "What's wrong with him?"

"Broken leg," said Jim. "I've gotta carry him out to the yard."

"I'll help you," said Lisa.

They set Jake out on the grass between two big patches of snow. Jim held up Jake's hindquarters with a towel so he could go to the bathroom, but he just looked at them and panted.

"Don't you wanna do anything?" said Jim.

"He looks really sad," said Lisa.

"The vet wanted to put him to sleep, but I wouldn't let her," said Jim.

"Maybe you should've."

Jim hoisted Jake back into his arms, grunting with effort, and stared at Lisa. "What do you mean? I should let someone kill my dog? Are you nuts?"

Lisa petted Jake's head and held his chin in her other hand. "What do you think? If you could talk, what would you do? Would dying be better than this?"

Jake closed his eyes. He felt heavier than ever.

As they walked back up the steps to the house, Lisa said, "I'm sorry. I shouldn't have said that, Jim." In the kitchen Lisa stood next to the cupboard, chewing on her bottom lip and fidgeting with one of her earrings. Jim carefully set Jake down on the floor near his water bowl. Then Lisa continued. "When my mom started getting so thin and weak, my dad could barely stand it. He was always saying, 'Would dying be better than this?' I wanted to strangle him! I mean, how could you want someone you love so much to die? How could he give up on her like that?"

Jim leaned against the sink and folded his arms across his chest. Did Lisa expect him to answer? He didn't know what to say.

"Every evening before dinner," Lisa said, "I would sit with my mother and read to her. I'm sure she was listening, even though she couldn't talk anymore. My sisters, all they did was cry like she was already dead. They'd cry right in front of her! At dinner my dad would always say stupid stuff like 'I hope God takes her soon.' But I wasn't going to let God take her without a fight! I kept right on talking all regular to her right up until . . ." Lisa's voice trailed off. She looked as if she were concentrating very hard. "But you know something? Maybe in some strange way my dad was right. I didn't know how my mom felt. She probably hated being so sick. I only knew what I wanted. I wanted my mom alive. I mean, how can death possibly be better than life?" Lisa was staring right past Jim at some point on the refrigerator. "It's really confusing," she said as she bent down to pet Jake. "Of course you don't want to die, do you, big fella?"

Jim wiggled his left foot and then his right. What could he say to Lisa? I'm sorry about your mom? My grandmother is really sick and might die soon? The other night when Dr. Mazer had called about putting a feeding peg in Nana's stomach, Mom had said something that really bothered Jim: "Nana wouldn't want to live that way. I think she'd rather die." Suddenly Jim wanted to tell Lisa, but what if she started crying right here in his kitchen? Then what?

"I talk to my grandmother in a regular voice," Jim said to fill the silence. "Everybody else in my family talks to her like she's hard-of-hearing and really dumb all of a sudden."

"I'm sorry about your grandma," said Lisa. "I thought she was really nice."

Silence again.

Jim wanted to talk about Nana's stroke language and about the list of words he was making, words like *drubbly, riskling, drubbish*. He wanted to tell Lisa about the way he sometimes heard Nana's voice even though she was far away in the hospital. He even wanted to show her the laptop and the stories, especially the one about Nana's grandfather. He suddenly felt heavy, as if he were carrying big rocks in his pockets and needed to take them out and put them on the kitchen table. But he didn't have the right words to start, especially with Lisa Mondini. What if she laughed at him and then went and told Frankie and he told Matt? Pretty soon all the guys at the lunch table would be making fun of him.

"Where do you want to work?" Lisa said.

"Let's go upstairs."

"Wow!" said Lisa when she saw Jim and Pete's bedroom. "This is a kickin' room!"

Jim really didn't understand what was so great about it. There were windows and a closet and all these posters, sports on his side of the room and rock bands on Pete's. The paint was cracking in one corner of the ceiling, and the English muffin wrapper was still flapping over one of the windowpanes.

"You can go first," said Jim.

He sat on his bed while Lisa arranged herself on the far side of the room near Pete's desk.

"Why are you standing so far away?" Jim asked.

"To practice projection, the way Ms. Durbin told us," said Lisa. She carefully pulled down and smoothed her sweater. "Okay, here it goes!" she said. Her hands were empty.

"Where's your essay?" asked Jim.

Lisa pointed to her forehead. "Up here," she said. "I know it by heart.

"There was once a woman with the strength of Hercules and the beauty of Venus. She was graceful and smart and very kind to everyone."

This sounded like the beginning of a fairy tale. Lisa looked taller than usual. She clasped her hands together by her waist and stared beyond Jim at some point on the wall behind him. "This woman ran as fast as the wind. She made the best lasagna in the world. She always beat my dad in chess. She could make thirty-four foul shots in a row. Her name was Angela L. Mondini, and she was my mother."

Lisa spoke loudly, as though she were in front of a vast audience. She went on to tell her mother's life story, about how she had grown up on a farm on the outskirts of town, the place that was now a development called Clover Dell Estates.

"Every morning before she went to school, my mom had to collect the eggs from the henhouse. She hated all the squawking in there and said the chickens were a bunch of old biddies who never got along. She also felt sorry for them because all they did was eat and lay eggs.

"One day her brother called her Chicken Legs, and she got so mad she punched him in the nose. 'I'll show you what these chicken legs can do!' she screamed at him. That's when she began running everywhere. By the ninth grade she was the fastest runner in the whole high school."

But not fast enough to get away from Mr. Mondini, thought Jim. He wanted to hear about how Lisa's mother ended up with a loser like Mondini, but all Lisa said was "My mother met Alfred Mondini in the eleventh grade in chemistry. They were lab partners. Two years after high school they got married."

Lab partners? That would be like Pete marrying Kristen Lubell, that geeky genius he had for a lab partner. Scary!

Lisa stopped for a moment and looked at Jim. "Am I going too fast? My sister Stacy says I talk too fast and garble the words."

Lisa's eyes were bright, and even from way across the room Jim could feel them trained on his like lasers. She looped her hair behind her ears and looked hopefully at him. Jim suddenly felt embarrassed that Lisa was here in his room.

"You're doing f-fine," he stammered.

Lisa smiled and continued. She went on about her mother's basketball career in high school and college, about how smart Mrs. Mondini was and how she could fix anything, including an old toaster. Lisa described one Christmas when her mom made all these dolls for her four daughters and how Lisa's doll was wearing a basketball uniform, complete with high-top sneakers. But when she got to the part about her mother's cancer, Lisa swallowed hard. Her face drained of color, and her eyes narrowed just like Mr. Mondini's. She took a deep breath as though she were about to jump off the high diving board at the town pool.

"Before she got too sick to talk, my mother told me lots of stories about the farm and about playing basketball in high school and about marrying my dad. She made me write stuff down, so I wouldn't forget anything. My mother told me that words float away into thin air when you say them, like dandelion fluff, but if you write them down, you can hold on to them and the stories live forever. And she thought that stories need to be passed along. Otherwise, what good are they? She said, 'Lisa, I want you to keep talking to me even after it seems like I'm not listening. Hearing is the last of the senses to go. I will hear you. I will always hear you.' That's when I started to write just for fun, not only for school. I made up poems. They were pretty dumb, but my mother loved them. She made me promise to keep writing. Then when it hurt too much for her to talk, I told her stories about school, and I read her a poem every night before she went to sleep. My mother was the best and strongest person I ever knew. I miss her every day."

Lisa stopped. Jim thought it was the end of the essay and he began to clap for her.

"I'm not done," said Lisa, putting a finger to her lips.

"This is a poem I wrote for her recently:

"I dribble and shoot
A ball the shape of the world
When it goes through the net
I know you hear the *swish*
I remember every bit of your face
And I remember everything you told me
Especially about playing with my whole heart
You may not be here to clap for me or hug me anymore
Like the other mothers who cheer us on
But what I do best and know best
I learned from you
My mother who knew that a circle is perfect
No beginning and no end
And a ball is the shape of the world."

Lisa finished and took a bow. She didn't look sad the way she had in school the day she announced her essay topic to the other contestants. She didn't look angry or sullen the way she did so often at basketball practice. She looked radiant and pleased and very proud, as if she had just been named the MVP of the Pineville Tournament.

"What did you think?" Lisa asked.

"It was good," said Jim. He didn't know what else to say. Lisa had done it perfectly, but he was too shy to tell her he thought she could win the contest. And a little part of him was jealous.

That night while Jim was trying to fall asleep, he kept thinking about Lisa Mondini. Why had he shown her Nana's laptop? What if she told her sister and then her sister told Pete? What had come over him? She had promised not to tell a soul. She had crossed her heart and hoped to die. Jim didn't know why, but he trusted Lisa Mondini. He even wanted her to come over to his house again.

Mom took a rare day off from going down to the hospital. She had piles of Nana's mail and papers on the dining room table that she needed to sort out. She also had phone calls to make and a list of nursing homes to visit.

"Mom, Nana doesn't want to go live in some nursing home!" said Jim when he heard about it. "She always said she'd rather die than do that!" Jim couldn't believe it. He sounded like Mr. Mondini! *Would dying be better than this?* He sounded like Mom! *I think she'd rather die.* Lisa was right. This was very confusing.

"I'm sorry, honey, but there's nothing else I can do," said Mom. "They want her out of the hospital, and she hasn't progressed enough for rehab and she needs two people to get her in and out of bed and the wheelchair." Mom rubbed her forehead as if it hurt. There were rings of gray under her eyes. "We wouldn't be able to get her through the doorways in our house or upstairs to the shower. I hate to do this, Jim, but there's no other choice right now."

Jim didn't want to look at the brochures Mom laid out on the dining room table that evening when she got home from touring three of the nursing homes.

"Hey, this one looks like a regular country club!" said Pete as he thumbed through a folder for a place called Happy Hills.

"You don't want to put her all the way up in Chester, do you?" said Dad, pointing to another folder.

"I think this is the best place I saw," said Mom. She held up a color photo of a gray stone building with a bank of geraniums along the wall in front of it. "They said as soon as a bed comes available, they'll call me. It's called the Burnside Home for the Aged. It was very clean, and they have lots of activities like bingo and sing-alongs."

"Nana never plays bingo, and she can't even sing!" said Jim indignantly.

Nobody paid attention to Jim. They all were busy studying the pictures of old men painting pictures and old ladies sitting at a table listening to someone read them a book. Jim thought it looked like a nursery school for senior citizens.

"Well, I'd better go call Tante Sarah so we can make a decision," said Mom.

"At least she's making some progress," said Dad. He followed Mom out of the dining room.

"Why do you always have to be so negative about Nana?" Pete said to Jim. "This isn't easy for Mom to do, you know! Why don't you just grow up?" Pete left Jim alone in the dining room.

Jim stood there looking beyond the nursing home brochures to the neatly stacked piles of bills, magazines, letters, and catalogs—a month's worth of Nana's mail. Then he saw a stack of unopened mail. He absentmindedly flipped through it until a cream-colored envelope caught his eye. It was from the museum in Washington where Nana was supposed to give her speech. Jim held the envelope up to the light with both hands. He could not make out what the letter said. He saw the letter opener lying there, the one from Nana's drawer, and he carefully slid it across the top edge of the envelope.

Dear Mrs. Wallach,

We deeply regret that you will not be able to join us for our conference next month. However, we understand that you are ill and wish you a speedy recovery. If, by any chance, you would like to have another member of your family present your speech, please contact me at your earliest possible convenience. We will be printing the programs on March 18th.

We all wish you the best during your convalescence.

Sincerely yours,
Miriam Schwartz

Jim froze with the letter in his hands. All month Nana's mail had been accumulating on the dining room table. He had not bothered to look at any of it. But here he was with the letter about the conference. There had to be a reason he had stumbled upon this important piece of information. Nana understood about the reason things happen, about signs and omens. Jim folded the letter and tucked it into the pocket of his baggy jeans.

T HE MORNING OF the Pineville Tournament Jake had to be rushed to the vet. He had been gnawing on his broken leg, and now it was bleeding. Dad wrapped him in an old bedspread and put him in the back of the car.

Just as Dad pulled out of the driveway, the phone rang. It was the Burnside Home for the Aged calling to say that someone had died last night, so there was a bed available for Nana, but she had to arrive by 3:00 P.M. if she wanted it. This threw Mom into a tizzy of phone calls. She told Jim he'd better call Josh for a ride to the tournament because as soon as Dad came home from the vet, they were going to have to rush down to the hospital and collect Nana and get her to the nursing home.

By ten Jim was standing alone in the kitchen, waiting for Josh to pick him up. It felt as if a hurricane had swept through the house, all the excitement of phone calls and Jake being whisked away and then Mom and Dad leaving in a flurry of kisses and good lucks. Dr. Hamilton had decided to keep Jake at the animal hospital because his leg was infected. Pete of course had slept through everything and was still sound asleep upstairs. The house was completely silent except for the old clock on the mantel. Jim looked down at Jake's empty bed, the uneaten biscuit from last night lying on the floor next to it, and a wave of emptiness came over him.

He heard a couple of car honks and looked out the window to see a shiny silver sports car. Jim thought it was one of Pete's friends, but then he saw the neatly shaved head and the wraparound sunglasses, and he knew it was Mr. DeLonga and Josh.

"Hello, young man," said Mr. DeLonga. "Let me put your bag in the trunk. It's going to be a bit tight for you there in the jump seat."

Josh smiled weakly but didn't salute or anything. He got out to let Jim fold himself into the tiny backseat. Jim had forgotten all about Mr. DeLonga's coming to this tournament.

"So Josh tells me you're the starting point guard this weekend," said Mr. DeLonga before they had even pulled out of the driveway. It sounded as if he were challenging Jim to explain why.

Jim didn't know what to say. Josh had been acting funny all week. Now Jim realized that he had probably been worrying about his father's coming to the tournament, expecting Josh to be a big superstar on the team. Jim could see Josh's profile and how tense it was.

"Uh-huh," Jim said.

"Well, you must be pretty darn good, Jim," Mr. DeLonga said, "because I know Josh can play the pants off boys twice his size."

"Dad!" said Josh. "Stop. Jim is my best friend."

When they got on the highway, Mr. DeLonga cranked the engine into high speed, and Jim thought he was going to throw up. By the time they reached the Pineville High School parking lot, Jim felt lightheaded and his legs were starting to cramp.

"What's wrong, Jim?" said Mr. DeLonga. "You don't look so hot." He almost sounded hopeful.

"I'm fine," said Jim, bending his right leg to stretch his muscles. *What a loser! Maybe if he'd bothered to come to any of our games, he'd know that Josh has started every single one!*

"I'm sorry about that," said Josh as they walked to the front door of the school ahead of Mr. DeLonga. "I've been stressin' all week, wishing he wouldn't come. He's so obsessed with being number one in everything."

Jim looked at his friend. Josh did look pale and tired. Jim considered asking Mr. Mondini to let Josh start the first game of the tournament, just so he could get his father off his back. But then he thought, *No way, José! I deserve this!* He remembered Dad telling him before the tryouts to forget about all friendships when you are competing in a sport. As Dad said, "In the heat of battle it's every man for himself. If you want to play, you have to make the coaches notice you." Mom had chided Dad for being too harsh. But then Nana had chipped in her two cents: "I learned a long time ago, you can't be timid in this life, my Jimmy. There's nothing wrong with being a little pushy; otherwise no one notices you. Whatever you do, don't be a nebbish. You don't get anywhere being a nebbish." Marco was the "un-nebbish" of this team. Look at what he had done in the few short weeks of the season so far: gone from being a serious benchwarmer to starting over Mondini's own daughter!

As they entered the lobby of the school, a couple of women dressed in matching turquoise warm-up suits greeted them. They were sitting at a lunch table with a cigar box and a stack of programs.

"Are you guys players?" asked the plumper one.

Jim and Josh nodded, so she handed them each a program and stamped a red happy face on the backs of their right hands. "Good luck, boys."

Mr. DeLonga had caught up with them. When he tried to pick up a program, the lady with the cigar box said, "That'll be two dollars, please."

"Kinda stiff." Mr. DeLonga said as he pulled out his wallet. "I'd better get to see my kid play some significant minutes at these prices."

Josh yanked on Jim's sleeve and said, "Let's get outta here."

They found Mr. Mondini and Mr. O at the registration table handing in their rosters. "Hey, fellas, top of the morning to ya," said Mr. O cheerily. "Ready to bring home some hardware?"

"Go over to that small gym and start getting warmed up," said Mr. Mondini, barely looking at them.

The only player missing was Lisa. No one knew why she wasn't there.

A lot of the fans from the first game between the Rockets and the Comets stayed to watch the Thunderbirds play the Warriors of Pineville. The bleachers were packed and noisy. A kid at the scorekeepers' table had a boom box, and it was blaring a hip-hop song. Jim thought this was the closest he'd ever come to playing in a big-time arena. He half expected Tricia Van Huff, Andrea Mondini, and the rest of the high school cheerleaders to come dancing out of the locker rooms.

"Home court advantage," Mr. Mondini was saying to them in the pregame huddle, "is not something to sneeze at. It's a real factor, so you have to block out all the external stuff and just focus on your game. This is a tournament, so there won't be much subbing. Sorry, but that's just the way it is. If we win, then everyone gets to go home with a nice trophy. If we lose, we just go home with some dirty socks."

They all put their hands in. "Key word is *execute*," said Mr. Mondini. They all grunted "together" in unison.

As he jogged out onto the floor, Jim heard a baby squeal and then saw Mrs. Brooks standing there in the first row holding Cherise with one arm and pumping her other fist. "You go, Thunderbirds!" she yelled. For the first time all season Jim wished his family were there to cheer him on. Here he was starting, and none of them would even see it. He remembered Lisa's poem to her mother, who could never come to another basketball game. Jim looked up into the crowd, stupidly hoping to see Dad giving his dorky thumbs-up sign or Mom waving like a little kid or even Pete smiling his sarcastic smile. There was an elderly lady with poofy blond hair being helped into the second row of bleachers. She was wearing a fur coat. He blinked. For a moment Jim thought it was Nana. He could hear her yelling, "Go, my Jimmy! Go, my handsome American grandson!" Then the lady turned, and Jim saw a stranger's face.

"What are you gawkin' at?" said Marco, coming up behind him for the tip-off. "Is there a chick I need to check out?"

"Nah," said Jim. "She's too old for you!"

The ref blew the whistle, and the game began. Jim could see right away that the Warriors were good. They had discipline and confidence, and they played clean. The other point guard was short and square, built more like a running back with very quick hands. Jim felt the adrenaline pumping. This was going to be tough.

The Thunderbirds won the tip-off, thanks to Frankie. He got the ball to Jim, who decided to dribble to the right because he didn't think the bullish kid had a left hand. Jim called, "Kentucky," because it was the play he knew his team could usually execute perfectly. And wasn't "execute" Mondini's theme for the day? As soon as he made the call, everyone started moving on cue, Marco switching with Matt, Slade coming over for the ball, Frankie stepping just outside the paint and then dodging his defender in time to get the pass from Slade. *Swish*. The first two points were scored.

By the half the Thunderbirds were up by ten points. Mondini told them he wanted to keep the starters in. "Ten points is nothing against a team like this," he said. "We want a win under our belt going into the second game."

Jim took a swig of water and saw Josh looking at him. "You're doing awesome," said Josh, and gave Jim his little salute.

Jim knew how hard it must be for Josh to sit there on the bench while his know-it-all father was fuming somewhere in the stands. How could Josh be so calm about it? Jim sometimes wished that Josh could get angry, really angry, and stop being so loyal. Maybe *loyal* wasn't the right word. Maybe it was *wishy-washy*. Josh always did as he was told, followed orders, from Mondini, from his mom, his dad, even from Jim. Josh could be bossy or loud or surprised or goofy, but he never was angry even when he had a right to be.

Josh did not get into the game at all. The Thunderbirds won 62–58. Mr. Mondini told them all to get something to eat because their next game was in an hour.

Jim and Josh walked down the hall toward the cafeteria. They saw Lisa coming from the lobby. She was waving and smiling, but she looked very pale. "How'd we do?" she asked eagerly.

"We won!" said Josh. "It was a good game."

"What happened to you?" asked Jim.

"You don't want to know!" said Lisa, grinning. "I puked my guts out last night. It was nasty! My sister Andie decided she was going to cook dinner. She made spaghetti with clam sauce. My dad still tried to get me up this morning! He told me I was letting the team down if I didn't come. Do you believe that? Oh, God, there he is, Mr. Basketball himself!"

Jim and Josh turned around to see what Lisa was staring at. Mr.

Mondini and Mr. DeLonga were talking to each other just outside the doors to the gym. Mr. Mondini was holding his clipboard in one hand and the bag of basketballs in the other. Mr. DeLonga's face was red, and he was waving his arms around.

"Who's that man yelling at him?" asked Lisa.

"My dad," Josh said in a quiet voice. "Look at him! He's out of control!"

"Come on," said Jim. "Let's get something to eat. Don't worry about it."

"Do you want me to find out what's the matter?" said Lisa.

"No," said Josh.

The three of them entered the cafeteria line. There were bagels and egg sandwiches and bananas and doughnuts. Jim was starved and grabbed a bagel with cream cheese and a container of chocolate milk. Josh took a banana, and Lisa said, "I can't even look at food!" They found an empty table near the windows.

"I can't believe my father sometimes," said Josh. "Why did he have to come up here anyway? Why did my mom ever marry such a loser?" Josh spoke in a slow, sad voice. "Why doesn't he just go home and burp his stupid baby?"

Josh peeled his banana, but then instead of eating it, he just stared at it. Lisa and Jim exchanged looks. Jim thought of all the times Josh had slept over at his house, how Josh had his favorite place on the couch when they watched basketball on television with Pete and Dad. Dad always said, "Josh, you must be a corporate sponsor to get a box seat like that!" and Josh would answer, "I pay good money for this seat, Mr. Malone!" And they would laugh away. Josh was a charter member of the House of Sports, Dad liked to say.

"I bet you'll start the next game," Jim said to Josh.

"Well, I don't want to start if it's only because of my dad and his big mouth!" said Josh.

Jim saw Mr. DeLonga first. He walked up to where they were sitting, his face still red, his sunglasses on top of his head, and said, "Josh, let's go. We're leaving."

For a moment no one said anything. It was like one of those tense moments in a movie thriller. Jim stared at Josh, trying to beam anger into him. Don't let him push you around! Be tough! But Jim realized that even with all his stupid outbursts at home, he was basically a little mouse himself when it came to speaking up.

"What are you talking about, Dad?" said Josh. "We have three more games, maybe four." Josh did not sound angry, but he did sound determined.

Jim was impressed. He wanted to say, Yeah, Josh, you tell him! but of course he sat there in silence.

"I don't have to waste my time at a basketball tournament where all you do is sit on the bench. Your coach is a dunderhead who doesn't understand the game. Probably never played it to begin with." Mr. DeLonga had his hands on his hips. He cast a shadow over Josh.

Dunderhead? Was that some kind of southern word?

Jim caught Lisa's eye, and they started to laugh.

"My father may be a lot of things, but he's definitely not a dunderhead!" said Lisa with mock seriousness.

"What exactly is a dunderhead?" said Jim in a fake English accent. "A type of shark?"

"No, I believe that would be a hammerhead," said Lisa. "A dunderhead is completely different. It's a type of extremely dumb mammal."

The three of them burst out laughing. Mr. DeLonga looked like they had just tried to serve him poison. He obviously had no sense of humor.

"Come on, Josh. Get your bag," he said. "We're leaving."

Josh looked at his father in disbelief. But Mr. DeLonga meant business. He started to pull the chair out from under Josh.

"Hey, Dad, what are you doing?" said Josh.

"If you want to leave," said Lisa, "go ahead. My dad and I can drive Josh home."

"Thanks, Lisa," said Josh.

"We're leaving now," said Mr. DeLonga in a shrill voice. "Now!"

Another moment of tense silence. Josh stood up as Jim knew he would. No matter what Josh said about his father, good or bad, he believed in him. Josh carried hope around in his heart like a secret potion, thinking that if he sprinkled it on his father enough, the man might soften up and show him some real affection. The guy could drop into Josh's world like a surprise parachute and bump into things and knock stuff over and make a mess of his life, and Josh would still welcome him.

Jim wondered what it would be like if Dad just up and left the family. How would he ever be able to forgive him? He thought of something Nana had written about her father, about how she had never given up hope that he would return to their family, even as the months of his absence turned into years: "It isn't easy to give up on your father even when it is obvious he doesn't want anything to do with you. You can't recite the Kaddish for someone who isn't dead, and still every day is like *yahrzeit*, because you keep the flame of hope burning from morning until night. 'My father will return,' you keep repeating as if you can make it so. A child will always find a way to explain and forgive her parent because otherwise she might lose her anchor and spin out into the scary, empty darkness of feeling alone in the world."

Jim had never thought about how Josh and Nana had this in common, disappearing fathers. When he looked at Josh's face, all twisted yet trying to smile, Jim could picture Nana as a little girl waiting for her father to come back. He thought of Nana now, her old face twisted from the stroke. Jim wondered if she had forgotten about her father leaving her family and how she had believed it was because the Nazis made her quit swimming. Jim wanted to tell Josh this story. He wanted to say, "Look, Josh, it's not about you and basketball; it's about your dad and his other wife." It suddenly became very clear. Jim wanted to tell Josh not to be afraid. He didn't need Mr. DeLonga. Jim would hold on to him so he wouldn't spin out into the darkness. He suddenly regretted his own selfishness. Why hadn't he let Josh play in the first game? Jim knew he could've faked an injury. Then none of this would be happening. With his mind racing, Jim still sat there unable to say anything.

"Don't go!" said Lisa.

"I've gotta go," said Josh. "Later, you guys. Good luck!" He followed his father out of the cafeteria.

Lisa and Jim sat there for a while without speaking. Jim wasn't hungry anymore. He looked at his half-eaten bagel and pushed it away. He didn't feel like talking. The rest of the day stretched before him, a lot more basketball, and he should have been happy, but some of his enthusiasm had walked out the door with Josh. For the first time Jim realized that basketball was not separate from the rest of his life.

Nana moved to Burnside, Jake died, and the Thunderbirds won the Pineville Tournament, all on the same day.

Jim put his trophy on the kitchen table next to the day's mail and Jake's tags. Dad put Jake's bed and all his toys in a black plastic garbage bag and took it out to the garage. Jim kept staring at the empty floor under the table and the dark stain on the wall where Jake had rested his back. Gone. Vanished. In a moment Jake had disappeared. The old fella, the great one was being cremated.

In the end Jake had been put to sleep. After cleaning up his leg, Dr. Hamilton had run some tests on Jake and found that his kidneys were failing. She had strongly advised that Jake "be put out of his misery." So while Jim was playing in the Pineville finals, scoring his season-high nineteen points, Mom and Dad had made the decision. Jim knew they were right. Still, he wished that Jake had just died on his own while sleeping under the kitchen table.

Mom was tired from helping Nana get settled in the nursing home. "Did she seem happy?" asked Pete.

"I couldn't tell," said Mom. "I mean, she kept saying, 'Wow, wow!' but she didn't smile. The ride in the ambulette really wore her out. When I left the home, she was sleeping."

"Don't worry, Mom," said Pete. "At least she's really close now, so you don't have to spend so much time on the train."

Dad wanted to hear all about the tournament, but Jim wasn't in the mood. This was probably the first time ever Jim hadn't wanted to talk about a basketball game.

"Jake had a good life," said Mom as if she could read Jim's mind. "He had so many adventures, and he knew we loved him very much, especially you, Jim. You took such good care of him right up until the end."

"Yeah, bro, I've gotta admit, you did more than any of us," said Pete. "I can't believe how you hauled him in and out every day! You're stronger than I thought!"

Jim smiled weakly. He could still feel the weight of Jake's body in his arms. He could almost smell the wet grassy odor of his back. It didn't matter how old your dog was, thought Jim, you never want him to die. But maybe Lisa was right: Jake had been pretty miserable these last few weeks. He must have been humiliated, such a big, strong fella having to be carried in and out by Jim. He couldn't chase a squirrel or a black crow out of the yard. He didn't like the taste of his biscuits or dog food anymore. All that sleeping. He must have been dreaming of doggie heaven with its barking and scratching and chasing of Frisbees.

"Can we bury his ashes in the yard?" said Jim.

Dad nodded.

"We can mark the spot with a circle of rocks," said Pete.

"There's that old piece of slate out by the garage," said Jim. "Maybe we can use it for a headstone."

"Remember the time he brought back that live mouse, Mom?" said Pete. "He had the tail between his teeth and this little gray thing was dangling there and you kept screaming, 'Leave it, leave it!' but he kept trying to get closer to you?" Pete and Mom started to laugh.

"He was so proud of himself," said Mom.

"He wanted you to take it from him," said Pete. "It was a precious gift for you!"

"Some gift!" said Mom.

"What about when he ate that entire box of fancy chocolates from Nana?" said Dad. "Remember all the foil wrappers strewn on the floor? We couldn't figure out how he unwrapped them!"

"And they had liqueur inside! He was definitely a little tipsy!" said Mom. She started laughing again.

"Eating was his favorite hobby, I think," said Jim. "Remember how he used to root around in the garbage when no one was looking? I once caught him with butter wrappers and a couple of yogurt containers on his bed. He looked at me all innocent, like he had no idea how they got there."

"Jake had the best face," said Pete. "Didn't he look like he was ready to speak sometimes?"

Mom, Dad, Pete, and Jim laughed and told stories until their stomachs hurt from laughing so much. Jim had once had a parakeet that died. Just keeled over and fell off his swing and died. Jim remembered how hard he had cried, all afternoon. That was the only death he had ever experienced before today. He never thought that death could make you laugh like this. Jim was sure that Lisa and her sisters hadn't sat around telling funny stories about Mrs. Mondini the night she died. He felt a little guilty for laughing. He hoped Jake understood that it meant they loved him.

For the first time in ages Jim didn't feel the creeping dread. For a little while everything here in his house felt normal again. They were sitting together around a table, having a good time. It seemed weird that something as un-normal as Jake's dying could make Jim feel as if it were just another regular night with his family.

Maybe this was bad thing number three. Maybe now he could shake off the spooky premonition that something terrible was waiting to happen. Jim felt a glimmer of hope for Nana. Maybe she was going to recover at Burnside. Maybe by this summer, or Thanksgiving, she would be talking and walking again. By next winter she might even be coming to basketball games when Jim made the eighth-grade travel team. But before all that, maybe, just maybe, Nana would be able to come to Washington and hear him, her handsome American grandson, read her speech to the Holocaust conference.

Lisa had actually been the one to call Miriam Schwartz, the woman who had signed the letter from Washington. When Jim told her he was too shy to do it, Lisa copied down the phone number and said,

"Well, I'm not shy. I'll tell her I'm one of Nana's grandchildren, and we have chosen my brother to read the speech. As long as you're not going to chicken out!"

Jim crossed his heart and swore on the Webster's dictionary in the school library. They were there waiting for Ms. Durbin and her final pep talk about the essay contest.

When she arrived, she was carrying a coffee can, which she placed in the middle of the table. "To decide in what order you guys are going to read at the contest," Ms. Durbin said, "I want each of you to pull out a number."

That was how it turned out that Jim would be last. He groaned when he saw the number eight. He had really wanted to go first and get it over with. "Can we trade if we don't like our number?" he asked.

"No," said Ms. Durbin.

Lisa called Jim every night the last week before the contest. Pete made fun of the calls, but Mom said, "They're both nervous. I think it's great that they're trying to boost each other's confidence."

Actually, they hardly talked about the contest at all. One night Lisa called to say she had left a message for Miriam Schwartz at the museum. The next night she called to say Miriam Schwartz had returned her call and agreed to let Jim make the speech. "She wanted to know how to spell your name for the program." The next night she called to talk about how they would get to Washington. "You don't mind if I come along?" Lisa had said. Lisa was getting more psyched about this than he was! Jim wondered why he had ever thought it was so important to present Nana's speech. He knew he was going to have to tell Mom and Dad sooner or later.

Friday after school, the day before the essay contest, Jim and Mom drove over to Burnside. Mom had been there every day, but it was Jim's first visit. It looked just like the picture, a big gray building with a wall, but there were no geraniums and no leaves on any of the trees or bushes. The lady at the visitors' sign-in window greeted Mom like an old friend.

"How are you today, Mrs. Malone?" she said. "Is this your son? Awww, what a good-looking young man. How old are you, 'bout ten or eleven?"

"I'm almost thirteen," said Jim. What a dumbbell.

Nana lived on the fourth floor. Mom explained that the sicker and more feeble residents lived on the lower floors, and the higher you went, the more independent the people were until you got to the fifth floor, where they pretty much took care of themselves. Jim figured Nana must have seriously improved since the last time he saw her.

The elevator opened on the second floor, and Jim saw a woman in a wheelchair who looked like a skeleton with eyes. She was staring right at him, and he shuddered. Mom put her hand on his shoulders as the door shut. "Some of these people are in pretty bad shape," she said. "I'm sorry."

Why was she sorry? It wasn't her fault these people were so old and nasty-looking.

When the doors opened on the fourth floor, Mom walked briskly out of the elevator and waved to a male nurse standing by the nurses' station.

"Afternoon, Gabby," he said. Another old friend, thought Jim.

"Come back here, Jerry!" came a loud voice from around the corner.

An elderly man dressed in a plaid sports jacket and bow tie came shuffling toward them. He was carrying an armload of clothes on hangers.

"Jerry, dear, stop right there!" A woman came running up behind him.

The man smiled at Mom and tipped his hat. Then the male nurse stepped between Jerry and the elevator and said sweetly, "Where are you going, Jerry?"

"I'm going home now," Jerry said, still smiling. But the nurse cupped Jerry's elbow and turned him around.

"Not today, Jerry," said the nurse. "Let's get all your clothes back in your closet. That's a good fellow."

Jim wanted to know why Jerry couldn't go home. He seemed fine to him. Before he could ask, Mom said, "Look, there's Nana!"

They stood on the threshold of a large room that looked like a hotel lobby with all these sofas and chairs and tables. A television tuned in to a cooking show was hanging in one corner. There were old people everywhere, some in wheelchairs, some on the armchairs and sofas. A few of them looked up at Jim and Mom and nodded as if they knew them. Jim didn't see Nana anywhere, but Mom did. She walked right into the room, wove through all the furniture, and bent down over a wheelchair in the far corner. The person in the wheelchair whose head had been tucked down on her chest suddenly looked up and said, "Wow, wow!" It was Nana.

Nana looked smaller and skinnier than ever. The skin of her face seemed to be pulled back, making her chin and nose look all sharp and pointy. Her eyes seemed bigger, maybe because her face was so shrunken. Oddly, her hair was all done as if she'd been to the beauty parlor, poofed up with hair spray, and she was wearing a pale blue sweater with rhinestones. "Come, come!" she said.

Mom leaned over to kiss her cheek, but Nana kept staring at Jim and pushed Mom away. "Pete, Pete," she said.

Jim looked at Mom in confusion, but Mom said, "It's okay, Jim. She calls me Sarah sometimes. I figure it's close enough."

Jim kissed Nana's small soft cheek, and she made a happy groaning sound, sort of the way Jake did when you rubbed his belly in the old days. He noticed a bit of crusty orange stuff in the corners of her mouth, the way the cottage cheese had been stuck there what seemed like ages ago.

Nana waved at the doorway with her left hand and said, "My accountant, my accountant, drubbly, go, go, go."

"She wants to get out of here," Jim said.

Mom unlocked the wheelchair brake, and together they pushed Nana. As she passed the other old people, Nana nodded and waved as if she were Queen Elizabeth greeting her subjects. In the hall she let out an enormous sigh of what sounded like relief.

"Jim wants to see your room," Mom said loudly into Nana's left ear. "Let's go show him your room."

Here Mom goes again, thought Jim, talking to Nana like she's some two-year-old. The hall reminded him of the hospital, but when he looked into the passing rooms, he saw afghans and braided rugs and stuffed animals. They were almost like the dormitory rooms they had seen on their tour of Villanova.

Nana's room was plainer than the others. Her roommate wasn't there. There was a vase of yellow roses on the windowsill and framed pictures of him and Pete, Mom and Dad. It startled him to see his face here in this strange room.

Nana began struggling to get out of her wheelchair.

"Wait, Mama," said Mom. "Let me find an aide. I can't get you back in bed by myself."

Mom left the room, and Jim sat on the chair by the window. Nana looked at Jim and said, "Pider, Peter, budder, schlumplfl!"

"I'm not Pete, Nana," said Jim. "I'm Jim. *Jim!*"

Nana grimaced. She laughed a deep donkey-type laugh Jim had never heard before. "Very good. Very good."

At least she isn't trying to get up, thought Jim. She motioned to her mouth and then to her limp right hand. "Nothing, nothing," she said, sadly shaking her head.

"It's not nothing," Jim said. "You still have a lot. You have your left side, you can eat again, you have Mom and Dad and Pete and me. . . ." Jim felt as if he was trying to convince himself.

Nana shook her head wearily. She put her chin down but continued to look at Jim as if she were scrutinizing him over the top of eyeglasses.

"Nana," said Jim, "I have a surprise for you."

Nana's expression didn't change.

"Tomorrow is the essay contest, but that's not the surprise."

Still no response.

"Remember your speech?" said Jim. "Well, guess what! I'm going to read it at the Holocaust conference. Me. I'm going to Washington!"

Nana frowned. She seemed to be trying very hard to understand him. "Really, really!" she said.

Jim was encouraged. "Do you want to come to Washington?" he said hopefully.

"Plopf, plumpf, give me some. I need it!" she said. "Hurry!"

Jim remembered that he had brought a small notepad and a pencil to write down some of these strange words Nana said. As soon as she saw him writing, she became agitated. "Hurry, hurry. Stupido!"

"Look, Nana, see," said Jim walking over to the wheelchair. "I'm writing down what you say so I can try to figure—"

Before he could finish his sentence, Nana pulled his hand, the one holding the pad, into her mouth and tried to bite it.

"Nana!" Jim said, pulling away. "What are you doing?"

Jim looked down at this little old woman in a wheelchair who seemed like an impersonator and wanted to say, "What did you do with my grandmother? You're not my nana. Who are you?" She was a bird, a squawking, flailing bird trapped in this monstrous thing called a stroke, flapping her wings, trying to set herself free. He looked into her brown eyes, and there, very far away, he caught a glimpse of his old nana, the nana who adored him, her handsome American grandson. But Jim also felt a cold, dark cloud slowly cross his mind, a cloud heavy with dread. Nana was drifting farther and farther away. It was undeniable. Soon she would disappear completely. And then what would he see when he looked into her eyes? Maybe Nana had been wrong. Maybe bad things didn't come in groups of three.

Jim's eyes opened at six-thirty the morning of the county essay contest. He had not slept well, and he woke up in a sweat with his pillow on the floor. The dream had been so vivid he was afraid to close his eyes again, so he got out of bed.

When he walked into the kitchen, he said, "Hey, old fella—" and then caught himself. He looked out the window to see the sky was pink and yellow. He unlocked the door and stepped outside onto the sagging back porch, where he noticed Jake's leash still hanging. The cool air felt good on his hot cheeks. Maybe he had a fever. Maybe he wouldn't be able to compete.

On the other side of the driveway he saw the purple flowers that were pushing through the little mounds of leftover snow. The color reminded him of his dream. In his dream Nana had been wearing a long purple robe. He turned and went back inside.

A few minutes ago the whole dream had been real, a complete and terrible nightmare, but now only fragments remained. Nana sitting on a throne in a purple robe. A wide beach with gangs of dogs, all kinds of dogs, running like crazy. Then people in wheelchairs, not old people, but kids and Mr. Mondini and even Lisa all racing along the edge of the water. And then Jim climbed up a lifeguard's chair, but when he tried to speak, nothing came out. He had to warn them . . . about what? He couldn't remember.

Jim poured himself a bowl of cornflakes and milk. As he sat eating, he absentmindedly stretched a leg under the table, reaching with his bare foot for the warmth of Jake's back. Jim hoped he wouldn't freeze up when it was his turn to read his essay. He hoped he wouldn't faint. He said to himself, "This is ridiculous. How can I be nervous three hours before the contest even begins?"

Jim tried to distract himself. He flipped on the television but could find only cartoons and weather and some grainy old black-and-white movies. He looked at a couple of recent *Sports Illustrated*s to see if he had missed any articles, but he had read them all cover to cover. He reread the article entitled "When Parents Forget to Be Fans" and cut it out for Josh.

Josh had been acting as if the incident with his father at Pineville had never happened. At lunch on Monday, Frankie had asked Josh, "What happened to you on Saturday? You split after one game? What's up with that?" Josh had made up some excuse about feeling sick and even though a few of the guys had seen the shouting match between Mondini and Mr. DeLonga, they left it at that. But when Josh didn't show up for practice Wednesday night, Jim called him to find out why. After all, they still had a couple of league games left to play and another tournament at Mountainside.

"I'm quitting the team."

"What are you talking about?'

"My dad is making me."

"You can't quit the team!" Jim was furious. "Just because of your father! You've never quit at anything, Josh!"

"Aw, it's no big deal—"

"It is, too, a big deal!" Jim cut him off. "Look, the Thunderbirds need more than one point guard, and you know Damian is useless. You can't just leave us in the lurch like that. Did you tell Mondini?"

"Not yet . . . but my dad said I have to quit . . . he wants me to start playing tennis. You know, take lessons and stuff. He even signed me up at this ritzy tennis club over in Warwick."

"Give me a break," said Jim. "Tell your father to go back to Atlanta and leave you alone."

Josh laughed. "He's already gone. You know my dad, the phantom."

"Listen, Josh, you're going to play the whole game on Saturday. Lisa and I have that stupid essay contest."

"Okay, okay," said Josh.

"And—" Jim paused because he wasn't sure he wanted to tell Josh.

"And what?"

"And I'm going to miss the Mountainside Tournament . . . 'cause I'm going to Washington."

"What for?" asked Josh.

"It's a family thing," said Jim. He wasn't ready to fill Josh in on all the details, especially since he hadn't even told Mom and Dad yet. "Okay, so you're not quitting, right?"

"I guess."

"You're not quitting or else you can forget about coming to the House of Sports to watch the NCAA tournament or the NBA play-offs or anything else," said Jim. "Your box seat will be turned over to another deserving fan!"

"*Okay!* I won't quit the team!" said Josh.

Pineville had not been the same without Josh there. Sure, Jim played every game and hung out with Lisa and Frankie and Marco between games, but in the back of his mind Jim couldn't stop thinking about how Josh had been yanked out of there. Jim felt powerless, and if there was one thing he hated, it was that feeling. Why couldn't he have convinced Mr. DeLonga to leave Josh at the tournament? Why hadn't he even tried? It was like what Dad said about basketball: "Don't be afraid to take your shot." Or as Nana said, "Speak up for yourself. Don't be a nebbish!" Why was it all so much easier on the basketball court and so much harder everywhere else? He didn't want Josh to think he didn't care about what had happened at Pineville.

Jim showered and dressed. He combed his hair and brushed his teeth. He took his essay downstairs and practiced reading it two times in front of the mirror in the bathroom. Both times he messed up on the names of the characters in *Madama Butterfly*. He tried one more time and read it perfectly. He looked at the clock in the living room. It was 7:45.

The contest was being held at the County Center, a large white building in downtown Warwick. It was used for concerts and antiques shows and the high school all-county basketball tournaments. Last year Dad and Jim had come here for the basketball finals. There were marching bands and cheerleaders and hot dogs for sale. Jim remembered thinking, In a few years I'm going to be down there on the floor playing in the finals. But now here he was in a pair of khakis, a light blue shirt, and a tie instead of a basketball uniform and big white high-tops.

"I got a space all cleared in our room for the computer, Squeak, so get out there and bring home the bacon!" said Pete. He lightly punched Jim's arm.

Mom hugged Jim, and Dad said, "Good luck, son," like something out of one of those corny old westerns he liked to watch late at night.

Jim left them with their hopeful faces in the lobby and followed the signs that read CONTESTANTS down a long hallway around the perimeter of the main hall to the back of the stage. There was a crowd of kids, and they all seemed to be talking at the same time. The teachers from the various schools were holding up signs with the names of their schools. Jim found Ms. Durbin. She was wearing a Chinese-style dress with a high collar, and she had her hair pulled up in a bun.

"Jim, you look very handsome," said Ms. Durbin.

Frederika and Vishnu were showing each other these secret handshakes while Malcolm kept asking Ms. Durbin, "Is my hair sticking up?" Then Mariah walked over, and Jim couldn't believe his eyes. She had little rhinestones all up and down her braids, and she was wearing this flouncy white dress that made her look like Cinderella. This is just an essay contest, not a royal ball, he wanted to tell her. Finally Lisa got there.

"Sorry I'm late," she said to Ms. Durbin.

"You're not late at all," said Ms. Durbin.

"What are you staring at?" Lisa said to Jim. "Haven't you ever seen a girl in a dress before?"

Jim looked away in embarrassment. He had been staring. No, actually he had been gawking at Lisa. She wore a dark red velvet dress with a lace collar. Her hair was partly braided and pulled back and partly long, hanging over her shoulders. There was a gold chain with a small heart-shaped pendant around her neck. She was wearing lipstick to match her dress.

"I like your tie," she said to Jim.

The schools were called into the auditorium one at a time and seated together on metal folding chairs on the stage. Jim could not believe the sea of faces looking up from the audience below.

They were going to announce the schools in no apparent order. Jim worried that Hollow Hill would be the very last, and then he would be the very last contestant of the entire contest. The judges might be dozing off by then. Everyone rose for the national anthem, which was sung by some girl from Maple Grove Middle School. As she sang "and the home of the brave," a few kids in the audience whooped it up the way people do at baseball games, and Jim heard a distinct *"Go, Hollow Hill!"* Then the mayor of Warwick made a boring speech about "the future of our nation" and "the leaders of tomorrow" and the superintendent of schools in Pineville made a speech that she must have thought was hilarious, because she kept stopping to leave room for the laughter even though there wasn't much. And then finally the contest began.

The first school picked out of a hat was Casey Middle School. It had only three contestants. Jim watched the first, a tiny girl, walk up to the lectern. She must have been a sixth grader who had skipped a few years. There was a small step stool ready for anyone who couldn't reach the microphone. She gracefully hopped up on it, introduced herself as Mary Elizabeth Hanratty, and dived headlong into her essay, something about gardens and insects and winning a blue ribbon at the county fair. Jim lost interest and started to daydream. He was thinking about where they could bury Jake's ashes when he heard the applause that meant Mary Elizabeth was done bragging about her prize pumpkin and it was someone else's turn.

Up and down, up and down, every shape and size of kid seemed to be competing. Every kind of voice: nasal, husky, high, and squeaky. Every imaginable subject—"Firehouse Etiquette"; "How I Saved My Cat's Life"; "The Summer Solstice and I"; "My Grandfather, the Man Who Invented the Three-Hole Punch" (yeah, right!)—and on and on until Jim felt his head was stuffed with cotton. His fog was suddenly cleared as the mayor of Warwick announced, "Hollow Hill Middle School."

Mariah let out a little panicky gasp. Ms. Durbin stood up and strode confidently to the lectern. A couple of catcalls and whistles exploded from the audience. Ms. Durbin did a short pep talk about the school and then called Malcolm, who was first. "Why I Want To Be an Entomologist." This should really put the judges to sleep, thought Jim.

All through the first three essays Jim stayed pretty calm. But then it was Lisa's turn, and he started feeling nervous for her. Why? They were going to love her. She was a sure thing for one of the big prizes.

Lisa pushed the step stool aside. She stood straight and tall, the way she had that day in Jim's room. She cleared her throat and began. Her voice was bright and steady without any hesitation. The audience hushed in a way it had not done for any of the previous contestants. As Lisa recited her poem, you could hear a few muffled sounds and someone blowing his nose. Before she had finished saying, "Thank you," the audience erupted into enthusiastic applause.

Lisa turned, and as she passed Jim's seat, she put a hand on his shoulder and whispered, "Good luck."

Later Jim could not remember hearing his name being announced, walking to the lectern, or even introducing his essay. It was as if he were sleepwalking. He woke up when he was on the second sentence, and his voice sounded incredibly loud. He looked out at the audience and saw a couple of people covering their ears. The mayor, who was sitting next to the lectern, yanked at Jim's elbow and whispered, "Move back a little from the microphone." Suddenly the fact that here he was, Jim Malone, on a stage in front of a zillion people, reading something he had written for an English assignment, hit him like a tub of cold water. He started to laugh. He imagined them in their underwear. He laughed again.

"Jim!" He heard Ms. Durbin's worried voice behind him.

"Let me try that again," he said. "Sorry, I'm really nervous." There was laughter in the audience. Jim felt his heartbeat slow from a gallop to a trot.

"I have written about a visit to my grandmother when she took me to my first opera." Jim paused and took a deep breath as Ms. Durbin had instructed them to do before they began, a cleansing breath, she called it. She had told them it would send lots of oxygen to their brains, making it easier to speak. Cleansing breath or no cleansing breath, Jim could feel his nerve starting to ebb, so he began reading his essay before it was completely gone.

He didn't think about what he was reading; he imagined himself taking foul shots, one after another as fast as he could. He read the words on the wrinkled piece of paper in front of him. He followed the punctuation and kept going like a train speeding through a dark tunnel. His last sentence, "I promised my grandmother that I would go to another opera with her very soon," was a bright light at the far end of the tunnel, and he couldn't wait to get there.

The audience applauded loudly, though not as enthusiastically as they had for Lisa. Jim didn't care. He had no idea what he had just read. It could have been the instructions for a microwave oven for all he knew. But it was over, and his entire body felt like warm honey. He had never known such relief in his life. As he sat down, Lisa leaned over and said to Jim across Mariah's lap, "That was terrific!" Mariah gave Jim her fakest smile and looked away.

Jim was so happy that he actually started listening to some of the remaining essays. There was one about basketball by a boy with a thick pair of glasses. He looked familiar, even from the back, those narrow shoulders and bony arms, and then Jim remembered. It was the google-eyed kid from the Kings who had beaten them with his three foul shots. It was an interesting essay with all kinds of statistics and stories about college basketball, but the ending, which sounded as if it had been tacked on later, was about "the best thing" that had ever happened to him while playing basketball. It didn't take long for Jim to realize Google-Eyes was talking about the Kings-Thunderbirds game, but luckily, though he described the foul and his three good foul shots in excruciating detail, he never mentioned Jim by name.

The mayor got up to thank all of them "for representing your generation with such dignity and intelligence" and to announce the winners. He really dragged it out as if it were the Grammys or Miss America contest. The third prize went to Mary Elizabeth, the pumpkin girl. She looked thrilled about receiving the scientific calculator. Vishnu and Frederika must be crushed, thought Jim. Then the mayor announced the second place. It was Mariah! Of course, she jumped up with her hands to her throat acting all dramatic and squealed, "OhmyGod!" over and over. We'll never hear the end of this, thought Jim.

Finally it was time for the big prize, the computer, and the whole place was hushed as the mayor said, "My, my, isn't this surprising! Our grand prize winner is also from Hollow Hill! This has never happened before, two winners from the same school. May I congratulate Ms. Selma Durbin, their adviser, for doing such a remarkable job." The audience applauded as Ms. Durbin took a bow. Then it was quiet again. "The first prize winner of the seventh annual countywide public speaking contest is . . . Lisa Mondini for her essay titled 'My Mother.'"

Lisa seemed to be glued to her chair. Mariah leaned over to hug her, but Lisa just sat there, her eyes as round as Oreos. Finally she stood up and looked helplessly around. Ms. Durbin took her hand and led her to the lectern. The mayor hugged Lisa. It looked like someone hugging a tree because Lisa just stood there straight and tall with that goofy I-can't-believe-this expression. The mayor asked her if she would like to say anything.

Everyone quieted as Lisa spoke into the microphone. "Thank you so much. I know my mother is listening to this. It feels like a ball going *swish*!" People started applauding again, and Jim thought she would sit down, but she waited there at the lectern for the audience to quiet down. Then she said, "I wanted to thank my dad and my sisters . . . and also my practice partner, Jim Malone, who is a really good basketball player and an even better listener."

Jim didn't care about not winning the contest. He was just happy it was over. Of course, Pete was disappointed about the computer and needled Jim most of the way home in the car.

"Your essay was really good, Jim, but why did you read it like a friggin' robot?" said Pete. "You didn't have to rush through it like that! A brand-new, fully loaded computer could be sitting in our trunk right now heading for the space I cleared on my desk!"

"Pete," interrupted Dad, "your brother did his best, and we're all proud of him."

"Jim, I know you hate to get up like that in front of so many people," said Mom. "But you were wonderful! When you laughed, it broke the tension, and then you seemed so confident. The next time it should be much easier."

The next time would be sooner than Mom knew. Jim felt a surge of confidence. I did it, he kept thinking. I did it! Now he knew he would be able to give Nana's speech in Washington. He was ready. But first he had to break the news to Mom and Dad.

THEY STOPPED FOR lunch at Norm's Diner on the way home from Warwick, even though Pete complained that he had to get back for a "study date" with some girl named Amanda. He and Tricia had broken up one week ago.

"Your love life will have to wait," said Dad. "Today belongs to your brother. Competing in the countywide essay contest—that's quite an accomplishment. We want to celebrate."

"Congratulations, Jim. I know how proud Nana would be," said Mom.

They sat in a booth near a window overlooking the parking lot. Every booth in the diner had its own mini jukebox. Pete began flipping through the lists of CDs.

"Talk about 'retro'!" he said. "Whoever heard of this one, 'Sadie'?"

"I love that song," said Mom. "By the Spinners, right?" Mom began to sing the first few bars.

"Stop, Mom!" said Jim. "Please stop now!"

"Okay, okay, I don't want to embarrass you," said Mom with a laugh. "Today is your day!"

The waitress handed each of them a menu the size of a road atlas.

"Hey, Jim, how about the chipped beef," said Pete. "Mmm, now that sounds tasty."

"No, I think the chop suey à la Norman is what you want," said Jim.

Pete and Jim both started to laugh.

"That's the trouble with these places," said Jim. "Too many choices. I guess I'll have a bacon cheeseburger since I never get that at home."

Normally Mom would have said something like "Think about the grease! The fat!" But today she said, "Whatever you want, sweetie."

Jim figured that while Mom and Dad were still feeling all warm and fuzzy about the essay contest, he might as well tell them about Washington. Pete would find out sooner or later. And if anyone got upset, at least they were in a public place so no one would go ballistic on him.

"Mom, Dad, remember that speech Nana was going to give in Washington?" Jim said. "Well, uh, I'm going to give it for her."

"Jim, that's a lovely gesture, but we don't have Nana's speech," said Mom. "And I doubt she would be able to tell us where it is."

"I have it," Jim answered sheepishly.

Mom and Dad looked at Jim with puzzled expressions. Pete was flipping through the jukebox again and didn't seem to be listening.

"Where did you find her speech?" asked Dad.

Jim took a deep breath. He knew he had sworn to keep the laptop a secret, but he was sure Nana would understand. After all, she wanted him to share her stories.

"See, a few months ago Nana bought herself a laptop computer and—"

"A laptop computer!" interrupted Pete, turning abruptly from the jukebox. "Nana owns a laptop computer! How come I never heard about this?"

"It was a secret," said Jim. "She was writing all her life stories on it. She showed it to me that weekend I went to the opera with her."

"Maybe we should go down to her apartment and get it," said Mom.

"I already have it," said Jim. "It's under my bed."

"You mean, you've had Nana's laptop stashed under your bed and you never told anybody?" said Pete.

Mom, Dad, and Pete all stared at Jim. They seemed to be waiting for him to finish his story. So Jim explained how he had taken the computer because he wanted to keep it in a safe place. He told them about reading the files, about how Nana had written twenty whole pages for the Holocaust conference, and about how it was a really amazing speech. He didn't tell them about Nana's voice in the driveway or about why he was sure Nana wanted him to give her speech.

"But I called and told the people at the conference Nana would be too sick to attend," said Mom.

"Well, we called and told them I could do it," said Jim.

" 'We?' "

"Lisa. Lisa and me. We decided together, and she called the lady at the museum."

"Lisa?" said Mom.

"What is the exact date of the conference?" asked Dad.

"Uh, April second."

"That's next weekend, Jim," said Mom.

"My name is on the program," said Jim.

"Don't you have a tournament next weekend?" said Dad. "At Mountainside?"

"Yeah, but I'd rather go to Washington," said Jim.

"Are you sure you can do this? Get up in front of all those people?" said Pete. "You can't go rushing through like you did today. I mean, a Holocaust conference, that's a big deal."

Jim was sure. He was absolutely positive. He could ride through that scary tunnel again, especially if it meant that the world would get to hear Nana's story. The more times he read it, the more incredible her story became. She had lost everything, not once but twice! Two whole families blotted off the face of the earth. Then, for some reason, God had given her family number three. Mom, Dad, Pete, and Jim were what she called her gift from God. Maybe that was why Nana believed that everything came in threes, good or bad.

Jim had spent a lot of time trying to figure out what Nana's crazy stroke words meant, why she tried to bite him, and what her eyes were asking him to do. He had figured it out this morning while he was waiting for everyone else to get up. She was angry because Jim was writing down the stroke words instead of listening to her. Those spoken words were gibberish. The real words were in her eyes, and those real words were growing fainter, almost impossible to hear. Soon the only words left would be the ones in the laptop and the ones in Jim's head. Then, like a thunderbolt, it hit him. The voice in the driveway was clear: "Take care of my stories." Jim had made a promise he knew he had to keep.

Jim was looking out the window at the parking lot. He saw a blue minivan pull into a space on the far side of the lot. A man in a dark suit emerged from the driver's side. Then Jim saw one, two, three, four girls hop out of the van. The tallest one was Lisa.

As the Mondinis approached the door to the diner, Jim said quickly, "Lisa wants to come along, and I told her it was okay. I mean, she helped me set this all up. I know I can do this. I want to do it. I have to do it!"

"Well, I suppose if you . . ." said Mom. Her voice trailed off. "Oh, look, there's Lisa and her family."

Nana began refusing to get out of bed. The nurses and aides tried everything, but whenever any of them got close, she tried to bite them. The doctor came by to see her on Thursday and said she seemed unusually tired, so he ordered some tests. Mom shook her head and said, "Poor thing, she has no veins left to poke; she's black and blue all over her arms." Mom went to Burnside every day, but she didn't see any reason for Jim or Pete to go because Nana was mostly sleeping.

At the diner Mom and Dad had agreed to allow Jim to go to Washington. Mom had said, yes, of course, Lisa could come along, and Dad had said he would call his friend Phil and borrow his video camera for Mom to bring. The more they had talked about it, the more enthusiastic they had become. Even Pete had seemed pumped, but Jim wasn't sure if it was because of the speech or just because of the laptop computer.

Mom and Dad had decided that one of them should stay home and keep an eye on Nana. And when they had asked Pete if he wanted to go to Washington, he had said, "No, I've got midterms next week. I'll catch the videotape." Jim figured that meant he had a date with Amanda, which suited Jim just fine. Mom, Lisa, and a roomful of strangers. Jim was sure he could handle it.

Mr. Mondini dropped Lisa off on Saturday morning just as the sun was coming up. Lisa was still on cloud nine from winning the contest. And Mr. Mondini was not as squinty-eyed as usual. He wasn't even mad at them for missing the tournament.

"Good luck, Jim!" he said as he helped Lisa get her backpack out of his car. "Wish you didn't have to miss today, but some things are more important than basketball!" What had come over Mr. Mondini? "I think Josh will do a good job."

Josh, who never broke a promise, had not quit the team. Saturday night, after the essay contest, Jim had called him to hear about the league game. Josh told him all the details, about Frankie's fouling out with a minute left, about the overtime, and about how, surprisingly, Kenny had really come up big for the Thunderbirds.

"Did you talk to your dad?" Jim asked.

Josh's breathing filled the receiver until he finally said, "My mom told me she thought I should finish the season, that I had made a commitment. She said she'd talk to him."

It wasn't exactly the showdown Jim had imagined, but he was happy that Josh had not quit. And it felt as if this whole basketball season had worked out okay for both of them. Now Josh had a tournament to play in just the way Jim had had Pineville.

Lisa gave Mr. Mondini a hug and said, "Thanks, Dad. I'll see you tomorrow night."

Something had definitely changed between them. Jim had noticed it at the Wednesday practice. Maybe it was because the season was almost over, or maybe it was because of Lisa's essay, but Mr. Mondini was easing up on her. He didn't snap when she made a bad pass, and he did clap her on the shoulders after a small-sided scrimmage, saying, "Top-notch, Lisa! Truly top-notch!"

"Have fun!" Mr. Mondini called from his open window as he backed out of the driveway.

The train was crowded.

"Do you think all these people are going to the museum?" joked Lisa. "Uh-oh!"

Mom had brought along her quilting pieces. She had a bagful of colorful hexagons. She was stitching them together, side by side by side. The quilt was going to be for Nana, she said. Lisa was fascinated.

"Ooohh, I like this one," she said, holding up a piece of green fabric with tiny purple kites. "And that one is cool. Look, Jim, it has faces on it."

Jim couldn't care less about Mom's sewing. It was just a bunch of scraps as far as he was concerned. He looked at Mom and Lisa with all these patches on their laps. Mom was wearing her reading glasses and trying to thread a needle. Lisa offered to help her. Then Lisa asked if she could sew, too.

"My mom taught me when I was little," said Lisa.

So Mom gave Lisa a few hexagons and her own needle and thread, and the two of them sewed away and talked and talked. They were as happy as two sparrows splashing in Mom's birdbath! Well, why not? They aren't going to do anything but sit in the audience and listen to me, thought Jim. Mom hadn't even read the speech yet.

Lisa and Mom were having a regular sewing bee, yucking it up like sisters. Jim was sitting there with nothing to do. He stared out the window at the passing scenery, the river with its choppy peaks of water, the sheer gray cliffs on the other side, the bridges, the factories and red-brick buildings. Nana had left Germany aboard a night train. "It wasn't because I was so smart and I could see the future. I left because I was following my boyfriend. If I had known that I would never see my parents, brothers, aunts, uncles, cousins, or grandparents ever again, I'm not sure I would have made the same decision. As I sat on that rumbling train, passing through the pitch-black night, I had no idea that everything that was familiar and dear to me would be destroyed and lost forever. Even what I was rushing to, my future husband, my child to come, my new home, would be violently ripped away from me, leaving me as I was that night on the train, alone and only looking bravely ahead." Jim could picture Nana with her ratty cardboard suitcase, sitting alone on a train. He wondered if she ever remembered that ride when she took the train up to visit them.

Nana must have known she was going to have this stroke. Otherwise why had she bought the laptop and started writing everything down? Like Lisa's mother, making Lisa write all her stories down when she knew she was dying of cancer, Nana wanted to make sure no one would forget her.

Mom said that nobody really dies as long as other people remember them. But what happens when those people die? They take their memories with them, Jim supposed. Unless it was written down somewhere. Jim thought about all the people in Nana's family who had died during the war. There was nothing left of them, not even a small photograph or letter, nothing except for Nana's memories.

Jim had decided to read all of Nana's folders in the laptop. At first he felt funny, as if he were snooping, but then he realized reading Nana's writing was like having her talk to him, and he longed to hear her speak again, in words he could understand. All the stories took place in Europe. Some were familiar. Some he had never heard before. She described her mother with her many keys tied around her wide waist, the keys that locked the pantry and the *guten Stube*, the parlor room, to keep out her boisterous children. She described her father, his strict discipline at the Sabbath meal, his long, dour face bent over the food in prayer. There were her three brothers, and all the goofy tricks they played on her and their baby sister, Sarah. There were Nana's grandparents, who were the most respected members of her large family. Nana really loved her grandfather.

"He had a long white beard and sharp blue eyes. I believed he knew everything there was to know because he studied the Talmud and spent his free time discussing it with his friends over glasses of hot tea. He was the wise center of my family's universe. My *opa*, as I called him, took me aside one day and told me I was the smartest of his grandchildren, and although I was a girl, he wanted me to get a serious education. He paid for me to go to the best school for girls. When I could not swim anymore because I was Jewish, and my father walked out and my mother cried all day in bed, it was my *opa* who loved me best of all. When the girls at school began to tease me and call me *Jüdin* or the teachers made me stand outside the classroom while the other children prayed, my grandfather taught me to ignore the prejudice and to respect myself. I didn't tell anyone in my family that I was leaving Germany to elope with my boyfriend. That was the one mistake in my life that I really regret, not saying good-bye. The last I heard was that my grandparents returned to their hometown in Poland as they tried to flee the Nazis. No one ever saw them again. I hope my *opa* wasn't disappointed in me. Of everyone in my family, I miss him the most, even today so many years later."

The scariest part of Nana's stories was how everyone seemed to disappear. How could so many people just vanish! Jim wondered what he would do if tomorrow he woke up and Mom, Dad, and Pete were gone without a trace. It made his heart race just thinking about it.

Maybe that was why Nana always looked at him so deeply and hugged him so strongly. She didn't know if she would ever see him again. Saying good-bye to Nana was always such a big deal. Maybe that was why she slept with all their pictures hanging on the wall next to her bed.

The conference took place in a small auditorium with staggered gray seats. The floor was carpeted, so the atmosphere was hushed and quiet. To Jim, it felt like the inside of a church. Miriam Schwartz, dressed entirely in black except for a wide lime-colored belt, met them at the door.

"What a particular pleasure and honor it is to have you here with us, young man," she said to Jim, vigorously shaking his hand.

An honor to have me? Jim thought. This woman is nuts. But he smiled and shook her hand back just as vigorously.

The auditorium was only about one-third full when Mrs. Schwartz escorted Jim up to the stage, where there were four chairs arranged on one side of a long table, all facing the audience. She introduced him to the three people standing near the lectern, the other panelists: two women, bent and leaning on canes, and a man with sparse black hair combed over his bald spot. The three of them all peered at Jim as if he were some exotic bird.

"And you, young man, tell me, vat are you going to talk about?" said the man first.

"My grandmother. I'm reading her speech. She's very sick. She had a stroke so I'm—" but before he could finish, one of the women grabbed his arm and said, "Such a good boy! I should be so lucky with my grandchildren."

"You must give your dear *bubbe* many *naches*," said the other. "You understand Yiddish, darling?"

Jim nodded. He had never heard anyone but Nana use the word *naches*. He felt a pang of longing for her.

Only a few more people came in to sit in the audience. Almost all of them looked pretty old. Jim relaxed. This would be a piece of cake compared with the essay contest. He saw Mom and Lisa sitting in the first row, gabbing away. Mom was getting Phil's video camera set up on her lap.

Jim and the other speakers sat down. Mrs. Schwartz tapped on the microphone a few times and asked everyone please to get settled so they could begin. Jim unzipped his book bag and pulled out the manila envelope with the printed copy of Nana's speech. Dad had taken the laptop to his school, hooked it up to a printer, and made this copy for Jim.

"As the population of Holocaust survivors grows smaller and smaller, we must make every effort to let their stories be told and recorded and preserved for all the future generations," Mrs. Schwartz began. She introduced the panel as "German Jews who survived the war in other European countries" and said, "They will share with us their harrowing tales of narrow escapes and how the kindness of others helped them through those dark days." Jim looked at the people sitting beside him and tried to imagine them running through the woods or down alleys. "Our young panelist is actually the grandson of Erna Wallach, who unfortunately became ill and could not join us. Let us welcome James Malone!"

A spattering of applause rose from the audience, and Jim walked to the lectern. He arranged the papers before him, cleared his throat and began without looking down, "How I Survived the War by Erna Wallach." Then he glanced at the first page. The title across the top was "My Grandfather and Me." What was this? He flipped through the sheets and saw it was all about Nana and her grandfather!

"Um, excuse me," Jim said to Mrs. Schwartz. "May I look through my book bag? This is the wrong paper." He walked back to the table and heard murmurs in the audience. The only other paper in his bag was his essay on the opera. Where was the speech? Then he realized Dad must have printed the wrong file! Why hadn't Jim even looked inside the envelope when Dad had given it to him?

Jim walked slowly back to the lectern. He felt as if he were coming down with a serious flu. Now what? Mrs. Schwartz was looking at him with concern. The people in the audience were all gazing up at him with puzzled faces. Jim had to do something! He somehow had to tell Nana's story. He imagined her sitting in bed, straining to bring her face closer to his, urging him to speak. "Jimmy, take care of my stories. Don't forget!"

"I . . . I . . . seem to have brought the wrong papers with me," Jim began nervously. He stopped to clear his throat.

Mom had the video camera covering half her face, so he couldn't tell what she was thinking. Lisa was smiling hopefully and nodding her head. She was sitting with her shoulders back, her legs crossed, and her hands clasped on her lap. He heard her whisper, "Go ahead, Jim!"

Then something else came into his head: A picture of a basketball hoop. *The object of the game is to get the ball into the basket. You can't be afraid to shoot.*

"I know what my grandmother wanted to tell you," Jim said. "Ever since I was a little kid, my grandmother, who I call Nana, told me her amazing stories. Sometimes I couldn't even believe they were true. I mean, they were about war, and I only know stuff about war from the movies." The people in the audience had settled down. They were listening carefully. No one was covering his or her ears, so he knew he was far enough from the microphone.

"In the speech my Nana wrote, which I forgot to bring, she talked about how, when she was a little girl, she never thought anything bad would ever happen to her or her family. She had three older brothers and a little sister, and they lived in a big apartment with their parents and a housekeeper. Every Friday night they had a Sabbath dinner with candles and the good plates and silverware. On Saturdays they visited their grandparents, and on Sundays everyone got together, all the cousins and aunts and uncles. It was a regular life just like I have.

She said sometimes she overheard her uncles talking about the Nazis, but it seemed like something far away.

"Of all the people in her family, Nana loved her grandfather Leo the best. She said he was quiet and very intelligent, and he always wore black clothing. Nana brought her grandfather her poems and drawings, and he always told her she was as smart as her brothers. Many years later, after the war, when Nana finally saw her sister, Sarah, again, Sarah told her about Opa's last words before he boarded the train for Poland: 'I may never see my darling Erna again, so you must promise when you do, you'll tell her that I love her and pray for her every day. She has given me great *naches*, and I am so proud of her.' "

Jim felt a lump growing in his throat. He took a sip from the glass of water Mrs. Schwartz had placed on the lectern for him. He had only just started, and he still had all the wartime to talk about when Nana had hidden in the mountains in Italy, about her husband being tortured and killed, about being shot and captured and escaping again, about her son dying of tuberculosis. He knew it all by heart from reading it over so many times, but he felt seized by the sadness of Nana never seeing her grandfather again and by his own enormous grief for Nana, who seemed, at this very moment up there in her bed in Burnside, to be boarding another train, her final train. He didn't think he could go on until he saw Lisa looking up at him with her wide brown eyes. Lisa, who knew all about grief. Lisa, who also knew all about expressing her deepest feelings without shame or stupid red ears!

Jim continued, and his voice grew stronger. Near the end of the story he added something that wasn't anywhere in Nana's original speech.

"Sometimes I don't think we realize that our grandparents have such a big impact on us. I'm almost thirteen, and lately, I mean, before my grandmother got so sick, I was really getting impatient around her and always complaining about how slow and clueless she was. But she never got impatient with me. She always believed in me and was really proud of everything I did. And she shared her life with me so I could . . . I guess, so I could learn that if you're confident and smart and lucky, you can manage to make it through anything. You don't have to be big and strong. I mean, if you could see her, my nana is a pretty small lady. But look at what she did! She survived the war! And she asked me to take care of her stories. She gave me a big responsibility. I wish she was here today because I would tell her, 'Nana, you always say I make you so proud, but you know what? You make me even prouder.' Thank you very much."

The audience applauded long and hard. Jim put his head down and stumbled back to his chair. He blinked, trying to keep the tears inside his eyes, behind his eyelids where no one could see them. As he sat down, the elderly man sitting next to him leaned over and handed him a clean white handkerchief. "Here you go, son," the man said. "No shame in crying. We've all shed rivers of tears."

J IM WAS DREAMING about a new puppy. The puppy, a blur of brown fur, was running across the yard and trying to keep up with Jim. *Yip! Yip! Yip!* The dog's baby barks filled the air. Jim stopped to let the pup jump into his arms, when he heard Dad calling his name, "Jim, Jim!"

He opened his eyes, and there was Dad standing over his bed in the dim early-morning light.

"Jim, you need to get up now," Dad said. "The nursing home just called, and it seems Nana took a turn for the worse overnight. Mom wants us all to go down there and see her."

Jim and Mom and Lisa had gotten home late last night. Their train had been delayed outside Philadelphia, so they missed their connecting train and had to wait another hour. Jim's clothes were lying in a heap next to his bed. He wanted to sleep.

"Come on, Jim," said Dad. "Pete, buddy, you, too, come on. Time to get up."

The four of them hurried out the kitchen door in their rumpled jeans and sweatshirts. Nobody said a word. Mom drove.

They had to ring the doorbell. Burnside was shut down and not really open for visitors, but the head nurse had promised Mom they would be allowed in. A custodian unlocked the door for them. They walked silently down the hall to the elevator like a bunch of sleepwalkers. Dad and Mom were holding hands.

The sun was just coming up outside the window next to Nana's bed. She was lying on her back with a clean white sheet pulled up to her chin. Her body had gotten so thin that it almost looked as if there were only a head resting on the empty bed. Her eyes were closed.

"Mama," said Mom. She leaned over and gently kissed Nana's forehead. Nana opened her eyes immediately as if she had been waiting for them to arrive. She looked around, letting her eyes linger on each face.

Jim tried to figure out what Nana was thinking, because except for her eyes, all her features were frozen. Nana's eyes didn't look angry, the way they had the day she had tried to bite him. They didn't look exactly loving either. They were searching for something. Maybe it was like the night during the war when she had studied her bed and the leaves on the tree outside the window. Maybe she was trying to memorize their faces before she began her journey.

A nurse came in carrying a cup of apple juice. "I'm so sorry," she said softly. "She won't drink at all, but we keep trying. We could put those needles in her legs, you know, to hydrate her, but at this point it would just make her more uncomfortable." She cranked up the top half of the bed to raise Nana's head. Then the nurse put the Dixie cup to Nana's lips, but she drooled the bit of juice, and it rolled down her chin onto the sheet. "Okay, Erna, it's okay," said the nurse. "I'm not going to force you, sweetheart." The nurse looked sadly at Nana's face. "I'll leave you with your family, Erna." Then she walked out of the room.

Mom pulled a chair over and sat next to Nana. She gently lifted back the sheet. Nana's arms looked like bones with the sheerest covering of skin. Jim had to look away. He felt like gagging. Mom took one of Nana's small hands in hers and touched it to her cheek. Nana, with a slight groan, pulled her hand away and closed her eyes. Then Mom laid her head on the bed next to Nana's shoulder and began to cry softly.

"Hearing is the last thing to go," said Jim. He didn't mean for his voice to sound so loud.

"What are you talking about?" said Pete.

"When a person is dying, hearing is the last sense to go," said Jim. "Lisa told me."

"So?" said Pete.

"So instead of just standing around staring at her, we should be talking to Nana," said Jim. "She can still hear us."

Dad went to the other side of the bed and spoke into Nana's ear. "We're all here, Nana!" he said. "And we're not going anywhere!"

Pete and Jim took turns mumbling something into Nana's good left ear. Jim didn't know what Pete had said, but he whispered, "I won't forget. I promise."

Then the room was quiet except for Mom's muffled cries. Jim hated the sound of Mom crying.

"Nana, I did your speech in Washington. Everyone there really liked it. A lady from the newspaper even interviewed me." Jim wanted to drown out the sound of Mom.

Nana's eyes remained closed. Her breathing was deep and uneven.

"Mama," said Mom, hiccuping now. "My beautiful mama!"

Jim could suddenly picture Lisa sitting stoically next to Mrs. Mondini, reading to her from a book. He imagined her sisters standing at the doorway, crying and blowing their noses and Mr. Mondini pacing in the hall. Jim was proud of Lisa for not sobbing at her mother's bedside. He remembered something Lisa had told him: "I didn't want a sad, ugly face to be the last thing my mother ever saw. I didn't want her to see my face all puffy and red and covered in tears." Jim needed to tell Mom to stop, but how do you tell someone not to cry? As if Mom could control her sadness. How do you say, "Look, Mom, this tiny, shriveled woman here on this bed who you love so much is about to leave the earth, and you should be trying to make it easier for her." Jim didn't want Nana to die, but he also didn't want her to live without her voice or her independence. Maybe dying *would* be better than this. Not for Jim, Mom, Dad, or Pete but for Nana.

"Lisa says you have to let her go," said Jim. Mom, Dad, and Pete all looked at him as if he were an alien. "Lisa says, when a person is dying and the people she loves keep holding on to her, then she can't die, and she's in this painful place between here and there. She won't go until we tell her it's okay to go."

"Oh, come on, Jim!" Pete said, but Mom cut him off.

"That makes sense, Jim. And Lisa knows, Lisa certainly knows."

Mom sat up straight and blew her nose. "Listen, Mama," she began in a quivering voice, "I'll be okay. I mean, I'll miss you every day, but you know I am surrounded by love with Mitch and Pete and Jim. We'll all be fine and help one another. You've done your job."

"We love you," said Dad. He sounded as if he were about to sneeze.

"Peace, Nana," said Pete. He gave Jim a skeptical look and shrugged.

Jim stood silently next to Nana for a long time.

"Why don't you tell her it's okay to die, Jim?" said Pete. "This was your idea."

Jim hoped Lisa was right. He hoped Nana could hear him because he still had something important to tell her.

"Nana," Jim began. He paused as if he expected her to answer, "What is it, my darling?" Jim had so many things he wanted to tell Nana, but his mouth suddenly felt dry. He wanted her to know that he had been listening when she said, "Jimmy, there are other things in the world besides basketball. You have many talents, my darling." Sure, he was still obsessed with playing hoops, but he was beginning to realize he could be good at other stuff. Jim watched Nana's face. Her expression remained frozen. He should have told her before, maybe when he had slept over at her apartment, but he hadn't realized it back then. The night at the opera seemed so long ago, before he got to know Lisa, before the essay contest, before Washington. He couldn't explain it to anyone, but lately he was starting to feel smarter. After giving the speech in Washington, for a few minutes there, Jim had actually felt like the intelligent and handsome American grandson Nana always bragged about. Why couldn't he get the words out for Nana to hear?

Instead, he heard himself saying, "So, Nana, I know you're going to miss the House of Sports, but we'll always have a seat for you on the couch during the play-offs." He wished Nana would just flutter her eyelids or move her lips, anything so he could be sure she was listening. "Nana, I have to to tell you one more thing . . . I'm glad you wrote down all your stories, and I promise I'll take really good care of them." Jim stared at Nana's white face against the white pillowcase. It looked like one of those plaster of paris face masks they had made in art class.

Suddenly Nana's head rose from the pillow, her eyes opened, and she took three loud, choking breaths.

"Mama?" said Mom, jumping to her feet.

But Nana's head fell back hard onto the pillow, and that was it. Her breathing stopped. It was as if a switch had been turned off. Jim had never seen a dead person, but he knew immediately that Nana was dead.

Mom said, "Mitch, do you think she's . . . ?" Then she stopped, unable to say the next word.

"I'll get the nurse," said Dad.

Pete, looking pale as a ghost, walked out of the room after Dad.

Mom just stood there, whispering, "Mama? Mama?"

Why couldn't Mom see that Nana was gone? In that instant of her last gasping breath, Nana had vanished, leaving only this body that vaguely resembled her. To Jim she now looked like one of those wax museum figures.

Jim looked out at the brightening sky. There was still a faint white smudge of moon. Even though he could not see a shadow flying away from the Burnside Home for the Aged, Jim knew, with his whole heart, that Nana was free and looking bravely ahead.

JIM DECIDED THAT for his thirteenth birthday he did not want a party. What would they do? Try to break a piñata? Wear party hats? Play Mom's favorite game, Unwrap the Wrapper, which was like Hot Potato and a grab bag all in one?

But Mom and Dad really wanted him to do something special. "Even if you just have a couple of friends over and we have a barbecue."

So to make them happy, Jim invited Lisa and Josh.

The three of them played basketball while it was still light. Next weekend their travel season would be over. Lisa had told them her dad was going to let her try out for an AAU team coached by this lady who used to play at Duke. Josh was going to begin tennis lessons right after the last Thunderbirds game. "Who knows? I may even like tennis," Josh had said. Jim was going to play lacrosse in the town league just for something to do until summer basketball began.

As they played, shooting and goofing on one another, they talked about the party Mariah was having and whether or not they should go.

"I heard she invited Ms. Durbin," said Lisa.

"Get outta here!" said Jim. "No way!"

"Well, I heard Mariah has a crush on Frankie, but he couldn't care less," said Josh. "So he said to her, 'Mariah, if you invite Ms. Durbin, then I'll come to your party,' you know, just as a joke, but she took him seriously and went and invited Ms. Durbin!" Josh let out a howl of delight.

Dad was on the other side of the hedge, starting up the gas grill. Instead of the usual chicken dogs and turkey burgers, Mom had agreed to regular old hamburgers and hot dogs. And potato chips and root beer. Mom came out onto the back porch to watch them play.

"What a beautiful spring evening," Mom said, stretching her arms over her head. "Listen to those peepers."

Pete walked out behind Mom. He had wanted to go to the movies with Amanda, but Mom had put her foot down, saying, "Family comes first. You have to stay home for your brother's birthday. Period!" Pete was wearing his crustiest T-shirt and a visor, both backward.

"You guys want to play a little two-v-two?" he asked.

"As long as I don't have to be on your team!" said Jim.

"Who said I wanna play with you, Squeak? You think I wanna lose?"

"Put your money where your mouth is, music man!" said Jim.

"Hey, fellas." Dad's voice came from the other side of the hedge. "This is supposed to be a party!"

Pete came over and punched Jim lightly in the arm. "Happy birthday, little bro."

On the other side of the privet hedge, past the biggest forsythia bush, and near the edge of the woods, was a circle of stones that marked where they had buried Jake's ashes. The piece of slate stood as a headstone in the middle of the circle. It had been Jim's idea to bury him near the path Jake had always followed on his daily adventures in the woods.

The other day a small cardboard box had arrived by Express Mail. Inside was an amber urn that contained Nana's ashes. It seemed too small to Jim to contain all of her ashes, but it was rather heavy. Pete said it gave him the heebie-jeebies, but Jim sat and stared at the urn for a long time.

"You know, Nana is not really in there," said Mom. "Those are just her remains."

"I know that," said Jim.

Of course Nana wasn't in a small amber urn sitting on the fireplace mantel. She was out in the air, in the sky, in the trees, always close enough for Jim to feel her presence. He remembered the word *animism* from their Scrabble game. There was a spiritual force separate from the things we could touch or see, and that force was what created life. Nana's body was still here on earth, even though now it was a pile of ashes, but her soul—what did Nana call it in Latin?— her *animus* had been released from these ashes, and it was out there somewhere. One day he would try to explain it to Mom and Dad, but for the time being he was content just to have the knowledge. Jim felt Nana's spirit when he was drifting off to sleep at night sometimes or when he was shooting baskets. He felt it most of all when he was reading Nana's stories on the laptop.

In a few months they all would travel to Italy to scatter her ashes from a bridge over the Tiber River. That was what she had asked them to do in her will. Then she wanted them to travel up to the small village in the Apennine Mountains to the place where the hospital had stood, the hospital where she had made her deal with God. She didn't say what she wanted them to do when they got there, but Jim was sure they would be able to figure it out.

Jim thought thirteen was going to be a good year. He hadn't told anyone, but this morning he had measured himself on the door frame of his closet. He did it over three times to be sure he wasn't making a mistake. But there it was. The ruler landed on the same spot each time. A quarter of an inch taller! It wasn't much, but it was a start.